KENDRA MORENO
Ferocious reads to fill your nights.

TRIGGER WARNING:

PROLOGUE

KAI

Months later...

"You lost me the moment you stepped through the wall, Cora," I whisper, the words falling from my lips before I can stop them. I feel her horror slam into me as she shakes her head in denial. My sister is the strong one. She always was and always will be.

She was cast to the Dead Lands and survived, and she fought to find me again. I'll never be as strong as her. Can she not see that?

Can she not see that I'm ruined beyond repair?

"No, don't say that, Kai—"

"Cora," I interrupt, my hands coming up to cup her face. Her eyes drop to my forearms where bruises stand out against my pale skin. I can't hide them. They were meant to be seen, just like the scars he placed upon my body and soul.

The king may be gone, but he still haunts me.

"Kai, it's going to be okay. Everything will change now," Cora continues, but her words only make me sink further into my misery. Things may change in the world around me, but I'm already far too broken for change to happen to me. Cora has always been a fighter, and she's always protected me, but she wasn't able to protect me this time.

Now, I'm ruined. Now, I'm nothing but the echo of the woman I once was. All the hopes, dreams, and future . . . they're all gone. All that is left is a pain I cannot live in, not even for her.

"Do you know what he did to me?" I rasp. Tears spill over my lashes and drip down my cheeks as the memories swarm me, reminding me that I'm broken, that I'll never be whole again. I will never be anything but his. He stole every inch of me. "Do you know what he made me do?"

Cora's face crumples at my words. "I'm so sorry, Kai," she says. I can see her agony written on her face. She tried to come as fast as she could. It is not her fault. Some fates are written in blood and we can't escape them. "I didn't know—"

"No. How could you have?" I ask, staring at her with tears rolling uninhibited down my face. "You were supposed to die." My voice is more of a croak now, all the pain spilling from me as I take a shuddering breath. The moment I lost my sister, I lost my fight. "I mourned you the moment you walked through the wall. No hunt survives."

"But I did," she says, her words so much like a plea that they hurt.

None of my pain is directed at her. It's not Cora's fault, but now she's here, asking me to believe in her, to heal, and I don't feel as if I can ever be whole again. There are pieces of me that are missing, that the king stole from me. Cora may as well be just another phantom, another reminder of what I'm not, of what I lost. She died, but then she didn't. She's here, but even I can see she's no longer the same.

She's stronger now.

Nothing is the same, and nothing will ever be again. I am not the Kai she remembers.

I'm a shell barely held up by my sister's sheer will.

"Kai," Cora implores again, "we can get through this. I can help you."

She is still trying to take care of me.

Cora is the best little sister.

Now, she stands before me, glowing with radiance despite her pain at realizing how broken I am. Monsters stand with her, and although they are terrifying, they are clearly in love with my sister. Even in the Dead Lands, she's managed to enchant them, her stubborn strength calling to them in a way my old beauty never could. I'm not the vibrant older sister anymore.

I died the day she walked through the wall.

She tried to protect me, taking my place when I would have died on the other side, and now . . . I died anyway, just not in the way I assumed.

"The wall is going to fall, Kai. Things will change. I can help you heal."

Cora isn't listening to me. She's so desperate to save me, she doesn't understand there's nothing to save.

My eyes go unfocused as the memories crash over me again. I sort through them, wondering which ones I should tell her so she'll realize it's no use.

I've experienced so much pain, so much ruination, how could she ever understand?

"He would force us to watch his slaughter," I croak, and she falls silent. "I saw one of the concubines, an older one, get brutalized for daring to flinch when he raised his hand." My eyes meet hers, and I make sure she can see the darkness floating in my gaze. "I was her replacement, so I had to take the jewels from her body while she breathed her last breath on the floor. I had to collar myself."

It was the most horrible shame. I walked forward, stole those jewels, and collared myself. I had no choice. I'm not a fighter like Cora.

I chained myself with a dead woman's trophies.

"Kai—"

"No, Cora," I spit. "You were thrown to the monsters and came back leading them." My eyes soften at the stricken expression on her face. "You were always so great at changing the status quo, but I'm not you. I was given to a monster, but I did not come out the victor." I choke on my next words. "I came out this . . . this . . . hollow shell. I'm no longer the sister you left behind."

"Don't say that!" Cora cries, still trying to convince me.

"It's true," I choke out. "You were always meant to be great, Cora." I release her face and take a step back. Cora's eyes are on me, and I can tell she's horrified at my words. "You sacrificed yourself for me and gave me a chance at happiness, but I was never going to be happy. I wasn't meant for that."

I take another step back, and another.

"Kai, what are you saying?" Cora asks, stumbling after me, her hand outstretched, but I recoil from her touch.

If she touches me, I'll stain her.

"You sacrificed yourself for me," I repeat, placing my hand over my heart as I take one final step backward. The backs of my thighs hit the wall along the edge, pressing against old bruises and scars that will never fade. "I won't let you sacrifice your happiness for me again. I'm not me any longer. The king killed who I was." I know my next words will hurt, but it's better that she understands everything. It's better that she hates me by the end of it all. "You were too late," I rasp. "I'm just another ghost to haunt these walls."

"Kai—"

"You were too late," I repeat. "I love you, baby sister. I always will."

Then, before she can stop me or understand what I've planned, I let all of my weight fall backward. Everything slows around me, the world pausing for a moment so I can focus on my sister's face. Her eyes widen as she reaches for me, her fingers too far away. Her mouth opens on a scream I can't hear as she reaches forward. Her face disappears when she throws herself after me, but one of her monsters stops her.

Good. They will protect her. They will heal this pain I'm causing.

Wind rushes past me, my hair whipping around my face as I plummet toward the water below. Above me, I see the gargoyle spread his wings, but I know he'll be too late. I'd hoped they would be.

As I fall, I close my eyes, holding Cora's smiling, radiant face in my mind, the newfound power making her glow. It's her I see before I plunge into the water and everything goes black.

Blissful, painless darkness claims me, and I float into the ether with a smile curling at my lips.

Free at last.

I'm free at last.

CHAPTER
ONE
KAITO

The castle has always been an interesting place to rest, since the fighters have trouble spotting me in the turbulent river that serves as my home, my sanctuary. The water always calls to me, softening the blow of the world around us, even if I shouldn't risk being this close to the enemy. I've long since given up any hold on life. When my time to die comes, I'll embrace it, but until then, I won't live by constraints imposed by humans.

This world belongs to no one. There are no walls that will hold me.

I'm a bit prejudiced toward humans after what the king did to me.

I'm nothing more than an experiment, just like many of the others who live beneath the Gilded Lands. Unlike them, I am neither monster nor man. I don't belong anywhere.

I'm an in-between monster that no one will ever claim.

Still, the powers I was given have come in handy so many years later. I may have the traits of the fey that live in the Dead Lands, but I have other traits as well. I can breathe beneath the water and control it when needed, and I can live beneath the surface undetected.

unbothered, and unchained—like I'd been before I'd escaped the castle.

They searched for me. The king didn't want word of his precious experiments to get out, especially since I was one of the first, but I knew not to run to the humans. I'd be killed on sight for my unsightly gray skin, the horns that grow from my temples, and the claws that tip my fingers. Though I still have human traits, they're not enough to convince anyone I was once human.

They see a monster, and they don't look deeper.

I escaped into the river and stayed here, going where I wished and stealing what I needed, and that's why I'm here today.

There are so many occurrences happening around this city. I hear screams and shouts. The fighters have all rushed away, leaving the river unprotected. It's odd for them. They usually patrol every area.

It isn't until later that I hear the whispers.

The king is dead.

A hunt has returned with monsters at her side and dispatched him.

The world is free.

I have a hard time believing that any human, no matter the monsters at her side, will rule this world any better though. The wall will remain, and even if it doesn't, there will be no place for the king's experiment in any realm.

It will be the same.

Slipping from the water to rest on the edge, I decide to simply observe and watch the events unfold, but movement at the top of the castle catches my eye. My vision is not nearly as good as a true fey's, but I can still make out a woman on the ledge. Her dark brunette hair swirls in the wind as she faces whatever danger comes near her.

Something deep inside me lurches toward her despite not knowing what's happening. It's a silly thought, since I belong to no one and I'm not worthy of anything.

I watch as she exchanges words I can't hear.

She tips backwards, and my gasp catches in my throat.

She plummets through the air at an impossible speed, not even trying to fight it. By the time the gargoyle leaps from the top to go after her, he's too late.

I'm closer.

I'm already in the water before I'm conscious of leaping in, rushing toward her position as she crashes into the river with a force that should kill any human. When I come from beneath and wrap my arms around her waist, her heartbeat barely thumps in her chest.

The gargoyle draws closer, and I make a split-second decision.

She will not die today. My instincts refuse to let her.

I cover her mouth with my hand, forcing air into her lungs just before I dive beneath the water with her in my arms. The gargoyle flies past none the wiser, searching for the lost woman.

"You will live, *amarta*. I will make it so."

I do not know if they wanted to hunt or hurt her, but she was obviously trying to escape them so I steal her away. I rush us to safety to protect the human in my arms.

She's far too injured to hear me, though, as I escape the Gilded Lands and reach the small cabin I often use in the Dead Lands, carrying her limp body until I can bring her inside and gently lay her down.

I begin to heal her, using the power forced upon me to save her life.

She sleeps and while she does, I promise to take care of her, whether she hears me or not.

CHAPTER
TWO

KAI

Warmth infuses my body.

It spreads from the center of my chest outward, until I'm aware of each limb and my fingers twitch with the feeling. My eyes remain closed for a few moments as I focus on the growing sensation. Why does it seem strange? Why is it so foreign?

"I love you, baby sister. I always will."

My chest squeezes as the memory comes back to me. I should be dead, but instead, I can feel my body.

I force my eyes open, blinking against the darkness as my vision adjusts. For a moment, panic winds through my chest. Where am I?

Am I dead?

When I finally get my eyes to work again, I see wooden beams above my head. My fingers curl into a similarly carved wooden table. Something soft is beneath my body and head to cushion me from the hardness. I can't feel much—no pain or happiness. I'm numb.

What happened?

My eyes close for a moment as I search my memories. It all comes back in a rush—the invasion, the king, Cora . . . the fall.

I threw myself from the top of the castle, so how am I alive?

I don't seem to have much energy, and my body isn't responding even though I want to jump up and demand an explanation, but I have just enough to slowly turn my head. It brings the rest of the room into view, and it is nothing like I have ever seen in either the Gilded Lands or the Shadow Lands. It is not dripping in riches or gold, nor is it sad and old. Beautifully carved wood frames a door etched with designs of monsters. Two stone windows sit on either side of it, the sun shining in and blocking my view. The floor is stone, appearing inviting and warm. The walls and ceiling are a mixture of stone and wood. I smell smoke—a fire maybe? The room I'm in seems small but well cared for and homey. Another scent reaches me then, salty and wild like the water I plunged into.

My heart stills for a moment as I remember the impact and the waves closing around me like a kiss goodbye. How did I survive that?

How could any human?

I meant to die, so how am I alive?

Something bright catches my eye. I have to blink to bring my vision into focus as I manage to lift my arm. My hand shakes from the force of the effort, but I grasp the bright thing and lift it to see it better. Strands of silken dark brown are interwoven with bright orange. Hair, I realize. It's as bright as the sun. I trace it up and it ends at my head.

My hair . . .

What is happening? My hand drops, as I'm unable to hold it up any longer, and that's when the wooden door opens. Fear courses through me, clawing at me to scream, to run, but I'm unable to. I lie here, watching as the monster freezes at the sight of me. Shock and fear are etched on his almost humanoid face, just as it must be on mine.

Both of us just stare at each other.

His skin is gray, with blue highlights of all shades. It's not the gray hue of a stormy sky, but the gray you find only in the deepest parts of the ocean, though I do not know how I know that. His bright aqua eyes are tilted up and shaped more like a cat's. His nose is not human, with just two slits above deep, blue, plush lips. He's tall and covered in muscle, and he wears a bit of cloth around his hips. Slits line his throat, and his nails are black and long like talons. His hair is a stunning mixture of blacks and blues, and it falls around his shoulders in wet strands that somehow still look kempt.

Fear pulses through me as I stare, but my confusion wins out.

"Where am I?" I croak, my voice so hoarse and deep, it almost hurts to speak. "How am I alive?" I sputter into a coughing fit, and it unfreezes the monster man. He rushes to my side and lifts a crudely carved goblet to my lips after helping me sit up to sip the fresh, clean water. I shudder at the wet feeling of the hand on my back. It's almost cold, unlike the warmth of this room, but the water washes away the sharpness in my throat, and I sigh in bliss as he carefully lays me down. It is a he? Because he could not be mistaken for anything else.

He's neither man nor monster.

He's something between.

"What happened?" I whisper, scarcely able to meet his bright eyes.

"I saved you. You fell. You were hurt, and I wasn't sure if you were being hunted, so I brought you to my home. You are safe." His voice is smooth and thunderous, like crashing waves against the rocky shoreline, but his words are disjointed, as if he's not used to his voice.

I suppose I have to speak like that now, more used to screaming than speaking.

"How am I alive?" I repeat. My brain is scarcely able to comprehend what is happening.

"I used the magic we all possess to heal you, but it can only do so much. You have been resting for weeks now. I was not sure you would ever awaken," he murmurs as he straightens a fur that is draped across me before hurrying away. I manage to lift my head to watch him as he ladles something that is simmering above an open fireplace into a bowl.

When he returns, I flinch, and he slows his movements, watching me carefully. When I do not move again, he sits me up, propping me on the table with pillows, and begins to scoop the food in the bowl onto a bent spoon before he lifts it to my mouth. I simply stare at him, my fear so strong, I almost choke on it, but as I open my mouth, all he does is carefully lay the spoon inside and feed me. At the first taste, I become ravenous, my hunger roaring to life, and he helps me eat the full bowl before bringing me another. My fear is still lingering in the back of my mind, but I quickly realize this is not a man, a human, to fear. This is a monster, and he has taken care of me for weeks. If he meant me harm, then he would have done it before now. It's what finally gets me to speak again.

"I'm full, thank you," I murmur, my manners slipping out.

His eyes jerk up to mine. "You are welcome." He cleans as I watch him, seemingly as nervous as I am before he turns to me. "Do you have anyone I can take you to? Any family? I was not sure if I should leave you with the humans or—"

"No!" I realize I almost shouted when he stumbles back, so I slow down and calm myself, breathing slowly. "I have no one," I tell him once I calm my beating heart.

It's a lie but also a truth.

Cora will think I am dead. Mother and Father never cared, but I can't break Cora's heart any more than I already have. No, it is better that she thinks I am dead. She can finally be happy and move on with her life and stop saving me all the time. Nothing good ever comes from it. "I have no one," I repeat.

We watch each other for a moment, wariness and interest sparking in his eyes. I am sure the same curiosity is in my gaze as well. After all, it's not every day you see a monster. We were told nothing but horror stories about them, yet here one stands, a monster who not only saved me but also nursed me back to health and protected me from those he thought were hunting me.

Maybe the monsters are not as evil as we were taught to think. The humans I know were certainly more cruel than I ever thought they could be.

Maybe everything was a lie.

I do not know how my sister survived here and how she went from distrusting the monsters to loving them. It is her strength, I realize. She has always been so strong, so sure, and she can withstand anything. I am not like her, and I never have been. Darkness closes in around me, a reminder of what I was trying to escape.

I would be better off dead.

It would be easier.

Then, for a moment, aqua eyes pierce that fog, and a deep voice pulls me back in. "What is your name?"

"Kai, Kai Black," I murmur, focusing on him to fight off the tidal wave of pain waiting to pull me under.

"I am Kaito. It is nice to meet you, Kai."

I swallow as I stare at him, unsure what to say or do. He turns away, tidying up before moving to my side once more and smiling down at me softly, revealing rows of sharp teeth that cause my eyes to widen.

"Rest now, Kai Black. I will protect you."

But who will protect me from him?

THREE

KAITO

The human, Kai, is different from the others.

She looks at me with fear, but not revulsion or disgust, and she spoke to me, not just around me, as if acknowledging I am a living being. It has been far too long since I conversed with anyone, either human or monster, and I find I like it. She needs to rest though. Her body is still healing. She had many broken bones, a deflated lung, and a cracked skull. It is a miracle she survived, or it would be if not for my magic, which was given to me by humans.

I am a curated creature, not a real monster like the other beings, but I am also not a man. Still, how could I ever be bad when I have the ability to save such a beautiful, pure creature and snatch her back from the brink of death?

I do not know, but I hover outside of my cabin, not wanting to disturb her since she seems unsure and fearful in my presence. She flinches when I draw too close, though I am unsure if she knows she does so. I make a note to move slower and not touch her without asking permission first, even if it is to sit her up to eat or drink. I guess I got used to her being out cold, where I could infuse her with my magic at regular intervals to speed up the healing process and pull her back from death.

Now that she is awake, she will need nutrients as well as time to heal. She will also need my protection here in the Dead Lands from those that would do her harm. It is clear she is . . . raw, which is the only word I can think of to describe her emotional state.

I check on her a few times, but she seems to be sleeping, which is good. Her body needs to rest, so while she slumbers, I move away from the cabin and the water, which is calling my name, and toward the woods that grow around my little sanctuary. The trees reach into the sky, blocking out the sunlight above me. I hear echoes of other monsters in the distance, but I ignore them. None ever venture this deep. They say it is home to a terrible creature.

They are not wrong.

Hunting is easy when you have talons and in no time, I have some smaller animals I can skin and make into a soup for her to ingest. I also harvest some plants to make a salve for her bruises and a tea that will stop any sickness or pain. I'm just heading back to the cabin, fearful of leaving her too long, when I see tracks.

They circle the perimeter of the trees, and they are too big to be caused by a lesser monster. No, this is something else. Crouching, I gather some of the dirt and sniff, wrinkling my nose at the smell. Yes, definitely a monster. Worried for my little human, I lay some traps that will alert me if others draw too close. It's long and tiresome work to circle the perimeter, but it will ensure her safety.

I am just setting the last trap when a scream pierces the air—a very human scream. Birds soar into the sky, silencing the forest around me. I race back before I can even think, hurrying through the door of the cabin, ready to defend Kai . . . only no one is there. Blinking, I carefully shut the door and frown. She thrashes around on the dining table I made into her bed, kicking at the furs. Her mouth is open in a continuous scream, and her eyes are clenched tightly shut.

She is going to hurt herself.

When I draw closer, I realize she is still asleep.

She is having a nightmare.

I carefully lay my hand on her head and push some magic into her, soothing her fighting soul. "Shh, Kai, I am here. You are safe," I tell her.

It takes some time, but she finally settles, breathing heavily as her eyes blink open. When she sees me, looks around, and understands what is happening, she crumbles. Water begins falling from her eyes and down her face as wounded noises escape her throat. The noises go straight to my hammering heart and rip it open.

I don't like them, and I don't like seeing her in distress, so I lift her up once more and embrace her like I have seen mothers do to their babes. "Shh, *amarta*, I am here. You are safe. It was just a dream," I tell her.

At first, she is stiff in my grip, but she soon relaxes. Those noises are muffled by my chest, and more water spills across my pecs as I rub her back to soothe her.

"Not just a dream. Memories," she mumbles.

I wonder what haunts my little *amarta* and how I can protect her from it.

I wonder if I'm capable of anything at all.

CHAPTER
FOUR
KAI

This cabin is quickly becoming my safe haven. Despite my initial fear of Kaito, it only takes me a few days to start to feel comfortable around him. It's difficult not to relax when he goes through so much trouble to take care of me. Every day, he brings me soup he makes himself, ensures I'm healing, and checks to make sure I'm okay. He never touches or even reaches for me without asking permission after the first time I flinched. He's safe and sweet, so the cabin becomes familiar and comfortable.

Because of that, the outside world, where the true monsters live, terrifies me all the more. At night, the sounds echo inside the cabin, making me shake in fear when the creatures make their calls. It doesn't take me long to realize I'm not in the Gilded Lands anymore, but it doesn't seem to be the Shadow Lands either, which leaves only one place—the Dead Lands.

Although I understand that someone has been lying to me and that the monsters aren't all bad since Kaito has done nothing but been nice when even my own kind hurt me, their screams and growls still frighten me. Kaito remains with me in the cabin each night, a silent sentinel that stops me from descending into a ball o fear. His monstrous but now familiar features bring me a semblance of peace, but as the sun rises on the seventh day I've been awake, my sentinel decides to speak, and his words bring back the fear.

"You should accompany me today," he says, glancing over from the fire where he stirs a pot, "and see where you're living."

My throat seizes, but I manage to croak, "I'd rather remain here."

Kaito straightens and studies me carefully. I shrink under his gaze, knowing he sees too much. "You can't remain in the cabin for the rest of your life. You're mostly healed now, and walking will do you good."

I clamp my lips shut and turn away from his earnest face. How strange that his appearance no longer bothers me. For all the stories I've been raised on, he should terrify me. He looks like any monster, but his kindness combats the fear I've been taught to feel. The outside world, however, doesn't have the same benefit.

"Kai," he murmurs, drawing my gaze back to him. "I understand if you're afraid, but I won't allow anything to harm you."

"Aren't there monsters larger than you?" I ask, studying him. He's big, but surely others are bigger.

"There are always greater monsters," he replies. "What matters is how we handle our fear of them."

Biting my lip, I look down, knowing my tone is morose. "I do not handle fear well, especially now."

He's beside me before I realize he's moved. Kaito offers me his hand, letting it hover in the air before me, imploring me to trust him. I only hesitate a few seconds before I slip my fingers into his slightly webbed ones, his cool skin making mine prickle.

"Fear is necessary to live. It's okay to be afraid, Kai." He squeezes my hand gently. "But it's not okay to sit in that fear for all our lives."

How do I explain that my life already ended? How do I tell this kind monster that my life was forfeited the day my little sister walked through the wall and sacrificed herself for me? How do I tell him that it ended time and time again with each atrocity I experienced, each time the king hurt me, and again when Cora returned with her monsters at her side?

How do I explain that I never wanted this second life and that I intended to end the first one so I'd never have to feel fear again?

"I fear the outside," I whisper, but what I really want to say is that I fear living. I fear what it will do to me if I walk the Earth with the knowledge that I don't intend to stay here forever. I don't want that pain. I didn't before I leapt off the castle, and I don't now. Presently, though, with this kind monster looking into my eyes, practically begging me to walk beside him, I war with my emotions. Yes, I am afraid, but I'm also deeply curious.

"I will be beside you for every step," Kaito offers like a gentleman.

I bend. "Will you . . . Will you stay close?" I ask weakly.

"As close as you feel comfortable with." He helps me to my feet and together, with slow, measured steps, we walk toward the front door of the cabin.

My body protests at first since it is the most I have moved, but it's soon drowned out by fear. My heart beats hard in my chest, thumping so loudly, I fear that Kaito will hear every nervous beat. I have to remind myself to breathe as we stop in front of the door, and I only remember when Kaito's fingers squeeze mine again. It also reminds me that we're holding hands, but I can't bring myself to release him, not when we're about to walk outside of my safe haven.

"Ready?" he asks, watching me carefully. "We'll go out, gather a few supplies, and come back in."

"No," I answer honestly, but I find myself nodding a second later.

I hold my breath as Kaito reaches forward and pushes the door. I flinch when it swings open, as if expecting every monster to come after me the moment I'm exposed to the outdoors. Nothing happens. There's no screech of some monstrous bird or growl of some creature waiting just outside to rip me apart.

"One step at a time," Kaito murmurs, waiting patiently for me to gather my bravery.

Listening to his soothing voice, I take a single step forward, and then another, and another, until I'm standing on the other side of the threshold. Taking a deep breath, I draw in the scent of the forest around me, the trees different than those at home. That's what makes me realize we're in the Dead Lands and not the Gilded Lands. The thought nearly causes me to freeze again, but I understand I couldn't have stayed there. The Gilded Lands are where I died. I'm nothing but a phantom now, waiting for death to finally find me, so it makes sense that I'd spend my time in the Dead Lands.

Despite what I know and what I've been told, the Dead Lands aren't as . . . well, dead as I expected. The trees are great, tall things that look both burnt and alive. They have dark leaves that speckle the branches, giving them a haunting quality that makes me shiver, and although the sun is high in the sky, it barely penetrates the canopy, casting everything in shadow. Some of the shadows shift and I flinch, but I realize they are only small creatures I don't recognize living amongst the leaves.

"It has started coming back to life," Kaito says as he leads me a little farther out, never pushing. He encourages me, but he doesn't force me to move. He waits for me to be ready. "Since the new monarch destroyed the wall, it's allowed the Dead Lands to find new life."

"I didn't expect it to be so . . ."

"Dark?" Kaito watches me closely, as if I'm going to flee at any moment. I still might.

"Alive," I reply, meeting his eyes. "It's all so alive."

Kaito nods and looks into the trees. "There is much that the Gilded Lands kept secret or perverted the truth about this world, such as the Dead Lands being dead or the monsters being bad. I've learned that monsters come in any form. It isn't how someone looks that makes them a monster, it's how they act."

I bite my lip at the profoundness of his statement. It resonates with me deeply, and I find myself squeezing his hand this time, offering comfort. "I understand," I rasp, looking up at him.

For a moment, our eyes meet and hold, but fear still makes me look down and hide from his searching gaze. The moment some-thing twitches in my chest, I'm reminded of my life, of the pain I live with, and I can't bear to look into eyes that stare at me as if I'm not broken. I'm no longer whole and salvageable. I am a million shat-tered pieces floating in a wooden bowl. At any given moment, what's left of me will spill out and there will be no more broken pieces to mourn. I'm not worthy of such a look. Not anymore.

Outside the cabin, just on the brink of where the forest starts to darken, Kaito reveals a small garden hidden by trees. I stare at the lush plants growing vegetables in surprise. He plucks a few, passing them to me before moving on to another plant. Once we both have an armful of food, he leads me back inside. The moment my feet cross the threshold, I feel safer and as if I'm able to breathe deeply again.

"That wasn't so bad, was it?" Kaito asks as he sets the vegetables on the counter where he plans to cut them.

"It was terrifying," I admit, emptying my own arms. "But . . . I did not mind so long as you were with me. The darkness unnerves me."

"There is good in everything," Kaito muses, beginning to chop the vegetables he brought in. No doubt he plans to add it to the large, boiling pot in the fireplace. "Even in darkness."

His words touch something deep inside me. The darkness has only felt like darkness to me. What must it feel like to see something else there? To be able to see in the darkness and live in it? I can't even fathom such a thought. I miss the light. My darkness is too thick for even monsters.

Rolling my shoulders, I pick up another small knife and start to slice a different vegetable. Kaito looks over at me in surprise.

"You don't have to help," he says, watching me carefully.

"You've shown me nothing but kindness," I reply. "The very least I can do is help you prepare dinner."

We spend the next few minutes in silence, only the sounds of our chopping breaking up the quiet. It's a comfortable companionship, so comfortable in fact, it makes me wonder exactly what I'm doing here if I don't plan to use this second life as anything but a stepping stone toward my eventual death. Still, Kaito makes something inside me force in air, even if I don't want to. Perhaps it's simply his kindness or the way he treats me like I'm a porcelain figurine in need of repair. Or, perhaps, it's the way he saw me flinch and changed his entire demeanor to make me more comfortable. Either way, there's a speck of light in the darkness because of him.

I don't know how it makes me feel.

I don't understand it or him or anything inside me. My emotions war with each other, begging for attention, but above all, that darkness suffocates me. It drags me deeper until that speck of light is so small, it might as well be forever out of reach.

But it's there. Shadows, it's there.

"You know, before I met you," I say, glancing up at Kaito, "I thought all monsters were, well, monstrous."

Kaito smiles. "And I thought all humans were cruel." He bumps his shoulder gently against mine, and it doesn't even make me flinch. "Seems we were both wrong."

That speck dances in the darkness like a ballerina on stage.

What I could have.

What I never will . . .

CHAPTER
FIVE
WEYLAND

Her scent finds me deep within the Dead Lands, the intoxicating aroma stroking down my fur and making me howl with desire. I know it's a female by the deep hints of femininity within the scent, the notes rolling together until I can pick out her gender. She smells like elderberries and the freshest of linens, a mixture that makes me imagine white sheets stained with the berries. The scent drags me away from my hunt and demands I follow it.

Who am I to deny it?

I am but a beast, a slave to my desires, and the scent beckons. I follow it before I'm conscious of doing so, running through the Dead Lands at a pace most creatures wouldn't be able to maintain, but I'm motivated by the scent and her allure. I run for days as long stretches of time bleed together. I lose count of how many days I run. The ache in my bones is easily ignored when I think of what awaits me at the end of the scent trail and whom I might meet. I don't know her or what she looks like, but I know I need to see her. My instincts demand it.

I run through the forest, across rivers deeper than I am tall, and pass creatures that look up in curiosity at the lycan racing past them, half afraid I'm being chased by something more imposing. I leap over smaller ravines and run until my legs scream at me to stop and my muscles beg for a break.

Still, I run.

The scent brings me closer to the Shadow Lands than I'd like. I normally stay as far away from humans as I possibly can. After all, they'd happily skin me and use me as a rug if they ever caught me. Today, I risk it in my quest for her, for the source of the scent—elderberries and fresh linen.

It drags me closer until a small cabin appears in front of me with soft light glowing from within. It looks cozy and quaint. Built roughly from wood and only one story tall, it's not much, but it looks comfy enough. Moss grows along the trunks used to build the house, giving it a light musky aroma that is somehow still pleasant. A few curtain-covered windows appear on the sides, and there's a single door in the front of it. I assume there's another one on the back. No monster would allow themselves to be trapped by one door.

The scent is stronger the closer I draw, but I'm not the only one who has smelled her. That is very clear.

A dozen other monsters surround the cabin, their maws salivating over the smell wafting from inside. They are a mixture of beasts that I can't remember the proper names for. She called them all here, their need to consume her so strong, they crossed the Dead Lands just as I did.

But she's mine. Whoever she is, I won't let them claim her.

The cabin door slams open, and a water creature steps out with a vicious snarl on his face as he leaps to battle them. He throws himself forward with a worthy bellow, alone, and then she appears in the doorway behind him. The light behind her almost blinds me, never mind her beauty. Her hair is a tawny darkness, intersected with bright orange flames near the front. Her eyes are bright and flash with fear and determination. She's tall, willowy, and beautiful but also scared. Her limbs shake in fear, and her eyes are wide with intense emotions. She holds a large club awkwardly in her hands, as if she's not sure how to use it. Despite her fear, she screams for the water creature and holds the club high as if she's ready to use it. My heart thumps at the sight, my claws growing longer as I crouch with a snarl that silences the trees and life around me.

Mate.

The echo is loud in my mind, a ricocheting thought that dances from one side of my mind to the other, and it seals her fate.

"Kaito!" she screams when the monsters attack, her small hands swinging the club when a smaller monster gets too close to the doorway she huddles in, half in the light of the cabin and half in the darkness of the woods. It hisses at her but backs off, confused that such a fearful creature would dare fight back.

Mate!

With a snarl, I leap into the fray, attacking the creatures that would dare attack my *bacca*. How dare they? My teeth are bared as I lurch forward. The water creature sees me and weighs me up, and when he realizes I'm helping, he accepts without a second thought. The Dead Lands have one very simple rule—you're either enemy or ally.

Today, I'm an ally, but I plan to be so much more.

The woman stumbles back in terror when I appear, her eyes so wide, I fear she'll never blink again. I rip one of the horrible monsters apart and turn to her to see the horror in the pupils of her eyes. She fears me. My mate fears me.

"I will not hurt you," I growl, and she flinches. I realize this is something that will take time because her fear is so palpable, I choke on it. I am a beast of a creature, so I need to be careful with my fragile mate who is very clearly not a monster. I soften my expression. "I will never hurt you, *bacca*," I murmur, trying to cover my canines with my lips so I don't scare her further. "Stay inside."

With a angry howl, I leap back in the fray, tearing the enemy creatures limb from limb and reminding those who may still come

29

that she is spoken for and that there are two creatures protecting her here.

My beautiful mate.

My elderberry. My *bacca*.

The blood of the creatures who dare come for her stains my lips as I rip them into pieces.

CHAPTER
SIX
KAI

We hear them before we see them. We'd just cleared away the evening meal, and Kaito is stoking the fire when the first call rents the air. I leap to my feet, stumbling at the beastly sound. Kaito is by my side in a second, clutching my arm to help me stand, our eyes going to the door.

"Kaito," I whisper.

"It's fine. Whatever it is will just be passing through or curious. You're safe," he murmurs softly. I relax slightly, but when a second call comes and then a third, I whimper in fear, backing away. The hair on my arm rises at the growls that seem to surround the cabin, almost permeating the walls, as if they are looking for a way in.

It's clear Kaito is not the reason they are here. It is me.

"Kaito?" I wrap my arms around myself, scared beyond belief. I want to die, but not like this. I don't want to be ripped apart by monsters. I want to go on my terms.

Hurrying to me, he cups my face, making my eyes widen. "Stay here. Stay out of sight. I will deal with this," he orders, his voice deeper than I have ever heard it. He almost vibrates with power. "I promise you, Kai, I will protect you. Tell me you believe me."

"I believe you," I whisper, and I do. His determination to protect me is in his eyes and every line of his face. This monster, this man who saved me, nursed me back to health, and showed me nothing but kindness would go out there and kill anyone who dared to even think of hurting me. Something about it gives me strength I didn't know I had anymore.

"I need a weapon," I murmur. "Just in case."

Frowning, he searches my face, but the growls are getting louder. Dropping his hands, he hurries to the corner of the room, and in a wooden chest I did not see prior, he digs about before revealing a crudely carved wooden club.

"I use it to get rid of snortwegllers, but it will do. Hopefully, you won't need it. Stay down." He hands it to me, searching my gaze once more before opening the cabin door and charging out with a snarl.

I hesitate, wanting to do as he asked, but I can hear the snarls, and something inside me pangs with worry for him. I need to see if he is okay so I hurry to the door, but I am unable to step over the threshold, my fear holding me back.

Monsters blot out any view of the Dead Lands I might have had before. They surge toward the cabin and Kaito with a singular purpose. They are small, about knee height, but most of their faces are taken up by huge mouths with razor-sharp teeth, almost like piranhas. They have four eyes, six arms, and move faster than I've ever seen anything move. They almost create a wave of monsters that envelop him completely. Covering my mouth in horror, I search for Kaito in the throng and find him holding his own despite the massive wave. He kicks and shoves them away, ripping them apart. Tentacles suddenly shoot from his sides and sweep out to throw hundreds of the creatures back. I blink. I cannot look away from him. Somehow, he grows impossibly bigger, his furious roar rumbling the ground. He's magnificent and terrifying at the same time. My sweet nurturer is gone, and in his place is a monster.

Gripping the club harder, I swallow as another noise reaches me. Something smashes through the underbrush before the cabin.

Whatever coming, it's huge, and I turn to see what it is. Before I can, a monster sneaks up on me, appearing out of nowhere, drawing all of my attention. I smash the club into it, almost screaming when it bites down on the wood with huge teeth before I fling it away. It takes surprisingly little effort to throw it. More turn toward me, and I have to focus on swinging and smashing to keep them back. I become so lost in the fight that I don't notice the wolf man until he's leaping into the masses before me.

My eyes widen, and I barely breathe, barely move, as its eyes lock on mine. I have no doubt it's ready to rip me apart and eat my organs, just as I've always been told all monsters do. Kaito either doesn't notice or is too busy to. I want to run away and scream, but I'm locked in his gaze, held hostage by the bright gold of his eyes.

Terror almost makes my heart leap out of my chest. My club won't do much against such a monster.

"I will not hurt you," he snarls, or at least that's what it sounds like he snarls, though it's hard to hear over the hammering of my heart. "I will never hurt you, *bacca*. Stay inside."

Unsure what to do or say, I watch as the huge wolf man turns and roars at the monsters before diving into their masses and ripping them apart one by one. I want to slam the door closed and hide, but I cannot leave Kaito. He has my loyalty. I cannot leave him when he needs me, so I stay here, locked in fear, fighting back any creatures that grow too close. Even that small rebellion costs me, my bones shaking so badly, exhaustion starts to close in at the edges of my vision. There's been so much adrenaline that my brain now fights to stay coherent.

The tide slowly turns as the wolf and Kaito work through the attacking monsters, their bodies littering the area until they realize they cannot win. With synchronized roars, the small monsters retreat into the woods. Panting, I check over Kaito, who only has a few small wounds on his body. I'm relieved that he's okay. I drop the club to the ground, the weapon suddenly too heavy to hold up, and then Kaito glances at me.

So does the wolf.

Two sets of eyes and two sets of expectations.

Two monsters.

Fear finally wins. I slam the door and lock it despite this being Kaito's home. I hurry over to the bed and wrap the fur around me like a child as I collapse in exhaustion and terror. Old memories fill my head, ones of similar eyes watching me and taking what they wanted.

It's too much.

I hide beneath the blankets like the weak creature I am.

DAYS PASS LIKE THIS. I huddle alone inside the cabin, my terror once more taking over. I am nothing more than a whimpering creature. Kaito is outside. I hear him, his gentle voice carrying through the door. I can almost see him imploring me to let him in, to let him take care of me, but it's the other one who is too much. The wolf stays with him, watching me with bright-red, hungry eyes and sharp teeth.

They bring me food and water and leave it on the doorstep, which I barely reach out and grab. I'm too ashamed to look into their eyes. My own self-deprecation fills my heart with hate for what I have become, for what I used to be, and for the man who did this to me. I tend to the fire and eat and drink, though I taste nothing. I mostly sleep when the nightmares will allow it. I peer through the window every now and again to see them clearing away the bodies and tending to their wounds before I duck out of sight.

I am weak.

I am useless.

I am broken.

It repeats in my head like a mantra.

You're nothing, the king's voice says, following me into my dreams. Even there, I cannot escape the monsters coming for me.

My eyes close as I huddle into the nest I have made near the rear of the cabin, away from the door and window. My club is held loosely in one hand as I fall into the darkness.

Hands slide under my dress. Mortification and shame color my face, which heats as the crowd looks on and laughs. I should be used to his demonstrations and games. I want to close my eyes and retreat into my head, but the scars on my back remind me of what a foolish rebellion that would be. He would see it and punish me. No, I have no choice but to endure. My teeth clench together so hard, I feel them cracking, and my heart speeds up until I almost hyperventilate.

The king's thick hand slides into my underwear, touching me in places I had given freely to only one man once before—a man I planned to marry, not this cruel one.

I must flinch, but I don't mean to. I swear it.

He freezes, gripping me until I cry out. "Bring the whip. This one still needs to be broken."

"No, please!" I scream.

My own scream wakes me. Tears flow down my face unchecked, and my throat is raw from screaming. That's when I hear knocking at the door. I'm surprised they didn't just kick it down, but I'm thankful they did not.

"I'm okay," I croak. I know they hear me because the knocking stops, but pain lashes at me. I am so broken, I can't even sleep. Memories cling to me even now, making me want to scrub at myself and scream.

That's when another noise penetrates my hazy senses—soft, beautiful singing.

A deep voice for sure, but no less mesmerizing. One of them is singing, and I don't think it's Kaito since I heard him singing the other day while he was cooking and it sounded like birds screeching. No, it must be the wolf. Lifting my head, I slide closer to the door, needing to hear better. Something about the sound settles my racing heart and soothes the jagged edges of my soul.

It grows in strength, and I almost weep until I realize my back is to the door to listen better. When it stops, I almost want to demand he carry on. For that short amount of time, I thought of nothing but his singing and the story he was weaving.

"Are you okay?" His voice still has a slight growl, as if he cannot help it, but it's also probably as soft as he can make it.

"Please don't stop. Sing, talk to me, anything, just distract me," I beg before snapping my mouth shut.

There's silence for a moment, and I almost shrink away in shame when his soft, growling voice comes again. "The vines are coming down at the wall. It means monsters are free. Some have left the Dead Lands in search of a better life, though I don't know if they will find it. Most are still scared of humans, and most humans still have not crossed the barrier, but I heard rumors, even deep in my den, that the new queen plans to change that and integrate the races." Cora. My heart softens at the mention of my strong, willful sister. If anyone can change everything, it's her. "I do not know how it will go, but things are changing with the humans, or so they say. Monsters are growing bolder, the magic here is free, and the land seems to be healing." He keeps talking, and I want to ask questions but I am too afraid, so I just settle back and listen to him share information about a land I planned to leave.

"The new queen is doing well. She holes up between castles here and there. Her monsters are always around her. I hope this means change, but I also know this could end badly. Only time will tell if history plans to repeat itself. I hear whispers that not everyone is happy with the change." I almost feel him shrugging through the wood. "It is better this way though, I think. Things should change. We have been trapped for too long." He sighs. "I know all about that. Even amongst monsters, I am an anomaly, the only one left—a lycan without a pack. Most can no longer change or have accepted the way they are. I seem to be stuck between. What is left of my pack mates who did not perish or give into the darkness rotting our souls have become nothing but beasts you hear the faint howls of. They died in an attack on our home. Others saw our weakness, our dwindling numbers, and wanted the safety of our dens. It is all about survival in the Dead Lands, or at least it was. I lost them all. I was the only one who survived, and I have been wandering ever since, alone and lost, almost giving into the monster like the others until the other day, when I smelled you. Something in me refused to give up and told me that I was needed. I'm glad I came when I did, and hopefully, when you feel like you can, you will open this door and we can get to know each other better."

I turn my head, pressing my cheek to the wood. I would like that. I misjudged him. He is just as alone and lost as I am. How could he ever be evil? He saved me. However, fear is a fickle and monstrous emotion to conquer, and like wars, it is fought one battle at a time.

His voice tapers off, and he slowly begins to sing once more, filling the night with a story of woe, loss, beauty, and love.

My eyes close once more as he sings, and I slip into a peaceful, dreamless sleep.

CHAPTER
SEVEN
KAITO

It has been days since I have seen Kai. I miss her hesitant smile, having her eyes on me, and being able to take care of her. I know she is struggling with the same thing that makes her fearful of touch and change, but I hope she trusts me and herself enough to venture out soon. Until then, I collect wood, food, and water to leave for her like clockwork. The lycan, who told me his name is Weyland, helps. I was wary at first and hesitant about what he wants from my Kai, but he has proven to be nothing but dependable. He gives her space, sings to her when her nightmares become too much, and has never once pushed her.

He is slicing wood with his claws while I prepare a fish when I hear the creak of the door opening. I freeze. I want to leap to my feet and rush to her, but I do not look at her, instead focusing on the fish. I know Weyland heard her too, his ears twitching before he continues slicing slower and softer, as if worried he'll scare her even with that.

For a moment, I hear nothing else, and then there is a shuffle. It is torture, worse than anything the king did to me, to not look, until her shadow falls across me. Only then do I lift my head and meet her hesitant eyes. Her hands are clasped before her, twisted in worry. She shakes ever so slightly, and her eyes are too wide, but she is here.

She is so brave and even more beautiful.

"Hi," she says softly.

"Hi, are you hungry?" I ask, unsure what to say, not wanting her to retreat. Weyland moves closer, placing wood into the fire we built. She eyes him with a hesitant smile but keeps her distance, her shoulders tense.

"We have not been properly introduced. I am Weyland." He holds out his hand like the humans do, his fingers tipped with long, sharp black nails and covered in the same fur as his body.

She watches it for a while before rounding her shoulders and laying her hand in his. It's a big deal for her, and watching her overcome her fear makes something inside me twist. I watch him shudder and close his eyes.

"I'm Kai. Thank you . . . well, for everything."

"Of course, *bacca*," he purrs.

Blushing, she pulls her hand away and frowns at him, but when she moves to my side, I almost grin in victory. "I was hoping to wash in the river if that's okay?" she asks me.

"Of course. I'll escort you and watch the area," I offer, slowly climbing to my feet so as not to scare her.

"I will come as well," Weyland states.

"Oh, um, great," she murmurs.

Together, the three of us cross the tiny distance to the shallow river, and when she eyes us expectantly, we both turn away from her. I hear the shucking of her clothes and ignore the tightening in my body, ashamed of myself for wanting her when she is so clearly suffering. When I hear the splash of water, I relax a little, scanning the trees for any more attacks. I had grown bold to think no one would find her and come for her.

It won't happen again.

While she washes herself in the river, we keep watch, our backs to her to give her privacy. "What happened to her?" Weyland murmurs too quietly for her to hear.

"I do not know. Something terrible, I think," I reply. "She was near death when I saved her. She bears many scars and is fearful of touch or fast movements."

"Then I will move slowly." He nods, and we share a look. We are still wary of one another, but it is clear he wants to keep her safe, and Kai needs it so I do not fight him, despite how much I want to keep her all to myself.

My head snaps up and Weyland's ears twitch when we hear screams in the distance. We share another look, but Kai seems oblivious. It was far away, so maybe her human hearing did not pick it up. For that, I am thankful. "That was a monster's scream," I mutter. Neither of us move to find what made the sound. Once, I would have, but I cannot leave my Kai defenseless, so I stay.

"Not like any I have ever heard. That was fear. Nothing makes monsters fearful," Weyland murmurs. "Not even when facing off with other monsters. Things are changing in these woods. We must be vigilant."

I nod my head in agreement, worried about what is coming.

"Done," Kai calls hesitantly, and we both turn toward her.

She shimmers under the foggy sun, her orange and black hair sparkling. Kai's eyes are bright and wide, and she wears a soft smile on her lips.

She is magnificent, and I know whatever is coming, it will not keep me from her.

Nothing will.

EIGHT

For the first time since Weyland appeared, I leave the cabin door open for both of them. They hesitate to enter at first, unsure if I need more time, but they have done nothing but protect me. While Weyland's visage is more terrifying at first than Kaito's was, he works hard to appear nonthreatening, moving slowly and keeping his growls to a minimum. He keeps his distance, understanding that I'm still working through my fear.

With the two monsters plus me inside the little cabin, it suddenly starts to feel smaller but no less comfortable. The fire burning in the fireplace keeps it warm, but surprisingly, the two men do the same. Though more growls and roars echo outside the walls, I'm less afraid with my protectors here, even if they bear resemblances to the monsters I sometimes glimpse outside.

I don't sleep as much, and I engage in conversation with them, but the memories come at night and more often than not, I wake to Weyland singing to me and Kaito watching me with a sad expression that breaks my heart.

"What's it like?" Weyland asks a few days later, his bright eyes watching me carefully. It should make me feel like prey, but instead, it's like a warm caress that traces my skin. He's sitting on the opposite side of the cabin, his fingers curled to hide his claws—something for my benefit, I'm sure. His lips cover his wicked teeth even as he speaks, no doubt another thing he does for me.

"What is what like?" I ask, glancing up at him from where I stir the pot. Kaito produced a larger pot once Weyland joined us, so now our soups are plenty big enough to feed all three of us. The wolf has a large appetite.

"The Gilded Lands." Weyland tilts his head. "Surely that's where you come from. You sparkle so brightly, and Kaito said that's where he found you."

I freeze, the reminder of the Gilded Lands making my heart stop briefly before I urge it to restart and pretend as if that name has no bearing on my soul and doesn't haunt my every waking moment.

The bruises have healed but, like my body, my soul and mind will always bear the scars of what happened to me within those golden walls.

Kaito watches from the table where he chops vegetables for the stew. His movements slow, as if he's listening, but he doesn't turn to look.

My mouth is dry, but I force the words out anyway. "I was born and raised in the Shadow Lands," I reply. "That was the place my family called home."

I told Kaito I have no family, and while I did that out of self-preservation, I don't know if I should reveal exactly who my family is. Cora will be well-known by now, her will and strength growing the longer she holds the kingdom, so that secret should remain with me for a while.

Also, a small part of me worries that if Kaito knows Cora is my sister, he will be . . . disappointed. She is brilliant, strong, powerful, and everything I am not.

"Do the Shadow Lands sparkle as much as the other one?" Weyland asks, watching me carefully. Something tells me he can see more than I'm revealing, but I don't question him right now. I don't know if I can bear that inspection.

"Have you never seen them?" I respond, tilting my head. "If the wall has fallen, surely you've visited."

Weyland shifts uncomfortably. "I am young by many monsters' standards. I was born after the wall was created, and I have not yet had the strength to visit lands that will not welcome me, but any land you once called home intrigues me."

My eyes crinkle and I look down, intent on hiding my reaction to the wolf. Both he and Kaito stir something inside me, something that frightens me, and I don't want to look too closely at the feeling.

Not yet anyway.

"The Shadow Lands do not sparkle," I begin. "As the name implies, we were in the shadows of two realms, the Gilded Lands and the Dead Lands. We knew nothing of either, received nothing from either, and we were treated as disposable rats by the Gilded Lands. It was a cruel life, but there was some good there, bright spots of time that make it seem okay." Like Cora. Like Merryl. Even the thought of him brings both grief and happiness for what we once had, for what we could have had, and it is only then I realize I never mourned for the life I lost.

"Women were not treated kindly. Our only hope was to marry well, to find someone who loved us just enough not to beat us, but while the Shadow Lands wears its cruelty on the surface, the Gilded Lands hides it beneath." Weyland and Kaito are fully listening now with something heated in their eyes. "There, the streets glitter with the gold of all the wealth stolen from the Shadow Lands, but beneath all that shine, monsters bear human faces."

The words echo in my mind. *Monsters bear human faces.* After all, isn't that what I'm learning? It's not so much appearance as what lies underneath.

"I should like to show you the Dead Lands," Weyland says after we're silent for long seconds. "Though the name implies it's long since buried, there is much beauty in this realm, especially now that it's growing back. We could protect you and show you how the rest of the world looks."

There's earnestness in his gaze, his expression appeasing even if his teeth glint in the low light as he speaks. With each passing day, I grow less afraid of the wolf who tries his hardest to be gentle for me. He's here to protect me. Each night I wake with a nightmare, I also wake to him singing softly under his breath for me, calming my frantic heartbeat. And Kaito, beautiful, kind Kaito always makes sure I'm well taken care of and comfortable. Both of these monsters have shown more kindness than I've ever witnessed outside of my sister. I don't know why, but I do not question it.

"I think I would like that," I whisper, looking down quickly, but I don't miss the sparkles that dance in their eyes at my answer. Their hope makes me afraid to let them down. I don't want to be so afraid that I can't step foot outside this cabin. I want to be able to keep those sparkles alive, but my brokenness is a constant reminder of what sort of monster I might be.

"You grew up in the Shadow Lands," Kaito says as he moves over to the pot to add more vegetables. "But I found you in the Gilded Lands."

I nod. "You did."

He meets my eyes. "I saw you fall from the castle into the river."

Weyland tenses at his words. Clearly, it's new information for him. I'm stiff as I perch on the edge of the chair, my eyes dancing between them. Panic begins to wind through me that they will figure it out and leave me here alone.

"Someone pushed you?" Weyland asks, his voice growly. "Who hurt you? Who did such a thing?"

His fury doesn't frighten me like it should, perhaps because it's directed at this phantom threat he perceives, but I can't allow him to be angry at something that isn't real outside of my own body.

"No," I reply. "No one pushed me from the castle."

Silence.

I can't bear to look at either one of them, so I stare down at my fingers where they wring together, desperate to distract myself from the weight in the room as they ponder my words.

When strong fingers touch my chin and lift it, I meet Kaito's too perceptive eyes. His gaze traces my face, stroking along my features as if he's using his hand, but his fingers remain gently on my chin.

"Did you stumble, Kai?" he asks carefully. When I blink up at him and shake my head, he sucks in a breath.

The air inside the cabin grows even heavier.

The weight of what they suddenly understand chokes me.

I am a coward, and I chose death rather than life.

I am broken.

"You wear your pain on your skin," Weyland murmurs. "I can see it as brightly as any paint. It does not fade. It will not. You are beautiful no matter the cracks in your heart."

Those words crash into me and sink in, and I feel tears pooling in the corners of my eyes. Such tender words, so kind and so unlike anything I've encountered before.

Kaito kneels before me, stooping to my level. He doesn't touch me, but when I reach for his hand, he freely gives it, the webbing between his fingers somehow giving me comfort—a reminder of what he is and the softness of these monsters versus the humans who once touched me.

"There is an important question," he says, his gaze soft. He's as gentle with me as he always is, but despite my admission, he doesn't look at me with pity. He still looks at me the same, as if I'm some flower that needs tending to. "Do you want to live?"

I open my mouth and close it, the words too thick to come at first. I want to give him the answer he wants, but something in his eyes begs me not to lie and I find I cannot. After swallowing a few times, I'm finally able to rasp, "I don't know yet."

The weight is still heavy, but some of it eases, as if they both feared I would say no. Something tells me that they would offer comfort no matter what, but my heart aches with the knowledge that I can't give any answer with certainty. When I jumped, I knew I wanted to die, but now . . .

"I don't want to go back to my home," I admit, looking down again, my wounds too raw and exposed to meet their eyes. "I'm more terrified of humans than I am of monsters." A small chuckle slips out at those words, at the preposterousness of it, and yet it's true. It's humorless, desperate, and afraid, and it reminds me that I'm in the presence of souls kinder than I've ever known.

"Is there someone we can . . ." Weyland takes a deep breath. "I would avenge your pain if you'd let me, *bacca*. You only have to ask."

His words remind me of the moment the king died, when my sister defeated the true monster, but I can't speak about those wounds yet. I can't speak about the trauma I wrap around my shoulders like a shawl, the pain weighing me down and making me feel as if I'm trekking through mud most days. It's still too soon, and I can't bear to speak of such atrocities in this cabin, my safe haven.

"There is no one left to hunt down," I tell him, glancing up. "But had there been, I might have accepted your offer."

What peace it would bring to watch the king be ripped apart by Weyland. What satisfaction it could have brought. Unless it didn't. I have no way of knowing what will ease my pain. I only know that if anyone deserved to suffer, it was the king.

Weyland offers me his hand, and although I'm already holding Kaito's with my left one, I reach for Weyland's with my right. Where Kaito is like the cool depths of the ocean, Weyland resembles the warmth of the deep forest, their contrasting feelings absorbing into my fingers and spreading. The tightness in my chest loosens just a little with their kindness, as if getting such a small admission out into the open lifts some of the weight.

I realize then that Cora saw something she was never prepared to see if her own monsters were half as kind as these. It makes me question everything I know and rethink my view of the world, and I relax into their touch instead of pulling away like I might have before. But then I pull back from both of them because although I may be healing, it's still frightening to bear my soul to these two monsters.

I opened up just a little and let them into the barest, darkest corner of my soul where nothing but cobwebs and pain lives, and for the first time in forever, the beginning of a spark starts to glow.

CHAPTER
NINE
WEYLAND

Her deep, gentle breaths are like cannons in my ears, each one reminding me of the pain she's suffered. We don't know what trauma she's survived or what monsters have harmed her, but it stirs fury inside me.

For her to have jumped . . .

"Your growls are going to wake her," Kaito warns softly, keeping his voice low so he doesn't do the same.

I immediately stop, not having realized I was growling in the first place. "My apologies," I murmur, shaking my head. "It's only—"

"I know," Kaito replies, his eyes trailing over to the beautiful woman as she sleeps.

She looks serene, missing the fear that mars her face when she's awake, as if waiting for an attack, one that will never come. I will ensure it until my dying breath. Although that fear sometimes infiltrates her dreams, right now, she is at peace, and it settles something inside me. She's content at this moment. It would do no good to go after the monsters that haunt her.

Her brilliant hair is spread out on the furs that make up her bed, a perfect nest created by Kaito. If not for the fact that he saved my *bacca*, I might have been jealous. What I wouldn't give to make her a nest, though one day, I hope to make one big enough to nestle more than just her inside.

"She said there was no one to hunt down," I say, glancing over at Kaito again, my brows furrowed. "My fury demands that someone should pay for her pain."

Kaito nods. "Perhaps that pain has already been avenged, wolf, but sometimes pain is too great to eradicate with one single action. Healing is a long process."

I tilt my head, studying this monster that isn't quite a monster. I realized it from the first moment I saw him but didn't think about it for long since the need to protect my mate was more important.

"You speak of healing as if you've done so," I comment, watching him.

When Kaito looks over at me, something about his stare unnerves me. "You're a smart monster, Weyland. I'm sure you've figured out certain details about me."

I hesitate. This is Kaito's home. I do not wish to be kicked out of it and away from my bacca. "Not monster, not human," I say quietly, admitting that I've learned his secret. "But it means nothing to me. All that matters is that you are kind to Kai and you protect her."

Kaito blinks at me and then looks back over at Kai. "You are a different kind of monster, Weyland. It makes sense that she would like you." He sighs. "I was the king's first experiment. I escaped into the sewers long ago around the Gilded Lands, but I found myself here, never fitting in with either side. I know plenty about healing because it took me a long time to realize that I didn't need to march back into the Gilded Lands to slaughter every human I came across. It took me years and years. It could take her even longer."

Fear has me shifting—the fear that I could still lose my mate to something I cannot fight, to something I cannot protect her from. I only just found her. What I wouldn't give to keep her safe and warm and whole. What I wouldn't give to heal her broken heart.

If I could, I would take her past and scars as my own.

"So what do we do to help?" I ask, knowing I'm no expert in this process. Lycans handle things with violence and fighting, but this situation will take neither of those things.

"Be gentle. Be patient." Kaito looks toward Kai with the deepest longing. I understand how he feels. "And above all, we should help her feel as if life is worth living by reminding her that she isn't alone."

I reach toward Kai. She doesn't flinch in her sleep. Her guard is down, and it makes me realize I'm reaching without asking for consent so I tuck my hand away. When she's ready, she'll search for my touch, but until then, I'll be her gentle protector, her songbird, anything she needs me to be.

I will spend the rest of my life singing away her nightmares, and if that is all I'll ever get to be, then that will be more than enough.

"We show her what life can be," I say, making the promise to myself as much as I am to Kaito. "We love her."

Kaito doesn't answer, but I know he feels the same. We will be the light to her darkness. There is plenty of darkness in me, and I fear that it will spill into her own, but the brightness she brings gives me hope that I can be the gentle beast she needs.

Until she needs a violent one.

Something tells me that day may come sooner than we're prepared for.

I settle into my spot and calm myself by watching her chest rise and fall.

She's breathing.

She's alive.

CHAPTER

TEN

KAI

It has been almost a week since the attack, and I find myself dusting off my behind as I stand after tending to the dying fire. The sun shines even through the fog, and animals call in the distance—not big beasts, but the little ones that inhabit the forest. Everything is good. I am sleeping and eating. I do not feel afraid at this moment. As usual, Weyland's and Kaito's eyes go to me from where they are placing traps.

I have been learning to be helpful as much as possible. Weyland showed me how to prepare fish the other day, though his claws made it easier than my blunt knife, which I have hidden in the folds of my dress. As they work on our protection, I work on our cabin, making it homier. I feel like I have a purpose, at least a little one, and that has helped me regain a bit of strength and confidence.

"You mentioned showing me this world. I think I would like to do that today," I murmur, but they still hear me. They always hear me. I could whisper that I need their help into the forest and they would always find me. Without even meaning to, they are destroying my walls one by one with their kindness and understanding, never pushing me. Even with Merryl, he pressured me a little, never more than I was comfortable with, but the stress was there nevertheless. My monsters want nothing but to help me. Maybe it is time I let them. I cannot die now without at least knowing I tried to live. Not for me, but for them.

"Are you sure?" Kaito, my soft protector, asks, searching my gaze as he washes his hands.

Steeling myself, I roll my shoulders back and smile as much as I can. It's soft but still there, and he grins widely at it. "I'm sure."

"Let me clean up, and then we can show you around. Just some close places I know of." He looks at Weyland to check and nods.

Weyland jumps up swiftly before freezing, his eyes going to me in panic, but I simply smile. He moved fast, but I know he would never hurt me. Still, guilt fills his eyes before he relaxes. Hunching his shoulders so he seems smaller, he moves to the water and washes his hands and fur before turning back to us. Holding out his hand to me, he swallows nervously and waits.

Strong, I tell myself. *Be strong.*

Taking a deep breath, I place one hand in Weyland's and my other hand in Kaito's, and we set off into the surrounding woods together.

I see hope in their hearts and eyes.

They want to save me, and part of me hopes they can.

"WHERE ARE WE GOING?" I finally ask as they lead me through the woods. We stop every once in a while for one of them to show me an animal, a plant, or a tree. I don't know what I was expecting, but it wasn't this place so filled with life. Even in the shadows and fog, it thrives. The darkness does not keep it down, and maybe that's what they are trying to show me.

I can thrive, even in the dark.

"You'll see. We're almost there." Weyland shares a grin with Kaito, and I simply smile and nod, trusting them to know where they are going because I was lost after the first minute of plunging into the forest. Every single direction looks the same to me, and I know I couldn't find the cabin even if I wanted to.

It means I have to put a lot of trust in them, which is a big step for me, but I'm determined to see this through. If not for me, then for them.

They tug me along after them, deeper into the forest. I tire quickly, my body not used to this much exercise anymore. Before the Gilded Lands, I worked the fields and spent all day toiling. It made my muscles strong, and I was fast and sure. The Gilded Lands, amongst other things, made me soft. It's just another thing I lost.

It's a sour reminder, and I'm about to demand we go back when we break through the trees and I get my first glimpse of the place they have brought me to.

There is so much beauty, it almost makes me want to cry.

Fog surrounds a waterfall, but the sun breaks through and shines down upon the sparkling blue water. It's cleaner than any water I have ever seen, and it almost looks unreal. Rocks surround the pool, and grass and flowers cover every square inch along the edges. It's gorgeous and magical, like a place from a fairy tale.

"They say the water here heals all," Kaito murmurs. "I don't know how true that is, but I like to believe that this place can heal at least a little with its splendor. After all, this world has so much to offer, don't you think?"

He's gently coaxing me and trying to show me reasons to live.

"It's amazing," I admit softly. "Can we—"

"Absolutely." Weyland grins, accidentally flashing a fang before he turns away and covers it. They lead me to the edge, and I only release their hands so I can crouch down and plunge my hand into the water, gasping when I realize it's warm.

"You can drink it," Kaito murmurs at my side, and as if showing a babe, he cups his hand under the water before pulling it out and to his mouth, sipping the warm water. I copy him, my eyes widening at the mineral taste.

Weyland comes over and, with a finger on his lips so I don't warn him, pushes Kaito into the water. I sit back with wide eyes, watching as Kaito plunges into the water, only to surge through the surface with a grin. "Oh, that's it, wolf." Weyland tries to run, but Kaito is too fast. He flies from the water, grabs the lycan's leg, and tugs him in as he yelps and claws at the edge. The water droplets splash me, and a tiny giggle slips out at their antics.

Kaito strides from the water to sit next to me as Weyland sputters and stands in the pool, holding his arms to his sides, his fur drenched and pushed back. I can't help but grin and for a moment, I think of nothing else but this.

This place with them.

We spend hours lounging and soaking in the beauty of this place before my stomach grumbles. "I didn't bring food." Weyland frowns, growling at himself in annoyance. "Wait here, bacca. I will catch one of these magic fish to feed you."

"You don't have to—" I begin, but he is already wading into the water, his eyes tracking the movement of the fish.

"Let him. He likes to feel useful," Kaito offers, plaiting my hair carefully.

"How do you know?" I ask, glancing at him then back to Weyland.

"Because I feel it too, the need to provide for you, so let him, *amarta*," he purrs.

I blush, ducking my head, but even through my lashes, I watch Weyland. The first time I saw him, I was terrified, but as I watch him carefully stalk the fish, I cannot be anything but awed. The sun catches the myriad of colors in his fur, including red, orange, brown, and black. His claws sparkle with murderous intent, even though I know they hold my hand softly.

He is beautiful.

He strikes, fast and sure, catching a fish and victoriously holding it up with a shout. I grin as I sit up, but the fish has other ideas. It flops in his hands, fighting for freedom, and with a yelp, he tries to catch it, his arms windmilling in his attempt. Only, it doesn't work. The fish flips up, smacking him in the face before it drops back into the water with a small splash.

Wide-eyed, he turns to me, and for a moment, we just stare at each other, and then laughter bursts from me. Unable to stop the overwhelming amusement, I fall back, laughing. The sight of this big, scary lycan being hit by a fish replays over and over in my mind until I cannot catch my breath. I am laughing so hard, tears fall.

They both join in, their laughter matching my own.

For one blissful moment, with laughter in my heart and the sun shining down on me, I feel like I once did—whole, complete, and safe. When I finally catch my breath, my side hurting from the strength of my mirth, I peer at them to see them both watching me with matching grins.

"Your laugh is beautiful," Kaito says quietly. "It's the most beautiful sound I have ever heard."

"Then I will try to laugh more often," I promise.

For the first time in too long, I mean it.

CHAPTER
ELEVEN

KAI

After recovering from his amusement, Kaito kissed my hand and offered to find us something to eat, something that wouldn't attack the poor lycan—his exact words. He plunges into the forest with a promise to be back as Weyland trudges to my side, flopping back with a groan.

"Not my most graceful moment," he mutters, but he's smiling, and since he's relaxed, he's not covering his fangs. I like it. It's . . . him. "I promise I can actually hunt."

"I thought it was funny." I smile, lying back in the flowers, my head turned toward him. He turns to me, and he snaps his lips over his teeth.

"Sorry, I forgot," he mumbles, lowering his eyes in guilt.

"Don't," I murmur, stretching out to cup his mouth. He freezes, his eyes wide as I peel back his lips so his fangs hang naturally. "They don't scare me. They are part of you. You never need to hide yourself from me, though I appreciate you trying not to scare me."

"You . . . You do not mind them? Even though they are monstrous?" he asks.

"I'm finding those who are outwardly beautiful are more

monstrous than any being in these lands, so no, they do not scare me. I like to see them. It's a reminder of where I am and who I am with," I admit softly.

He watches me carefully before relaxing his mouth. "I wanted to die too, you know," he randomly says.

I blink, freezing.

He looks away as if to give me time to compose myself, knowing how those words will trigger me. "My family, my den, was invaded and everyone was slaughtered. I could not save them, and I had to live with that guilt, but more than that, I did not want to live in a world without them, so I threw myself into battles, hoping one would kill me. It never did. I was too strong. The fact that I did not want to live gave me an edge and over the years, I've found reasons to want to live again. I cannot bring my family back or change the past, but I can learn from it. I believe the world does not give us more than we can handle. We just get a little lost sometimes." He peers at me. "You became my reason the first moment I smelled you—a new reason to fight and live. I could hear my family howling their joy at me finding you."

"Why me? Why am I so important to you and Kaito?" I question, needing to know. Some part of me already does, I guess. He looks away, and I turn his face back to me. "Please."

"I do not want to tell you. It must be your choice to live, Kai. Not because you feel like you must for us."

I can tell he won't share this secret so I relax, my eyes going to the sky. If he is doing it to protect me, then I trust him. He's right. I probably can't handle the reason yet, especially when the desire in their eyes when they look at me feels like it's too much. How could they desire a broken thing such as me? Is it because I'm simply the easiest option or because I'm a novelty?

"I lied to Kaito." I feel him jerk at my admission, but he doesn't seem angry, only surprised. "I have family, well, someone left, but I do not want them to know I survived."

"Why?" I feel his confusion but no judgment.

"Because if I decide I don't want to live, it would destroy them, so this is easier. The Kai they knew died a long time ago anyway. It is better this way," I admit.

"I cannot imagine a world where it is better when someone you love is dead, no matter what issues they have or how much they are hurting. If they love you, they would simply be overjoyed you were alive and would want to help," he reasons.

"Probably," I murmur, tears sliding down the sides of my face and into my hair. "But I'm not ready."

"Okay." He takes my hand then. There is no judgment or guilt, just understanding.

"I see the way you look at me." I turn my head to meet his gaze and he freezes once more. "I wish I could be the person who would act on those desires for you, but I can't. I'm broken, Weyland. All I feel is pain with random bursts of happiness around you both. The darkness has me, and I'm not sure it will ever let me go. Not enough for what I see in your eyes."

"I do not want anything from you, *bacca*. This is enough and always will be. Simply being near you and moving through life as your protector makes me happy," he admits. "I cannot change the way I look at you when you are the most beautiful creature I have ever seen, but I would never act on my desires for you if you do not wish it."

Part of me settles at that while another part of me mourns for the selflessness of this man, this monster, who so clearly wants me. Even knowing what he feels for me, I feel safe with him. Odd, I know. I must stare for too long because he squeezes my hand.

"I don't know what happened to you, Kai. Hopefully, one day, you can share with us, but if not, know this. Both Kaito and I will do everything to protect you, even from ourselves. You never have to worry about our intentions. We might be monsters, *bacca*, but we have honor."

"More than most humans," I reply, meeting his eyes. "I don't know if I will ever be able to put into words what happened to me.

63

Everyone always said talking helped them, but for me, ignoring it helps. I tucked it deep into my mind, but maybe one day, I can try for you and Kaito."

"Then we will await that day, and until then, know that this is all I want. I will gladly take every inch of you that you offer, and I will hold it close and protect it. We will not fail you, not like everyone else."

Isn't that the truth?

Except for Cora. She never failed me.

My poor, sweet sister just wanted to protect me, but some destinies cannot be avoided and neither can pain.

Pain means I am alive, though, and for the first time, I am beginning to see why life might be worth fighting for.

TWELVE

The small creature I manage to capture after a quick hunt should be plenty to feed Kai, judging by the size of it. There will be enough for her and perhaps for me, but unfortunately, I don't think it'll stave the lycan's hunger as much as I hope it will. I want my mate to know I can provide for her, so when I reappear with the bounty, I grimace and hold it up.

"I do not think this is enough, but I thought to bring it back so it can begin cooking while I hunt for more," I declare, taking in the sight of Kai sitting close to Weyland without a trace of fear in her eyes. There are small tear tracks on her cheeks, but they don't appear to be from outward pain. They must have talked and something touched my *amarta* deeply.

For that alone, the lycan is an asset.

I know he would rather rip out his own heart than hurt her. After all, I feel the same way.

Kai has slowly started to open up and be less afraid. Her fear has faded away when it comes to us, and something inside of me wants to probe deeper even though I won't. Everything must come from

Kai. Weyland and I are in agreement. We'll move at her pace, and we'll follow her wherever she goes, even into her own darkness.

"Don't bother," Weyland says with a grin. "I deserve a chance to earn my pride back. I'll go capture something else to add to the meal. You start the fire so Kai is not so hungry by the time I return."

I watch as the lycan smiles gently at Kai, which she returns with a soft grin, before he bounds off into the forest, hunting for another source of food. I don't know how long it will take him, but I suspect it won't be as long as it took me. Surely, wolves are better hunters than a . . . whatever I am. I'm formidable in the water, but in these woods? They are more his hunting grounds than mine.

I hold up the creature in hopes of impressing her anyway. "Lopes are much like rabbits, but they are a little tastier if you ask me. I found some leaves that are good for spices that should give it more flavor."

Kai leans up to rest her arms around her knees as her eyes soften. "It sounds lovely. Would you like me to help you build the fire?"

"Absolutely not. You remain there, and I shall build one for you," I reply. My mate will want for nothing.

Mate...the word came naturally.

It feels right and warmth blooms in me as I repeat it in my head, even if she never hears it.

She sits in her spot, watching as I move around, collecting wood. It doesn't take me long to get the fire going, the flames crackling as it reaches the correct temperature. Once I have the meat roasting over the fire, I take a seat next to Kai. I make sure to give her ample space, but after a few beats of silence, she moves a little closer, her eyes dancing to me and then away.

Our Kai is still shy, but she isn't afraid.

It eases something in my heart to know that she no longer fears us. It's progress, even if she doesn't realize it, and with that small show of strength from my mate, I want to bellow in victory but I restrain myself.

"It smells so good," Kai murmurs, her eyes reflecting the flames in a way that makes me want to move closer and hold her, but I resist. I want her to reach for me, and it's still too soon for such things. Kai is still healing, and if she never reaches out, then I will be okay with that. My only hope is that we can show her that life is worth living.

"The leaves are something I've only seen in the Dead Lands. Most monsters leave them be, but those of us with a certain palate utilize them. I find my taste buds hunger for more of the human flavors I used to smell while in the Gilded Lands, but I can manage with anything."

She hums under her breath, her arms still wrapped around her knees for warmth. Kai has started to put on healthy weight since staying with me. It was clear when I saved her that she was malnourished. Perhaps it could have simply been a lack of food in the Shadow Lands, but I don't believe so. Kai's shape is naturally curvy and her bones had been sticking out before. Now, she appears more sound—at least on the outside. It's the scars and pain on the inside that will take far longer to mend.

"You know," I begin, focusing on the fire so as to not scare her with my intensity. I can still see her from the corner of my eye, and I keep a careful watch on her reaction as I speak. "I saw you . . . when you fell."

She flinches, but when I glance to see if it's too much, I find that she's watching me carefully. She doesn't say a word, but her eyes tell me to continue.

"I was in the river below the castle. I was often there because some intrinsic part of me brought me back time and time again. Perhaps it was because part of me yearned for the human side of me to make a difference. Now, I think something pulled me there so often in order for me to see you." I sigh. "At first, I considered not moving. I watched you plummet from the top, but before you were halfway down, I was already swimming. I did not consciously make the choice to save you, but something urged me to save you nonetheless."

"I had no intention of being saved that day," she whispers, and the pain in her words makes my chest ache.

The idea of a world without my Kai? Unthinkable. Even now, I nearly shudder in horror at almost being too late.

"I know that now," I reply, glancing at her. "But then, I only knew you needed me, and so I was there." I turn the meat over the fire, making sure it's evenly roasted before continuing and meeting her eyes. "I know now that you jumped, but when I look into your eyes, I see a spark there that makes me want to climb up to the top of that castle with you. It makes me want to wrap you in my arms and be your reason to live. That feeling is so thick, it almost chokes me sometimes, and I want to destroy whatever hurt you."

She blinks, and I startle when I realize I've made her cry. Guilt eats at me, but when I open my mouth to apologize, she holds up her hand.

"Don't apologize," she rasps. "Your honesty moves me."

"I did not mean to make you cry." I grimace. "A beautiful creature like you should not be brought to tears."

"They are not sad tears," she admits. "I just . . . never expected to meet someone like you and Weyland. I thought I knew everything about this world I needed to, but I was wrong. I don't know what that means yet. I can't understand the inner workings of my mind still, but . . . I appreciate what you've done for me and what you continue to do for me."

Those words nearly knock me over, and hope blooms in my chest so fiercely, I have to swallow to keep it down. It's progress, but I can't push her too soon. Instead of shouting at her admission, I offer her my hand. When she slips hers into mine without hesitation, the buzz under my skin settles.

If given that chance, if Kai decides that this world is too much for her, then perhaps she will not be leaping alone the second time.

Perhaps our lives are so intertwined that whatever existence she chooses, I will choose too.

When Weyland reappears with another lope and a large, happy grin, both of us smile at the lycan. Some part of this, though I've never had it before, feels a little bit like home.

We eat so well, we have to lie near the waterfall for hours before we decide it's time to head back to the cabin.

THIRTEEN

The meat Kaito cooks fills me to the brim. My stomach distends with how full I am, and I'm forced to lie back against the soft moss and grass and watch the sky as it settles. Part of me wants to lie here forever, and I imagine closing my eyes and falling asleep and simply never waking up again. The flowers would twist around my bones like an intricate piece of art. The moss would carpet my resting place and cushion me for eternity. I would be a permanent part of this place that feels like something more than just a waterfall.

With Weyland and Kaito beside me, it feels like something more.

Perhaps it's the magic of this place that soaks into my veins and begs for more. Perhaps it's the two monsters who watch me with rapt attention, offering nothing but protection and kindness so as not to startle me. Either way, this feels like heaven far more than anything else has in my life.

There is only one other memory that comes close—Cora and me when we were younger. Father had been gone for a few days to tend to some issues in the fields and he had to sleep out there. It left us and our mother alone and for the first time, it had been peaceful. Cora and I had woken up to find Mother had cooked for us. It wasn't anything fancy, just a few eggs and some toast that had gone dry, but it wasn't about the food. It was about the way it felt as the three of us sat around the table in companionable silence before Cora made some joke about the bread being perfect for soaking up stomach acid. We all laughed, and it was brighter in the home for a matter of hours before Father returned. But that moment, that peace, had felt like heaven. Now, this space in time feels the same, only without the fear and anticipation of Father interrupting it.

Now, I fear something else.

Kaito and Weyland both say they are here to protect me, that they won't push, but can I really force them to walk on eggshells around me for the rest of their lives? Is it worth it to them to watch as I struggle and break over and over again? And at what point will it be too much? Will they look at me with all my cracks and see the darkness leaking out?

I'm afraid of what they may see, of what they may witness in my worst moments. Mostly, I'm afraid they will witness it and no longer see me as beautiful and leave. They say they aren't going anywhere, but I still fear it. My mind repeats over and over again that I'm not worth their attention or care. What if those intrusive thoughts are right? What if I'm not worthy of anything?

As the hazy sun begins to sink in the sky, Kaito stands and says it's time to head back to the cabin. At night, the Dead Lands come alive in ways that still frighten me, and I chastise myself for forgetting that we aren't as safe as I felt. Being out here in the open, even with my protectors, should put me on guard, but I had forgotten because of Weyland and Kaito and because I enjoy their company.

Weyland offers me his hand, his claws carefully tipped down, and I take it without hesitation. Something flashes in his eyes, as if he's proud of me, and I walk a little straighter as they lead me back through the trees. This time, I don't let go, not even when we reach the cabin. This time, when I settle in for the night, my eyes trail over to my monsters, my protectors, and I slip quickly into sleep.

As I sleep, though, I swear I hear Weyland singing softly. It's a lullaby that eases something else inside me and makes this feel like home.

The nightmares never come that night.

CHAPTER
FOURTEEN
KAI

There is peace in my soul as we go about our days, falling into a familiar routine. They hunt while I prepare the fire and herbs to go with the meat. We clean at the river where Weyland carefully picks out the knots in my hair for me while Kaito dives deep and offers me treasures. We talk until the moon is high in the sky, and when the sun shines, they show me this world of theirs. I begin to relax and understand their reasons for wanting to live, even when everything seemed bleak. After all, they were trapped here with no way out and they found hope, so maybe I can too.

It's a small, fragile flame burning in my soul, and every day I spend with these men makes the flames grow brighter, as if they are huddled around it, fanning it.

Today is no different. After a breakfast of nuts and berries I gathered for myself and meat for them, we head off into the forest. Only this time, I am not as scared. I look around as we walk, appreciating the beauty and splendor this once dead but now thriving land has to offer.

It is almost as if it heals as I do, but that's silly. My soul is not tied to this land, but I cannot help but look at it with understanding. I, too, was cast in shadows, and I still fight to free myself of them.

We pass our waterfall, which we visit often, and I find myself grinning at Weyland. "Where are we going?"

"You'll see soon enough," he starts, but then his eyes go wide and he raises his nose in the air. "Kaito!" he roars just as he pushes me behind him.

Kaito is at my side in an instant, protecting me as furry beasts burst from the underbrush, their claws dripping with liquid that seems to burn the ground. Small tendrils of steam hiss where it falls, leaving the smallest of craters behind in a pattern that almost feels artistic.

Weyland roars at the beasts, diving into their masses with teeth and claws as I huddle into Kaito, wishing I had brought my weapon with me. Cursing, Kaito turns to me, pushing my back to a tree. "Stay here. Do not move." He moves in front of me, kicking those that get too close.

I huddle into the rough bark, tugging at my dress as if that will somehow help. I'm watching the fight, terrified for my monsters, when something in the fog calls to me. I turn my face toward it in confusion and curiosity despite the battle taking place before me.

It echoes like a song of death, though I don't know how I know that.

So much pain and longing resonate in that song, I stagger to my knees and my chest tightens.

Before I can even consider taking a step in its direction, a creature bursts into the clearing, stomping on the furry beasts with huge, cloven hooves. It's as tall as some of the trees and as black as midnight, its luminous skin sporting a sheen riddled with blues and purples. Its eyes are a blazing red, both terrifying and intriguing. It looks like a horrifying version of the horses that used to till the fields. Bones show through its skin, and upon its head is a bone shaped into a sharp horn. The creature uses that horn to spear two beasts through their rib cages and then tosses them away with a bellow. Those red eyes turn to us, focus on my monsters, and then on me.

"Run!" Kaito yells to me as he stumbles back with Weyland. Both of them still hold off the furry creatures. I cannot move despite their insistence, fear planting my feet on the ground like roots, and I shake, watching as it rips apart the creatures as if they are nothing. One of the last creatures spits on it with that venom that seems to eat away at the ground. With a pained yell, the black beast kicks it into the forest, hissing as the skin burns away from the spittle.

When there are no more creatures left, it turns to Weyland and Kaito, who both look at one another before racing toward it.

They are intent on killing it, I realize. For a moment, those red eyes meet mine, and I see intelligence and acceptance as it watches death come.

More than that, I see hope that it will finally be the end.

It's a feeling I know all too well, and like Kaito saved me, I know I must save this beast. It's almost a threatening whisper in the wind.

Hurrying on stumbling feet, I throw myself between them and stretch my arms wide before the creature. "No!" I yell, my voice echoing through the trees around us like a war cry.

Weyland and Kaito freeze, their eyes wide in panic. "Kai," Kaito begs, glancing at the beast I feel stomping behind me. The hair on the back of my neck rises. "Slowly come toward me."

"No, I will not let you kill it," I tell them defiantly, and I see hurt in their eyes mixed with their worry as hot air blows across my scalp, making me shiver. Fear fills me, but so does determination. I won't let death steal another tortured soul.

I turn to face the beast, meeting its red eyes. "I won't let them kill you, but please don't hurt us." My voice is soft and shaky but there, and the beast lowers its nose with a huff. It blows my hair back as it meets my eyes.

"I mean you no harm." The words are spoken in a deep, throaty sound that runs across my skin and makes me tilt my head in confusion. The voice came from the creature, dark, smooth, and cold like death.

A male voice.

This is not just any beast. This is a monster.

A monster I just saved.

A monster that peers at me like he wants to eat me alive.

FIFTEEN

DADE

Never in all my years has another been able to bring me from the madness of my shift. The warhorse they call death is a curse upon my soul, one that controls every part of me, but here I stand, free of that control. I am bred to fight, to steal life, and to die gloriously in battle. As the last of my kind, I patrol the hills, searching for one such event to join the others. Instead, the wind carried a message upon it for me—her. I found myself rushing toward the sound of battle, only to discover the beauty so bravely standing before me when even other monsters cower.

A human, one with haunted eyes.

Yet one so brave, braver than any other being.

I see the lycan and the water monster behind her shifting closer in panic, and I stomp my feet to send them backwards and keep them away from my warrior. Her eyes narrow on me.

"Behave. They mean you no harm. Thank you for helping us." Her voice softens toward the end, a nervous smile curling her lips, and I feel the shift of magic under my skin, my form wanting to change back to that of a man. It is something I have not done in many years. After all, what is the point? I am no man, I am a beast, and I act as such. It is what I am, what I have always been, but for a moment, I ache to touch the softness of the being before me and feel the warmth of her skin and the strength within her brittle bones. There is pain in her eyes, pain I know all too well. It makes me want to roar in fury and demand to know how I can hunt down those responsible. She watches me like she sees into my soul and is witnessing the humiliation and grief of my past, like she is judging it, and when her hand drifts out, landing on my snout, I freeze. I scarcely even breathe, not wanting to scare her away.

"Thank you," she says once more.

I stare into her bright eyes, and a very human emotion fills me—want. I want this little creature. I want to experience what that kind of passion would feel like across my body, but then her hand falls away and she steps back, and it is like she takes all the goodness and light with her, once again draping me in darkness. The farther she moves from me, the more the darkness, the madness, takes hold once more.

Furious drums beat in my heart, demanding blood and death.

Demanding retribution.

"Let's go, Kai." The lycan holds out his hand, and giving me an unsure look, the beauty, Kai, takes it. With their eyes still on me, they ease into the trees.

I find myself following without deciding to. She brought me from my madness. She brought me back to life. She has given me a reason, and I find I am unable to stop. I do not hide that I'm following them, but I stay back, not wanting to frighten them. I can see them eyeing me with unease, but she offers me a small wave as they break out into a clearing with a little cabin built in the middle.

Curiosity has me watching them from the tree line.

I saw the same pain I live with in her eyes, the same darkness that haunts me, and for a moment, I had hope.

Yet I still linger here, shunned and alone once more, lost in the madness that ended my people.

CHAPTER
SIXTEEN

KAI

The next morning, the black horse beast still lingers in the shadows of the trees. He stays out of the clearing, as if being in the open frightens him, but he doesn't fall so far back that I can't see him from the open window. Those red, glowing eyes hold darkness and fear, and something inside me aches to reach toward it. It's a familiar pain, as if we would both understand each other. Something about this beast is so very human despite the skin it bears. He'd spoken, so I assume he has some humanity, but he holds his form. Perhaps that is what he is, what he always will be. Regardless, though, he's massive and imposing, but I'm not scared of him as he watches our cabin. Instead, I want to walk out there and talk to him.

Which is silly.

I'm already living in a cabin with two monsters. Why add a third?

Why not? a little voice whispers to me.

Kaito watches the beast the same as I do, but there's a nervousness to his countenance, as if he doesn't recognize what the beast is. Weyland, in contrast, looks less confused but even more afraid, as if he recognizes the beast in some way and that makes him even more scared.

"What is he?" I finally ask when I can't stand the nervous silence any longer. "Why do you look as if you've seen a ghost?"

Weyland glances at me, at the way I stand unafraid despite the clear danger of the creature. "Because he might as well be a ghost, spoken about in hushed, frightened whispers where no one can hear. We used to tell stories about such beasts around the fire, a tale to scare the pups, nothing more, and yet here death stands as if he's waiting to carry us away." He's tense, so tense I can see the corded muscles in his neck as he moves. He doesn't hide his fear, but his words feel as if they were meant to unnerve me.

They don't.

"How is he death?" Kaito asks. Whatever tale Weyland knows, it does not appear that Kaito grew up hearing the same stories.

I can feel that knowledge, the death song floating on the wind as the beast lingers. It's as if he comes to take your soul and carry it to whatever lies after, but it doesn't feel malignant. It feels . . . peaceful.

"The warhorses of the old world were feared in battle. They were great, hulking beasts lost to their madness with the first scent of blood and clang of war drums. They charged into battle, tore creatures limb from limb, and skewered them with their horns. They showed no mercy. They are not capable of it. They were created for war and nothing else," Weyland murmurs, his eyes on the beast outside pawing at the ground.

My head tilts in wonder. "And yet, he did not attack us when I stepped before him," I point out. "That doesn't seem so monstrous as what you're describing."

Weyland frowns, thinking over my words before replying, "You're right. It doesn't."

Which means some of the stories aren't entirely true. I don't doubt that this beast is dangerous, I saw what he did to the furry creatures that attacked us, but some part of me doubts this creature is a cold war beast with no thought. I heard his voice. There's pain in his eyes, but he is not completely lost. Not yet.

I don't know when I consciously make the decision. I just know one moment, I'm watching him through the window, and the next, I'm heading toward the door. Weyland and Kaito immediately spring into action, rushing forward to keep me inside where it's safe, where I can't be hurt.

But I'm tired of being afraid.

"That's not a good idea," Kaito says, his hands in front of him as if he's trying to reason with a child. "We know nothing about that beast out there—"

"We know he didn't hurt me when he had the chance. He didn't hurt any of us," I reason.

"Yes, but that doesn't mean he's not free to change his mind," Weyland growls, his shoulders filled with tension. "Stay inside where it's safe."

"I'm tired of trying to be safe. I'm tired of hiding," I retort, gesturing for them to move. "If you're so worried, come with me, but something tells me that I need to go out there and speak to him."

"Warhorses don't speak," Weyland replies, shaking his head in frustration. "They maim and kill and battle, but they don't speak."

"This one did," I argue. "He spoke to me before."

Weyland and Kaito share a look between them as if I can't see their disbelief through their coded glances.

It's Kaito who meets my eyes and studies me closely. "Are you certain?"

"Yes," I respond. "I heard his voice as clear as day. Didn't you?"

Another glance. "No," Weyland says. "We didn't."

That admission has me reconsidering my sanity. I know I heard his voice, but perhaps it had been for me to hear alone. That does not mean I didn't hear it. I know I did, but part of me needs to prove it to myself and really make sure I'm not finally losing my mind. After all this time, it's possible. When I was a prisoner in the king's castle, I'd fooled myself into seeing visions of my sister. Each time, I'd been disappointed. When she finally appeared, I hadn't been able to stomach her phantom, even if she was whole and real and alive.

Had I done the same to this warhorse? Or whatever he is?

"You can come with me," I murmur. "I'd prefer you to, but I need to go out there. I can't explain why or how I know I need to." I roll my lips between my teeth in worry. "I just know I need to."

Their silence fills the air around us before Weyland nods solemnly and reaches for the door. "If he appears like he's going to attack, then you get back into the cabin as quickly as possible," he commands, leaving no room for negotiation.

"I'm not foolish," I counter. "Of course I'll return if he attacks."

But I'll be afraid for my monsters if he does. Especially since we're going outside because of me.

Weyland opens the door, and both he and Kaito exit first, leaving me in the doorway to stare out at the tree line where red eyes watch me. I hesitate, wondering if this is really the smartest idea or if I'm making a mistake, but the more I study the feeling, the more this feels right. This creature will not harm me. I'm certain of it, just as I'm certain that the pain in his eyes is an echo of my own.

Part of me is frightened despite the certainty that I'm right, but I'm tired of being so afraid. What use has it been to me? None of these monsters have harmed me, not like my father or the king. Those men were true monsters. These ones are not. I still don't know if this life is worth living, but why not give it my all if I'm not afraid of dying? Why sit in the dark in fear if death is not so terrifying? Isn't being so afraid pointless in the face of all that?

The warhorse paws at the ground with its hooves, its red eyes watching me as I take a step outside. I keep my footsteps slow and gentle as I put more distance between the cabin and me. Weyland and Kaito stay on either side of me, their shoulders tense in case he attacks.

"We aren't going to hurt you," I say, holding out my hands to show him that I'm harmless, which is silly. I'm flanked by a wolf and a water monster and I'm trying to show him that I, the small, achingly human female in their center, is harmless. "I just want to talk."

The warhorse snorts and shakes his mane, his eyes never moving from me. He doesn't look toward Weyland or Kaito, as if they are not a threat. He's completely focused on me, my words, and my hands. That wickedly sharp horn glints in the light, drawing my gaze. The first traces of fear trickle inside me as I'm reminded of what he can do with that horn, but I push it aside.

I'm tired of being a mouse. I'm tired of being afraid of everything.

"Won't you come out?" I ask when the warhorse remains in the darkness. "We can hardly see you when you're hiding."

Weyland scoffs. "I can see him just fine where he's at."

"You must be hungry," I continue after shooting Weyland a look that quiets his protest. "We have some vegetables inside. Or other things. Do you like stew?"

The beast stills and then takes a step toward the clearing.

"That's it," I coo. "You're safe here. You can come out."

Another step, and another, until the sunlight that breaks through the clearing dances on his coat and highlights just how beautiful he is. Although he's a solid, inky black, there are colors that appear in the darkness when the light hits him, as if even in shadow, there's color. Blues and purples and pinks dance as he moves forward with slow, measured steps, moving along him like a wave as the sunbeams hit him, and his horn glistens like crushed jewels have been embedded inside it. The red of his eyes seems less threatening when he shines, as if he's simply a large horse with a menacing horn on its head.

It has been so long since I've had stew, he says, and I smile, glancing at Weyland and Kaito.

"Tell me you heard him," I say. "I knew I wasn't crazy."

Weyland shakes his head. "He must be speaking only to you, *bacca*."

I glance at the warhorse again as I hold out my hand. He hesitates before pushing his nose into my palm, allowing me to rub it. "Do you think you could speak so they can hear too?"

The beast pauses in his rubbing, his red eyes focused on me. *It has been so long since I have spoken out loud, little one. I do not know if I remember how to.*

My fingers brush along his nose, along the softness of his hair there. Despite the terror his visage should elicit, he's as soft as down feathers.

"There may be a bowl of stew in it for you if you try," I promise, smiling gently. "I'm right here. You're safe. You're free to speak."

Those red eyes blink. *Stew does sound nice*, he murmurs in my mind. *This may take a moment*, he warns as his hooves paw at the ground.

I go to move my hand back, but he snorts.

Will you keep your hand on me? On my chest? You . . . ground me.

"Of course," I reply, moving my hand down his neck to his muscular chest, resting my fingers there. To Weyland and Kaito, I say, "He's trying to remember how to speak out loud. He said it may take a few moments."

We all watch as the warhorse closes his eyes and focuses on whatever memory he needs to recall. His chest is warm beneath my fingers, and his heart beats hard enough for me to feel it. He's strong and fierce yet gentle as he shifts on his hooves. Whatever he is, he's not a mindless beast, that much is clear.

I'm so focused on my thoughts, on this reasoning that he's not a monster, that when the feeling of his hair beneath my fingers shifts to something else, it takes me a few moments to notice. Weyland and Kaito both make sounds of surprise, but my eyes widen as the warhorse changes before me, morphing from a giant, deadly horse into a very naked man.

I gasp, trailing my eyes up the chest my hand still rests against to a very handsome face. His skin is as black as his hair had been, and the sheen is still there in his flesh. His eyes are as red as they were before, so it's easy to realize I haven't gone insane and this is the same creature. A smaller horn, like the one he had before, rests in the center of his forehead, standing proud and deadly. My eyes trail down and . . .

Realizing I'm still touching him, I wrench my hand back and grimace. "I'm so sorry," I rasp, forcing my eyes to stay completely focused on his face. "You surprised me."

He opens his mouth and closes it a few times, as if trying to remember the motions of it. When he speaks, it's with the same voice I heard in my head, only now it feels more strained with disuse.

"There is no need to apologize, little one," he croaks and clears his throat. "Forgive me. It has been many centuries since I've spoken out loud."

"I . . ." I glance over at Weyland. "Was this part of the stories?"

Weyland shakes his head. "Not that I've ever heard."

"Right. Well . . ." I worry my bottom lip before glancing at Kaito for permission. When he nods his head just the slightest amount, I gesture toward the cabin. "I believe I promised you stew." My eyes dip down again and I flush, my face warming as I jerk my gaze back up. "Perhaps we can find you something to cover up with as well."

The beast, the man, looks down at himself in confusion. "I am wearing my flesh. Is this not suitable?"

"I, uh, umm, I don't know . . ."

"It is customary for humans to cover their nether regions," Kaito supplies helpfully. "It will make Kai more comfortable if you cover yourself."

The man's eyes widen in alarm. "Of course, little one. I would not want you to be uncomfortable around me."

And that's how I find myself in a cabin in the Dead Lands with not one, not two, but three monsters. Despite the change in plans, I'm able to sit down amongst all of them without fear, and although I recognize the pain in the newcomer's eyes, it does not trigger me.

I will not be afraid. I will not be afraid. Shadows, I don't want to be afraid.

SEVENTEEN

DADE

The human woman is intoxicating. I watch as she, along with the water monster, bustles around the small cabin to prepare a bowl for me. I do not remember the last time I felt kindness. I do not remember the last time I ate anything prepared for me or anything other than raw meat for that matter. The scents in the air make my mouth water almost as much as the sight of the woman does.

Kai.

She's so achingly small and human. So fragile. As she moves, her body strains as if she's still gathering strength to do the most basic of things. Though the pain is not flashing in her eyes right now, it lingers in the lines of her body, a sign that she'd been mistreated at some point—not by these monsters but by others. I understand those sorts of monsters all too well. The ones who made me were such beasts, monstrous beings who only cared for themselves and their prosperity. If I learn who harmed her, I'll slaughter her monsters just as I did my own.

I vow it.

"Luckily for you, Weyland is an excellent hunter," Kai says as she spoons stew into the bowl. "Kaito is also great at fishing, so we have plenty of food should this not be enough." She sets the bowl down in front of me. "I just add the seasoning."

"Which is a job in itself," the lycan points out with a smile. "The last time I tried to season the stew, we had to throw it out."

Kai smiles fondly, and I realize she cares for these two deeply. I want her to look at me like that. I want her to smile so big, the pain no longer echoes in her eyes.

"Yes, well, you can't dump a whole container of salt into something and expect it to taste good," she teases, and I like it. I like this little family they've created. I desperately want to be a part of it, to feel what such companionship feels like again.

It's been so long.

And Kai, achingly human Kai, calls to me in ways I've never felt.

The blanket wrapped around my waist reminds me that I had made her uncomfortable, but her eyes dipped to look down. It had taken everything in me not to stir, not to grab her in my arms and make her mine right there, but something told me that would have been the wrong thing to do. The pain in her eyes speaks of horrors, and like my own nightmares, they are not so easily conquered.

"Your kindness is appreciated," I say, a long-ago memory reminding me of manners despite the length of time I've only been a beast. "I thank you."

Her small smile aimed at me feels like a victory, more than any war I've won, before she settles in front of me. "What do we call you?" she asks. "You know our names, but just in case, I'm Kai. This is Weyland and Kaito."

I meet her gaze and study the shape of her face, the brightness of her eyes. She's beautiful, achingly so. I'd once been near queens and princesses who sparkled like the sun, but none of them compared to the woman before me. She glows from within as if some magic dances beneath her skin. She's perfect, even though I can see thin white scars marring her flesh. I've never wanted someone as strongly as I do her.

"My given name is Dade," I reply. "But I am open to whatever you would like to call me, Kai." The way her name rolls off my lips makes me shift in my seat. Kai. Kai. *Kai.*

Her eyes crinkle a little. "Do you enjoy the name Dade?" When I nod, she touches my hand. "Then that is what we shall call you. It's a pleasure to meet you, Dade."

"As it is the greatest pleasure to meet you in return," I say, and then I take a bite of the stew. It takes a moment for me to remember how to use the utensils beside the bowl, but I manage a clumsy bite regardless. When the flavors hit my tongue, I hum. It's delicious, far better than the meat and plants I've lived off of in my beast form.

"Are there others like you?" Kai asks, and I freeze. The madness dances at the edges of my mind, but when she reaches out to touch her fingers to my wrist, it disappears as if by magic. "I apologize if the question was too personal. I was only curious."

She moves to pull her hand away with those words, as if afraid she's being too forward, but I close my fingers around hers. Her fingers are swamped by mine, her smallness almost comical against my largeness. The lycan and the water beast tense at my hold. Kai flinches at the quick movement and shame fills me that I've acted as a beast.

"My apologies," I whisper, slowly releasing her hand. "You steady me, and I acted rashly to keep that magic close."

"It's okay," Kai replies, but shadows dance in her eyes, reminding me that I'm not the only one here with darkness. "I understand."

And she does, I realize. She understands exactly what I mean. Her eyes dart over to the others, and I see the healing in this family that has been happening before my arrival. If I want to stay here, I must be part of the healing.

"I should like to stay here," I say. "If you are comfortable." When there's silence, I decide it's best to list out my qualifications. "I am a great protector, strong and willful. No beast shall harm you while I am here." I glance at the others. "I am not a great hunter, but I am decent at foraging. If you would like to see my skills—"

"Dade," Kai interrupts, and this time when she places her hand on my wrist to stop my rambling, I do not grab her. I let her control the touch. "You do not need to prove your usefulness." She glances at Kaito, and I realize this cabin must belong to him. That glance is asking for permission. When he nods, my shoulders relax. "You're welcome to stay for as long as you need."

Forever, I think. *I would like to stay forever.*

But I do not say that out loud. Instead, I smile gratefully, take another bite, and say, "This stew is delicious."

CHAPTER

EIGHTEEN

KAI

After eating, we fall into a familiar routine of cleaning up the cabin, only for me to turn to see Dade there, standing with the blanket wrapped around him, watching us. "Please let me help," he murmurs. It's almost a plea. I can understand feeling useless, and at almost seven feet tall, that must not be a familiar feeling for such a creature.

His hair is as black as his beast, almost slick with oil. His muscles are even bigger than Weyland's, and he towers above us all, bending so as not to hit his head on the cabin ceiling. If we are collecting more monsters, we are going to need a bigger home.

I'm unsure what to tell him though. Luckily, Weyland steps forward. "I need to fetch more wood for the fires. You can help if you wish."

"Gladly." Dade stands straighter.

Weyland chuckles. "You might need pants."

"Wait a moment. I might have some that fit. I foraged when I arrived and there was extra clothing here that is too big for me," Kaito offers kindly, and after rummaging through a dusty trunk, he produces a pair of long, large leather breaches.

Dade accepts them gratefully. "I owe you," he murmurs before looking toward me. With a bow to me as if I'm some sort of royal, he turns, offering me his muscular back. That back is laden with scars that have my eyes widening in horror, but just as surprisingly, he drops the blanket, distracting me from the scars.

I let out a squeak and turn, but not before I see a very round, muscular bottom that has warmth spreading through me.

"I apologize, little one. I should have warned you. I am rusty at being around others, especially humans." When I peek at him, he is dressed and wincing as he watches me. "Can you forgive me?"

"Of course," I rush out, my voice nearly a squeak. My eyes drop down again before I yank them up. "Wood. You should get wood." My cheeks heat at that as Weyland chuckles. Dade, however, seems not to notice and with a bow, he heads out with Weyland.

I slump in relief, my cheeks flushed with embarrassment.

Kaito's arms wrap around me. "You are adorable," he murmurs as I blow out a breath.

"Clumsy," I mutter and take a seat with the needle I found, then I try to fix a hole in one of my shirts I stole from Kaito to sleep in. It's far too large for me, but it's warm and smells like him. Not to mention the way his eyes light up when I wear it.

"Beautiful," Kaito offers instead.

I duck my head once more, hiding my smile as I get to work. After all, here in the Dead Lands, there is always work to be done to stay alive.

Nothing here is given; everything is earned.

AFTER A LONG DAY of hard work that leaves me exhausted but keeps me occupied and feeling useful, we all collapse around the fire Dade and Weyland built when night descends. The slight chill leaves me huddling closer to the flames, the moonlight bathing us in its beauty. The cabin is cleaned, the clothes are repaired, and we have hunted and foraged enough food for a few days. We have an overflowing stock of wood thanks to Dade, and I managed to wash and untangle my hair and braid it back. I even helped Kaito fix a leaking hole in the roof, which was fun.

Sitting with the flames warming me, I lean into Kaito's side, his arm resting on the ground behind me to allow me to prop myself up. My gaze lingers on Dade across from me. His red eyes are locked on the flames and lost in memory, no doubt, but as if feeling my look, his eyes slowly rise and meet my own. As they do, I shudder. The power in his gaze is almost too much, yet I do not drop my own. Watching the flames dance in those red orbs as we observe one another, I feel like it's almost a religious experience, this acknowledgement of the monster he is contrasting with the gentleness with which he holds himself. How strange to recognize that and not be afraid.

I have so many questions, but for a moment, I let the peace stretch, enjoying their company.

It is then I notice I have not thought of my past or my need to enter death's embrace once today. Today, I simply existed.

"There are no others of me," he finally says under my perusal, his voice startling me because I was so lost in the spell in those eyes. "Not anymore. There was once a great many of my kind. Now, I am the last."

I feel Weyland's pain at that as he eyes Dade with something akin to understanding, that wary fear he had been watching him with lessening. "Me as well."

Dade nods. "I heard of the downfall of the great lycans. I am truly sorry for your loss."

"As am I for yours." Weyland nods, bowing his head in respect. "Tales of your kind were told to us since birth. I am sorry that is all lost."

"I am still alive, so not all is lost. Change is never easy. I grieve for those of mine that I lost, but that change also brought me freedom from the war chains and . . . now to here." Dade's eyes come back to me. "To you, the one who quiets the war drums and madness my kind is cursed with."

"Cursed?" I ask curiously.

"A story for another time. It is not a tale of happiness, little one," he admits, his arms pressed to his knees.

"I do not think any of ours are. Maybe that is why we were drawn together," I muse, bringing my eyes back to the fire, unable to meet his as I admit that. I feel his gaze once more and, taking a steadying breath, I lean back more solidly into Kaito. "I was hurt by the humans. By my own kind. When Kaito saved me, I was plummeting to my death quite literally. He nursed me back to health, but every day is hard. I bear and live with the scars they left on my soul and body." Swallowing, I look up then to see every eye locked on me. Shrinking slightly, I firmly place my gaze back on the fire, knowing they are all eager to help.

To know.

"The truth is, I was nothing before, and I am nothing now. I was a lowly peasant, destined to toil the fields and marry a man who would become my provider and the rule maker. I was happy with that life where others were not. I craved the simplicity of that existence and happiness. It all changed so suddenly, and although I ended up surrounded by riches and food that others only dreamed of, I was completely alone, and the price was far too steep."

"Who hurt you?" Dade practically growls, and it raises the hair on my arms even as it feels comforting.

You could carve the tension in the air with a blade for the way they all await my answer. "The king," I finally admit. Dade stands, and I peer up at him with wide eyes. "Where are you going?"

"To hunt this king." I see the truth in his eyes. He would hunt down a man on nothing more than my word and make him pay. It makes me smile as I sit up.

"Dade, although that is very sweet, it has already been done. The king is no more, and I am free."

"Not from the memories," he murmurs as he sits stiffly. "I know that too well."

I incline my head before sitting back and relaxing. "Very true, but nobody can save me from them."

"Watch us." Weyland speaks for the first time, and I meet his eyes. "Watch us save you from them."

The smile that blooms on my lips is fuller than any I have ever given before.

True happiness pours through me. And to think, all it took was being surrounded by monsters.

CHAPTER
NINETEEN
KAI

As the sun rises and the land around us awakens, I come to a decision. Today will be a good day. Today is the day I take control of my life. I have spent too long living for others. First my parents, then my . . . my lover, and then the king.

No more.

Today I will live for me. I will make the choice to live for me, even if it's too much. It is time to pull one foot from the grave and place it firmly on this earth. If these magnificent creatures snoring around the room can survive the clear pain they have endured and still find the strength to go on, then so can I.

Not once have they hurt me like my father or the king. Not once have they rushed or pressured me. They do not expect anything but my company. I'm so very tired of being afraid. That will change. I'm still not completely sure if I want to live. That question lingers in the back of my mind, but I'm not scared of dying, so why not give into this life and give it a try? Here, I can be reborn. Here, I can be whatever I want to be.

Here, I am free.

After eating, they leave me to tend to the flames outside and check for any tracks. Taking a deep breath, I dress in the stolen pants I hemmed a few days ago, one of their shirts, and my shoes, and I roll my shoulders back with bravery I'm still not sure I really feel before I step outside.

They turn at the noise, their mouths twisting in worry.

I do not know what my expression is telling them, but as I stop before them, I tilt my chin up in determination. My hands shake, so I quickly hide them behind my back, straightening my spine as I do. "I want you to show me."

"Show you?" Weyland replies slowly. "Show you what, *bacca*?"

"How to live," I admit softly. "But for now, I want to see what you are capable of."

If I know the truth, I won't be as scared, or that was my logic during the night as my mind refused to shut down. I'm driven by the bravery Dade showed. If someone like him, who has lost everything, and can still trust and survive, then so can I.

I can be brave for them.

They share a hesitant look, clearly trying to decide if it's a good idea. I stomp my foot and draw their gazes. "I don't need you to coddle me. I know my own mind." I soften my voice, knowing they are simply trying to protect me. "Please, I want to know you. I want to know everything. Can you show me?"

It's clear they are still hesitant, but Kaito drops the trap he has in his hands and wipes them on his pants. "Weyland first," he says as he watches me. "I will stay at her side in case it is too much."

I know they lessen their monstrous traits around me. They are so careful, but I want them to be themselves. They shouldn't have to hide it. I can either embrace all of them or none of them.

"If you are sure." Weyland still looks wary, but as Kaito guides me to sit on the grass and takes my hand, I nod and wait.

Dade moves to the side to give Weyland space, and with a slow breath, he changes. Magic seems to swirl around him as he transforms. His arms become longer, and his legs become bowed. The fur on his body grows longer, and his snout extends to a wolf's with huge, sharp teeth. A tail lashes the ground as his head falls back and he howls. When it stops, his eyes come to me, and I see the fear in his gaze.

Fear I will run. Fear I will reject him.

Standing, I move closer, even as I feel the others at my back. Weyland steps away, as if to escape my judgment, but I move closer once more. I raise my hand slowly, and when I go to touch his face, he flinches. Sadness fills me, but I keep my eyes on him as I stroke the softness of his fur.

"You're beautiful. I did not know you could change forms," I admit.

He dips his head slowly to give me better access, and I run my hand between his ears and scratch. His leg kicks out in a happy thump, making me giggle. How could I ever fear this?

It's just Weyland, although a different side of him, and he is still the same man who sang me to sleep through my nightmares.

"Who's a good boy?" I tease.

When I pull my hand away, he transforms back, and since I am so close, I feel the magic move across his body and almost stroke mine, making me gasp as something inside me seems to answer. He doesn't appear to notice. Instead, he grins at me before tugging me to his side.

"Your turn, water boy," Weyland goads, glancing over at Kaito.

I hold my breath and wait.

There is not much of me that remains hidden from Kai. Unlike Weyland and Dade, I have no secondary form. I appear as what I am. But when Weyland goads me forward, I raise my brow and glance down to the woman at my side.

"I do not transform," I tell her. "But I can show you part of what I'm capable of."

Her eyes brighten, and the looks she gives me twists my insides into knots. *I love her.* Fuck, do I love her. It's an instantaneous, emotional reaction. Seeing her healing oh so slowly makes a part of me want to sweep her inside the cabin and protect her from anything that may stop her progress. This moment, with her sitting outside with us all, wanting to see the more monstrous sides of us, shows me exactly what she's capable of.

My *amarta*. My brave little human.

Realizing I need water to show my tricks, I fetch the pail from inside the cabin before returning to her side. She watches me curiously as I set the pail in front of her and kneel. Her legs are tucked up beneath her, and her fingers are clenched tightly in her pants. Her eyes focus on the pail first before trailing up to my face.

"We've spoken of many things, but perhaps I should tell you of my origins," I murmur, reaching into the water pail. My fingers grow slick with the liquid, and part of me wishes they were slick with something else so I could show Kai exactly what she means to me through pleasure, but I immediately push those thoughts from my mind. She isn't ready. She may never be. It does no good to torture myself. "I was also a victim of the king, long before his fall."

Kai sucks in a breath. "You were?"

I nod carefully, preferring to stare at my reflection in the pail rather than look into her eyes. "Dade and Weyland were born monsters," I say, grimacing. "But me? I was made into one."

Dade shifts uncomfortably, as if he understands where I'm going with my story. Warhorses were also made in some respect, but Dade was likely not the first, even as he's the last. Warhorses were born at some point from those who were originally made.

"The king was always jealous of the Dead Lands, of the magic that permeates the soil. When the wall was erected, it caused the slow decline of that very magic, but the king sought to own a piece of it and so his experiments began." I tilt my head, my black eyes like inky pools of darkness in my reflection—eyes that somehow appear human despite the clear monster I am. "I was not the first experiment, but I am the first one to have lived. Part beast, part human. With that creation came many things." I twirl my fingers through the water and feel the magic there, the lingering remnants of what makes me who and what I am. "I yearned for freedom, which I eventually achieved when a guard wandered too close to my cage. I was filled with a thirst for knowledge that I never seem to quench and . . . the ability to control and survive in water."

With my words, the water begins to swirl up from the pail, coiling in the air as if controlled by some outside force. Kai's eyes widen in wonder even as Dade and Weyland suck in breaths behind me. I coax the water around Kai, letting it brush against her skin before allowing it to dance and wave. Once her eyes remain riveted on the water floating in the air, I force it into shapes. I make a lope run around her, sprinkling tiny water droplets on her face and bringing giggles from her lips. A snake coils around her, stroking the skin on her arm. Finally, my shape appears in the water, swimming. A human woman dips below the surface, languidly swimming, my form bursting around her. It's clear the two shapes mingle and dance, but before they can go any further as they embrace, I allow the water to drop back into the pail and sit back.

"I can also swim very fast and breathe under water." I shrug. "It's useless on land but a fun trick nonetheless."

Kai leans forward, her eyes fiercely holding mine. "Do not discount your abilities, Kaito," she says earnestly. "Thank you for sharing your gift with me."

Something inside me clicks and settles into place. Even as she keeps her eyes on me, I can't help but look away. During her healing, I'm realizing perhaps I have some healing left to do as well. Together, we can learn. Together, we can grow.

"Dade," I say, clearing my throat before picking up the pail and moving it out of the way. "Your turn."

Dade grins. "You have already seen what I can do," he tells Kai.

Kai, in her brightness, smiles at him. "Yes, but another look won't hurt, will it?"

And so the warhorse reveals himself in all his glory, and even I am filled with wonder at him despite seeing the monstrosities and masterpieces the king once made. The water in the pail dances as my magic seeps out and seeks the human woman beside me.

To touch, to linger, to love.

THE REST of the day passed without incident. No monsters came to attack the cabin. No new beasts came calling on Kai, refusing to leave once they saw her. Although the Dead Lands are alight with the sounds of monsters and creatures eager for meals, they do not appear. Perhaps it is because of the warhorse that now patrols our perimeter, or perhaps it is the lycan standing guard outside the door. Either way, I know I am not needed outside, so I find myself trailing inside to bring Kai the plate of berries I found.

The small berries are a rare find so close to the cabin. Traditionally found far deeper in the Dead Lands, I assumed I would never have the ability to show Kai just how sweet they are, but I stumbled upon a cluster of their bushes and immediately thought to bring them to my *amarta*.

When I step inside the cabin, I find Kai sitting up on the edge of her bed, her face pinched with some emotion I cannot place. I expected her to be asleep by now or at least lying down. Instead, she seems haunted by something.

Worried that today did indeed push her too far, I set the bowl of berries down and rush to her side. "What's wrong, Kai? Is everything okay?"

She glances up at me, her eyes filled with those memories that we want so desperately to chase away. Though we can never truly make her forget them completely, I hope that we can dull their existence. That is our plan, to help her heal and yearn for life. Even if she decides that she wants to live without us, we would accept it.

Love will have you do anything to ensure that the one you love is happy.

Kai sighs, her fingers wringing together with anxiety. "I'm scared," she admits, and my chest tightens. "I'm scared of everything, and I'm so sick of feeling so scared."

I search my mind for something to help. "Would you like me to leave? I can make you some tea and—"

"No," she rushes out, shaking her head. "No, please don't leave. I just . . ." Her eyes trail across my face, taking in the black of my eyes and the pale blue color of my skin. "I just want to feel something. Even for a moment."

I freeze, my heart beating rapidly in my chest. "You only have to ask it of me and I'll offer you anything you need, *amarta*," I whisper, unsure if I understand exactly what she wants. It's best if she names it so that I know.

Her fingers shake as she presses them to her cheek, her emotions flashing between fear and desire. "Will you . . . Kaito, will you kiss me?"

The thundering of my heart grows so loud, I'm certain she can hear it. I want to. Waters, do I want to kiss her, but Kai is still healing. Her soul is still shattered despite her progress, and today was already a hard day.

I would never want to push her.

I would wait a lifetime for a touch of her lips.

"I'm not sure that's a good idea," I murmur hesitantly. Although she asked, I'm afraid of what will happen should I give in.

"Please," she rasps, and my resolve completely crumbles. I cannot deny her anything, even despite my fear.

I grimace, but my body is already stirring at the thought of pressing my lips against hers. "One kiss," I say, more of a reminder to myself than her. If I start to kiss her, I worry I won't want to stop, and then I'll push her too far too soon. I want this action to be repeated in the future, and that won't happen if things progress too quickly.

"One kiss," Kai agrees.

Carefully, I take a seat beside her on the bed. Our thighs touch and she tenses, but when I offer her my hand, she immediately takes it, trusting me. I feel her tremble, feel the fear that tries to overrule her, but she bravely faces it down, her fingers tightening in mine until I'm certain she's stronger than I've given her credit for.

She leans in first, and I take it as a sign that she's ready. I reach up with my other hand and gently cup her jaw, tilting her face up to mine. Her eyes hold mine, focusing on me completely. As my heart beats loudly in my ears, I can hear hers doing the same. I lean down, lingering above her lips until her breath dances across mine. It's not meant to tease, only to give her a chance to decline. When she does no such thing, I press my lips against hers.

Tingles shoot from her lips to mine, like an electric shock that absorbs through my skin and takes hold. My magic spills from me, making the moisture in the air just as electric. I don't deepen the kiss. I only let our lips touch and I don't push any further. I stay there one second, two, three before I pull back just the barest amount and look at her face.

Her eyes are closed, and her lips are parted in such a way that I want to kiss her again. She pulls away from my hand and looks down, only opening her eyes when I can't see them.

"Thank you," she whispers, and my shoulders tense.

"Is there anything else you need, *amarta*?" I ask hesitantly, putting distance between us to give her space, not wanting her to have to reject me. I wouldn't wish to hurt her that way.

"No," she murmurs. "I think I'm going to sleep. It's been a long day."

I still can't see her eyes, and despite the pure joy I feel from the kiss, worry begins to scratch at my soul.

"Of course," I murmur. "I'll be just outside if you need me."

I had planned to stay in the cabin with her, but some part of me recognizes that she needs space to sort through her emotions. I want to hold her, to settle on her bed with her and offer warmth, but it feels like that would be pushing too far after so much progress today.

She nods and lies down with her back to me. Only then do I stand and head for the door. I glance back many times to make sure she's still there, that she's okay, but she gives nothing away so I slip outside and settle back against the door. Weyland glances at me as I exit, looking to the cabin and back to me.

"Is she okay?" he asks, worry in his voice.

"I don't know," I admit with a grimace.

That kiss sings in my soul, and I'm not sure if I should let it.

I'm not sure if it was the right thing to do after all.

CHAPTER
TWENTY-ONE

KAI

I wait until I hear the soft shush of the door closing before I give into the emotions boiling inside my chest. The moment he's gone, the first tear falls, and then another, and then another, until my pillow is stained with them. I clench the blanket between my teeth to stifle my sobs. I know they can hear far more than I can, so I hope it's enough as I cry silently in my bed, my body curled up tightly to keep myself together.

I feel as if I'm a million broken pieces held together by a string, ready to shatter at any given point, but I don't cry because of the fear still churning in my gut and wrecking me from the inside. I cry because the kiss felt normal. It felt nice, perfect even, but there was one thing missing—desire.

Am I broken? Have I completely lost every part of me to this fear that eats me alive? Will I ever be able to overcome it?

There's a connection between Weyland, Dade, Kaito, and me, but that uncontrolled desire I felt long before the king got his hands on me isn't there. It's all blocked by the fear that swirls inside me, my past haunting me like a ghost. I felt something, something small, like the barest flicker of a flame, but it was buried beneath the trauma of my past. I can see how it's being blocked, how I hold the key, but it's as if I can't see the lock keeping it all away. I desperately want them. I desperately want to feel again.

Images flash in my mind. I see the king sneering down at me, my naked body splayed out on the floor. I'd been hopeless, defenseless, and certain that I would die soon and hoping for it. Anything to escape the torture of feeling his hands on me. My body remembers his horrible touch and the feeling of him taking his pleasure out on me before unleashing his anger only a moment later. I was violated in every way until I was nothing but a shell. The fact that it still haunts me makes me flinch, but as I lie on my bed, tears trailing down my cheeks, I remind myself of what I know.

The king is dead. He can never hurt me again.

I am safe here in this cabin, my monsters protecting me outside.

I am cared for by Kaito, Weyland, and Dade.

If they can find the strength to fight again, then so can I.

With a shaky breath, I wipe my face with the back of my hand and begin to claw my way out of the memories that haunt me, one image at a time.

CHAPTER
TWENTY-TWO

KAI

I hated sleeping alone last night. They stayed outside of the cabin as if sensing my pain and guilt. I shouldn't have pushed Kaito for that kiss. Now I worry things are broken between us. Surely, he senses me pulling away. Kaito is an honorable man. He will feel guilty, and shame makes me hide until the sun is high in the sky.

Refusing to be cowed and hide away like I did when I was first here, I force myself to get up and get dressed. When I emerge, they carefully check me over but welcome me with bright smiles. There is some breakfast stew waiting for me, and Weyland hands it over, careful not to touch me, his eyes showing his worry. Dade grins at me and continues tending to the fire, but my eyes seek out Kaito, who is chopping wood. It's not usually his job, and he seems to be taking his anger out on it. Shame fills me once more at his obvious guilt, yet it does not stop me from appreciating the display of his glistening muscles. They shift as he chops, making my mouth turn dry before I force my gaze away. Shame once more heats my cheeks. I force myself to eat with rhythmic movements of the spoon but I

I hate this tension. I ruined everything, just like always.

When his shadow falls across me, I stiffen, unable to meet his eyes. Crouching next to me, he lays his big hand near my leg but doesn't touch me, and I hate the distance. I suddenly hate it so much, I could weep.

"I'm sorry, Kai. I let my desire for you overwhelm my senses. I never should have kissed you. I knew you were not ready. I did not mean to hurt you. Please forgive me."

When I glance over, his head is bowed and his shoulders are rounded in pain.

"I am the one who is sorry," I murmur huskily. "I knew better than to push it, but for a moment, when I looked at you, I just wanted to. I wanted to feel alive and normal. I forgot I'm not. I'm sorry that hurt you, but please do not feel guilty. That is and never will be your fault."

"How about we both agree we are sorry?" he responds, lifting his head, his eyes alight with hope as he watches me.

"I'd like that." I'd like to be able to move on, and the possibility that something between us could be ruined? I don't think I could live with that. Kaito was my first helping hand in the dark. He was and is my savior. If that were gone, if I were alone once more in the dark, I might just tumble into that waiting end once more. "How about we forget our jobs today and just go explore once more?"

I hope they say yes. I need to get away from here for a little bit. I need a reminder of why I continue to fight, even when everything seems so dark and hopeless. I need a reminder that there is good in this world, even if it doesn't feel like it right now.

"I say yes," Weyland says.

"I agree," Dade offers.

"Then let's do it." Kaito stands and hesitantly offers me his hand, hope still shimmering in his eyes.

Trying to reclaim this for myself, I lay mine in his and allow him to tug me to my feet.

I keep hold of him for warmth and comfort, needing it more than ever today.

~

WE TREK out farther than we ever have. Every time we go to stop, I insist we keep going. Something inside of me demands I push myself to see how far I can go—or maybe I'm just trying to run away from my demons.

"*Bacca*," Weyland warns.

"Just a bit longer," I plead, turning my big eyes on him and watching him weaken. It's cruel because I know they struggle to deny me, but I can't go back, not yet, and if you asked, I couldn't tell you why.

"A little farther, then we can go back and I'll show you a flower that glows if you disturb it," Dade offers softly.

All of them obviously sense my feral panic. Kaito is quiet and watching me carefully, and I hate that he's still blaming himself despite us talking about it.

I pushed it, me, and now he is paying the price.

The king's mocking voice follows me even now, and no matter how far I go, I can't seem to outrun it. It's as if he's chasing me, even though I know it's in my mind, but I still speed up my steps.

In my haste, I don't look where I'm going—another mistake. My feet catch on something, and my eyes dart down to see a tree root sticking up out of the earth.

I fall forward, the ground rapidly approaching my face, and I close my eyes automatically as my hands come up to protect me. Arms suddenly band around me, yanking me to a stop before I can hit the earth.

I breathe a sigh of relief when the arms adjust to hold me more securely, banding across my chest and slipping up to my throat.

The scent tells me it's Weyland, but my heart starts to race. The firm grip feels like a collar, like the old hands that used to hurt me.

Screaming, I jerk from the grip, hitting the spongy ground and scrambling backwards. I see blurs, shapes, and hands reaching for me.

Familiar hands.

Hands that hurt me.

Shadows grow around us, taking away all the light until I'm lost in the darkness of the shadows, completely cut off.

Alone.

Panicking.

Old memories wrap me in their mocking, cruel grip.

"Oh, how I missed you, my little pet," the king's voice whispers in my ear, and I twirl in the shadows, wide-eyed and terrified. His mocking laughter comes from behind me as I push to my knees and spin, whimpering in agony.

"Pet, little pet!" His voice comes at me from every direction.

Covering my ears, I start to scream, the panic choking me.

Suddenly something substantial, warm, and smelling faintly of fires and flowers wraps around me. My eyes open, and a hand, a black shadow hand, thrusts toward me, offering me a way out.

I grasp it with everything in me and pull.

TWENTY-THREE

The trees pass me by as I run, pushing myself, although I don't know why. No one can see me after all, not if I don't want them to. I could blend into the fog rolling through the Dead Lands or the ever-present darkness, appearing as nothing more than another shadow.

That's what they all think I am.

I am a bigger monster than most.

Even now, the world has a hazy quality to it, and when I smack my hand into a tree as I slide to a stop, it's nothing but black smoke formed into the shape. I could change into anything if I so wished, and I often do.

Boredom is my worst enemy.

I'm about to turn and find my way back through the lands to the cave I inhabit when a chord is struck. It's like music in the air, calling to me. I focus my powers on it, letting it wash through me.

There is so much delicious, vibrant pain, it beats within my soul. I could no more ignore it than I could the darkness. I let it guide me until I happen upon a clearing. My powers seem to react without my command, shadows crawling along the ground and foliage, obscuring it in darkness.

There are three monsters there, and they turn their horrified eyes to me, their whispers reaching me in the dark.

Boogeyman.

The horror and terror in that one word makes me smile. When the boogeyman comes, everyone runs. Ignoring them, I turn to the creature who called to me, and with the first look, I am struck by lightning, as if the sun has pierced my abyss.

She is a small, human female, but she exudes so much agony and fear that I could drink on it for days. I want to lick it away and taste every inch as she screams.

I find I do not like her terror, even if it echoes my own.

I drift closer, unable to resist, and emerge through the shadows as she spins. Her eyes are closed and unseeing, and her hands are over her ears as she screams. I look around for the cause and see nothing. Suddenly, her eyes open. Her big bright orbs freeze me in place, begging for an escape, for a savior. I have never been someone's liberator before, but something about this little human makes me want to be.

I hold out my hand, watching her, and when she lays her soft, small one in mine, I am lost to her completely, brightened by her sunlight and darkened by her pain.

I become hers.

TWENTY-FOUR

KAI

The darkness is so thick, it's practically impossible to see through. It echoes the darkness inside me, the memories of my past that torture me in my nightmares. Everything about this darkness should be terrifying and make me scream in terror, but it's almost . . . comforting, as if these shadows are darkness incarnate and also home. I want to wrap them around me like a blanket.

Lost in my panic, I did not hesitate to take the hand, a lifeline that was offered to me. I was drowning, gasping for air, and someone threw me a line. I did not pause to question it or wonder whom that hand belonged to. I was only prompted to take it. Something in my chest urged me to before I completely toppled into the darkness. The moment I took that hand, the darkness in my chest began to clear, but the shadows remain around me.

At first, I don't see him, but I can feel the hand enveloping mine. The shadows begin to swirl and fade, bleeding into the ground and leaving him before me in all his glory. His eyes are what strike me first. Initially blank in their whiteness within the shadows, the glow fades and reveals eyes as yellow as the fruit I used to collect back in the Shadow Lands. He's tall, far taller than even Dade who stands well above me. This being is massive, imposing in his stature alone, and it makes me gasp at the realization that this is a monster.

His skin is a deep gray mottled with shadows. He's both terrifying and magnificent, and my skin both crawls and erupts with goosebumps. I stare up into his face and his lips part, revealing pristine, sharp teeth that could easily rip my throat out. Sharp, pointed ears peek from his messy black hair, making me want to reach up and brush it aside.

As if I could ever reach.

"Hello, my little phosphene," he says, and his voice makes me shiver. It's deep and dark, just like his shadows. It almost echoes in the darkness, as if his voice is so powerful, it has no choice but to repeat itself. "My little oblivion."

My hand still rests in his.

Weyland, Kaito, and Dade all stand as still as statues to the side, their eyes wide in horror. A monster that frightens other monsters stands before me, holding my hand. Such a monster pulled me from my darkness and brought me back into the light. I should be equally as terrified of this monster who studies me so, his large hand swallowing mine, but something in me calls to him, as if we are the same and we wear the same kind of pain.

It's strange to feel so accepted and yet be afraid of it.

"What are you?" I rasp, watching him carefully in case he lunges forward. I won't be able to stop him should he attack, but I'm wary enough of him to think I can or that the others will be faster.

His shadows swirl beneath our feet, dancing and tickling. When they brush along my flesh, they leave behind a sweet coolness that begs me to lie down and let them cover me. It's like the fog Cora and I used to play in as children, providing the feeling of being blind and enjoying it while water droplets accumulate on your skin. His shadows feel like that, and it both haunts me with my past and makes me want to bask in the nostalgia. How curious.

He smiles, but it's more of a baring of teeth than anything else. It should be sinister, but I find the attempt endearing. "I am the darkness that dances in the forest. I am the shadows that kiss your feet. If you dive deep into your nightmares, you will find me there."

"I . . ." I snap my mouth shut. I had indeed found him in my nightmares, lost within the memories that haunt me, triggered by the hand of someone who will never hurt me.

"The boogeyman," Dade rasps, and I glance over at him.

The new monster follows my gaze, taking in the warhorse with curious eyes. "Yes, I have been called so many times."

"A story," Weyland murmurs. "A legend."

"Clearly not," Kaito points out, his eyes wide with fear as he focuses on where I still hold this new monster's hand. "Because he's standing right in front of us."

"Do you have a name?" the shadow monster asks me, focusing entirely on me and dismissing the others as if they are not a threat.

I hesitate at first, afraid that by giving him my name, he will keep it, but that seems like a silly notion when he just pulled me from my horrors. "Kai," I offer meekly, and the small sound makes me angry. Have I not grown bigger than my fear? Am I not holding the hand of a monster who frightens other monsters? Yet I still sound weak. "Kai," I say strongly, as if I'm proving to both myself and this new monster that I'm strong enough to face him. "I'm Kai."

"Kai," he repeats, voicing it like he's tasting the sound between his lips. "Kai, phosphene, oblivion." He leans down and peers into my eyes as if he were peering into my soul. "Kai, wielder of darkness, I am Rook."

Rook. It suits him, as if the name is as dark as his shadows.

The more I stare at him, the more his warmth seeps through the flesh of my hand and the angrier I grow until I'm seething and it begins to spill out of me. My heart beats wildly in my chest, fear making it faster, and my anger only amplifies that. Despite the casual nature of our conversation and knowing the others are here, that same fear consumes me from the inside out. When will it take me completely? Will I ever truly heal?

My fury turns to something else, something more potent. I am the darkness just as he said. I'm sick of being afraid. I'm sick of the nightmares that plague me whether I am awake or asleep. I move to jerk my hand from Rook's, but he holds fast, his large fingers tightening on my smaller ones.

"Let go," I hiss, fury spitting from behind my teeth.

"You're letting your darkness control you, little oblivion. You must control it in return," Rook says, still refusing to let go.

"You know nothing about me!" I jerk again and this time, the others see my struggle and take a step forward.

Rook shoots them a glare that freezes them for a mere second before they collect themselves and stalk forward.

"Release her," Dade commands, his lips parting over his teeth.

"Now," Weyland adds.

Rook only stares at them, unfazed. "If she allows the shadows to consume her, she will never be whole. It will kill her if she allows those shadows to fester."

They freeze, their eyes trailing over to me where I struggle.

"Let me go!" I snarl, lashing out at Rook, hitting his arm as if I have the strength to dislodge him. "Let me go!"

"Shh, little oblivion," Rook coos, and his voice echoes like before, offering comfort. "Fight the fear but don't fight so hard you grow tired. The key to defeating your darkness and controlling it is to first admit it is there."

I don't want to look too deeply into my soul. I don't want to see the oil that coats my memories and changes me into something else. I'm no longer Kai of the Shadow Lands. She died when I dove off that castle. In her place is something else, some other beast I'm not prepared to face yet.

"No," I whisper, tugging at my arm until it aches. "No."

"Yes," Rook counters. "Find it, see it, accept it."

The shadows around my feet begin to climb my legs, comforting me in a way that I've never experienced. The king's voice echoes in those shadows, demanding I obey and cower.

"No," I rasp, gasping for air, desperate to get away. "Please, no."

"That's enough!" Kaito snarls. "Leave her be!"

Rook doesn't even look at him. "You know nothing of darkness, half breed. I suggest you sit this one out." Weyland takes a step forward, but Rook shakes his head. "Your darkness is not as deep. Only the warhorse knows some of what she suffers, but none of you understand debilitating shadows like I do. I will not harm her. You have my word."

I've been looking forward to this, little pet.

Tears begin to fall down my face, spilling over my cheeks as I get a good look at my memories. I see Cora sacrificing herself for me and thinking I would only lose a sister, only to discover I was losing everything. A memory of Merryl as he watched the guards drag me away, doing nothing to save me, giving no protest follows after. He didn't even beg for me to be spared, so afraid of the king. The king tortured and touched me, then Cora reappeared in all her beauty, coming to vanquish my nightmares, but it was too late. They had already climbed inside my soul.

I collapse under the weight of my darkness, my sobs racking my body until I am torn into a million pieces. Strong arms wrap around me, the shadows holding me together despite the shards.

"I'm broken," I cry, my voice cracking and watery. "I'm so broken."

"Yes," Rook agrees, his large hand stroking my hair. "We all are, little oblivion." His chest vibrates with his hum in a way that soothes me. "But I'll tell you a secret."

I tilt my head up, meeting his yellow eyes, and I wait for his words of wisdom as the others come closer, offering their own comfort. "What?" I croak, holding my breath.

He smiles, and this time, it's not unsettling. "Those cracks are how the light gets in, little oblivion," he murmurs. "They are how the light gets in."

CHAPTER
TWENTY-FIVE
KAI

I don't know how long I huddle in Rook's arms, absorbing his shadows as if they are the warmth of a large fire. I only know that it's long past daytime when I stir and look up into the trees. There is no longer any sunshine, and whatever moon there might be this night is hidden behind clouds. I know nothing of the time, only that I've kept us all out in the forest so late. Shame fills me that I put us in danger for my own foolish hauntings and that I can't control them like Rook wants me to.

"I'm sorry I kept us out so late," I rasp, glancing over my shoulder toward Weyland, Kaito, and Dade.

We are so far from the cabin because I had been running.

I realize now that I had been trying to escape myself. I've been constantly running from myself.

Now that I see what I've been doing, I understand it, but I don't like it. Rook reminded me that I'm broken, but his sentiment about the light getting in surprisingly makes me feel better. If a creature such as him, so consumed by darkness and shadows that he is shadows personified, can find the light, then shouldn't I be able to?

"Don't apologize," Kaito replies with a shake of his head. "We were meant to be here when we were." His eyes dart up to Rook, who he holds me in his arms, and then away, as if he can't quite stomach looking at him for too long.

Weyland is watching Rook like a predator who meets one far bigger than he is. He's so incredibly tense that I feel as if his bones would creak with every movement.

"You need not fear me," Rook says, his cheek resting on top of my head. It's a comforting position, a soft one I didn't think a monster like him could enjoy. "As long as Kai wills it, I will not harm her chosen."

I sigh, sinking deeper into Rook's arms despite knowing nothing about him. I don't need to, not really. Our souls seem to speak to each other, and it feels like there is a tether between them that is as solid as his arms around me. I think Kaito was right. We were meant to be here to meet Rook. Why else would he feel as much like home as the others do?

I'm about to request we head back, prepared to invite Rook to come with us, when a scream rents the air and freezes each of us in place. Weyland holds a torch that I hadn't realized was there, but the light doesn't penetrate the darkness as much as I'd like. That scream had been monstrous, clearly not human, but it's rare to hear such a sound. Usually, the screams sound a bit more filled with humanity.

"What was that?" I whisper, tucking tighter against Rook.

Rook lifts his nose into the air as if he can scent the wind. When his face twists with murderous intention, he hisses, "Humans."

I blink. Humans? That scream had not been human in the slightest.

"Come closer," Rook snarls at Weyland, Dade, and Kaito. "I cannot hide us with you spread so far apart."

To their credit, the others immediately move in, the shadows swirling around us until they hide us from view. Disappointment at not being able to see the threat or where it comes from fills me before Rook nuzzles my hair.

"Do not despair, little oblivion. Look." I blink as the shadows lighten on our side, as if providing a window. "They will not see us, but we can see them," he says, knowing I was confused.

At first, no one appears, but the screams and sounds of movement grow closer. My ears aren't as good as Weyland's, who stiffens long before I hear male human voices laughing boisterously between themselves.

The torches appear shortly after, the soft glow spreading until the first one appears. I recognize him, not because I know who he is but by the way he carries himself like my father. He's from the Shadow Lands, although his weathered face doesn't strike my memories, but that isn't what makes me huddle into Rook.

More humans appear, many carrying weapons and joking between them.

"If the king could see us now, we'd surely be brought to his table," one crows. "Just look at our prize!"

"Aye, he would offer the finest wines and put their heads on spikes for all to see," another adds. "Perhaps the new queen's would be beside them, her mouth open in a scream forever."

I cover the gasp that slips from my mouth, my fingers holding it in, but the horror of these men praising a dead, cruel king isn't the worst of the matter. The cages begin to appear, carried by people I used to see working the fields in the Shadow Lands. I don't know any of their names, but I see a few faces I once knew before the king took me for himself. They look miserable as they carry large cages filled with dead bodies.

Bodies of slaughtered monsters.

Each cage is full and dripping blood, leaving a trail behind them. None of them live, so I can only assume the scream came from the death of another. Their prizes are innocent monsters slain for some proud, dead king.

The shadows in my soul almost take me, the horror of seeing those monsters in cages like I was kept in nearly triggering me. Only Rook's soft hand stroking my shoulders keeps me present as I witness this horror.

The last cage appears, and the monster inside is alive. The large snake woman tries to grab the people carrying her, but she can't reach them. She hisses and snaps, screaming her terror.

What's happening? The humans are hunting monsters now?

I clench my fingers on Rook's bicep, a request on my lips before I know I intend to speak. "Help her," I whisper.

What horrors are they saving this one for?

These men speak of the old king as if he's worthy of worship, as if they can bring him back to life. It's as if the Gilded Lands, Shadows Lands, and Dead Lands hadn't been dying under his rule.

As if he were not dead and only waiting for his rebirth.

"Help her," I repeat. "Please."

Seeing her in the cage makes me angry. It makes me want to rush out there myself and free her. Luckily, I don't have to. One moment, I'm being held in Rook's arms, and the next, the shadows around me twist and swirl. They crawl along the ground toward the group of humans. I think he's just going to go after the ones holding the cage, but I forgot that Rook is a monster whom other monsters fear.

Their screams begin to fill the air as Rook slaughters the humans one by one, these people far more monstrous than those they hunt. I stare with wide eyes as Weyland circles me in his arms while Rook makes quick work of the humans who have no awareness of the monster in their midst. When the screams stop, the shadows fade away, leaving only those at Rook's feet. The cage with the snake woman sits on the ground now, her eyes wild and feral.

I step forward, her eyes focusing on me. "We mean you no harm," I say, not sure if she understands me, but when I reach for the lock, Rook appears at my side.

"She may attack in fear," he warns.

I nod and pull the lockpin free. The door pops open, and I back up. "You're free," I tell her. "Your cage is open."

She hesitates one second, two before she slithers forth and leaves the cage entirely. Her long, lithe body is covered in wounds, as if she fought valiantly to be free. Those scales, a deep purple shimmer, reflect the light of the torch Weyland carries as she moves. She looks back once, meets my eyes, and nods.

"I am in your debt, human," she says before disappearing into the forest.

Kaito relaxes. "Nagas always put me on edge."

My eyes stay on where she disappeared, on where she found her freedom.

Something inside me sings at my action, as if I opened my own cage and found my own freedom and found my purpose, even if it's still the tiniest flickering flame.

The shadows stroke my flesh, and I look up at Rook, at this new monster who feels like everything I've ever wanted, and then I look at the four monsters I now consider my own.

"Let's go home," I murmur.

The tightest thread pulling at my heart loosens.

CHAPTER
TWENTY-SIX

KAI

While we walk back to our cabin, my mind wanders. My hand is still firmly held in Rook's, and I can't seem to let go. It's almost comforting to be hidden in his shadows.

Humans are hunting monsters?

Since when?

Why?

Are those the screams I keep hearing? What's happening out there in our world? I don't understand, and I suppose I never will while hiding away here. I can't bring myself to go back, not even for this warning. I don't know if that will ever change.

As we reach the cabin, I'm still distracted as I wash and prepare for bed. It's only when I'm lying down with my monsters surrounding me, filling the tiny cabin, that the truth hits me.

If humans are hunting monsters, is Cora in danger?

No, no, she can't be. She's queen now, not to mention the army of monsters she surrounds herself with. No human would dare attack her, and even if they do, her monsters will keep her safe.

But who will keep the monsters safe?

Unable to handle the stress, I start to clean even though I should be resting. I see them all watching me, exchanging concerned looks.

"Is this normal?" Rook whispers.

I pretend not to hear as I sweep, focusing on the methodical task to stop my mind from throwing up exactly what could be happening to Cora right now. One thing is for certain—if the humans get to her, it won't be pretty.

"No," Weyland answers.

"I see," Rook responds.

"What shall we do?" Dade hisses.

"Nothing. She will eventually tire. Let her work her way through this," Kaito finally offers, his voice soft and caring, and then without a word, he picks up the other broom, heads my way, and starts to help.

I shoot him a grateful smile, and hours later, when I'm covered in sweat and the cabin is sparkling clean, I collapse into my bed.

Weyland yawns. "It's about time."

"Goodnight," I tell them with a wince, realizing how late I kept them up with my troubles.

Within minutes, Weyland is snoring loud enough to shake the rafters, but it's a familiar, comforting sound that has me snuggling into my fur to keep warm. When my eyes close, however, my mind wanders once more, remembering the fear on the naga's face and the men joking about what they would do to her.

What about Cora?

Can I truly abandon her? She never abandoned me, but saving her wouldn't be easy if I traveled that path.

It would mean going back to a place I vowed I would never return to. It would mean leaving the safety of our cabin and the life I have found here. And what if she's fine? Then I would have faced all that for nothing. What if it's just a few odd hunters we have already dispatched?

"Sleep, little oblivion. Your problems will still be there tomorrow." Rook's voice is soft in the dark, a warmth that eases some of the tension.

The command in the shadows has me softening into my bed, and as Rook wraps his darkness around me, holding me in those comforting shadows, my mind relaxes long enough for me to fall into slumber.

No nightmares plague me that night.

TWENTY-SEVEN

WEYLAND

Kai is different today. She wakes with the sun, but instead of us forcing her from the cabin, she skips out of it. She reaches for my hand over breakfast, and there is something unguarded about the smile she gives me as we collect firewood. There was always a shadow there before, but now the shadow follows her. Rook is unable to leave her side, and something about having him there seems to have given her some confidence—or maybe it is the fact that he forced her to face her demons.

I don't know, but what I do know is that Kai looks happier than I've ever seen her. She appears unburdened, at least a little.

We fall into our routine and, surprisingly, Rook fits in well. He helps Kai with her chores before helping Kaito with the crops. It's as if he were always here, as if we were always meant to find her and be together. My eyes go back to her, and I realize we were.

She called us together. She made us a family.

The monsters nobody wanted.

The nightmares of even our own land.

The wanderers, the loners, and the lost.

Kai is the same, and maybe that's why we fit so well. I do not care about the whys, though, only the now. Kai is mine, and when she walks past me, grinning widely at me, I know my future is bright with her at my side.

For the first time in a long time, I have a family.

I have a mate, and I have a future.

"THE MAN I saw in your memories," Rook suddenly says, breaking the silence as we eat dinner. "Who was he?"

We all freeze, our eyes swinging to our Kai, ready to protect her. Her spoon clinks against the side of the bowl as she raises her gaze to his.

"The one in the fields with you," Rook clarifies.

When she blows out a breath, her shoulders relaxing, we all sigh in relief. We thought he meant the king, the one who hurt her. No matter who he is, I won't allow Rook to upset my *bacca* like that.

"Oh, that's Merryl," she whispers softly. "My ex."

"Ex?" My head tilts to the side, and she grins at me.

"You're adorable," she remarks, making my eyes widen. Clearing my throat, I ignore the wagging of my tail behind me. When it's clear I still want to know more, she slumps a little. "Someone I dated."

"Dated?" Kaito asks, puzzled like me.

Humming, she scoops another spoonful of stew as she seems to contemplate how to explain. "Unlike monsters, we don't know our mates. We find them. We often date, which means we get to know someone we like. If we are compatible and happy, then we marry."

"And you and he dated?" I want to growl. I'm pretty sure I show some teeth.

"For a while. We were even going to marry, which is a binding ceremony," she admits. "But that was before."

Wanting to take her mind off that and the darkness she has gone through, I cough to get her attention. "How did you date?"

"Oh, well, we did activities together that we thought the other might enjoy, or we ate together or worked," she starts.

"So we are dating." I nod, feeling happier now that I know. Her eyes widen and her mouth parts. "Aren't we? We do those things."

"Well, uh," she blunders, blushing adorably. "I guess, but you have to ask the other person on a date."

"Oh." I frown. I did not know I was doing this wrong with my mate. How foolish of me. If she needs human customs, I will offer her those freely. "Then will you date me?"

She giggles at my question, covering her cheeks as they redden.

"And me!" Dade raises his hand. "Date me more."

"I would also like to date." Kaito nods seriously.

"We are bound eternally, little oblivion, but I would also like to date," Rook adds.

Her eyes sweep across us, her cheeks so red, they must hurt. "Oh," is all she says.

"Did I ask wrong?" I frown, disappointed. "I'm sorry."

"No, no, no, I . . . um, yes. Yes, I will go on dates with all of you." She grins before it turns into the most adorable giggle. "When?"

"Now." I shoot to my feet. "Starting with me." I puff up my chest as she watches.

"Shadows," Kaito curses. "I should have been faster."

I stick my tongue out at him and hurry to her side, taking her hand and lifting her to her feet. My hands linger on her hips as she swallows, her eyes wide like the moon as they meet mine.

"Now?" she whispers.

"Now." I grin, removing my hands even though I don't want to, but I don't want to make her uncomfortable. "Come, *bacca*, let's date."

TWENTY-EIGHT

I hadn't expected Weyland to be serious about going on a date right this very second, but as soon as he grabs my hand and leads me from the cabin, I start to believe that's what he actually meant. His large fingers envelop mine, and I can't help smiling at his excitement.

"Where exactly are we going?" I ask, grinning up at him as he leads me into the forest. "The waterfall?"

He pauses and looks down at me. "Would you prefer the waterfall?"

I shake my head. "It's completely up to you, wolfie. Your choice."

A grin pulls at his lips, making my insides flip, and his fingers squeeze mine gently. "Wolfie, huh?" he asks. "I like it."

The flush that spreads across my cheeks is hard to hide, and it only makes him smile wider. Weyland is attractive with his strong jaw and bright eyes, but Weyland smiling? He's infinitely more sensual. His smile is free of strain and fear. He's simply existing, and everything about it draws me closer to him. When we first met, he didn't smile nearly as much as he does now. Perhaps I am changing my monsters as much as they are changing me.

We walk for about twenty minutes before Weyland stops at a particularly large tree. From what I can see, there's nothing special about it. There's nothing on it or in it, and there are no waterfalls or structures around us. I'm confused about why he chose this spot but decide he probably just wanted to be away from the cabin in general.

Determined I should encourage him, I pat the tree trunk. "This is a nice tree," I say. "Perfectly treelike."

Weyland snorts out a laugh that has my insides flipping again. "We're not there yet." He leans down and looks me in the eye, getting so close that his musk wraps around me and has me swaying into him. "Do you trust me, *bacca*?"

His expression is so earnest, I know my answer will make a huge difference. If I say no, it'll hurt him, but he also won't push, allowing me to have the space I need. If I say yes . . .

"Of course I trust you," I tell him with a smile. "Why?"

"I need you to cling to my back while I climb," he says hesitantly. "But if it makes you uncomfortable . . ."

Heights. I haven't been so high since the castle. My heart kicks in my chest, and I stare up at the tree. The top of it disappears into the rest of the trees, telling me it's much taller than the others. I should have been able to guess that considering how much larger the trunk is, but it still doesn't hit me until I stare at it.

"I . . . ," I trail off.

"We can go somewhere else," Weyland offers. "We don't have to—"

"I want to," I interrupt. "I do. Just . . . May I have a minute to gather my courage?"

"Of course, *bacca*," he murmurs, coming close to wrap his arms around me. The heat of his embrace relaxes me, his familiar scent holding me prisoner. "Take as long as you need, and if you decide we should go somewhere else, then we'll go. It's okay."

His warm hug immediately makes me feel better, but I still take a few minutes to breathe deeply and remind myself that Weyland will never let me fall. I once wanted to fall and now I'm scared to. How interesting. My mindset has changed so much these last few months, and it's all because of my monsters.

"Okay, I'm ready," I whisper, leaning back to look up into his face. "Would it be better if I climb myself?"

There's no way I can scale that trunk, but I would try if Weyland preferred me to.

He laughs. "No. When I lean down, wrap your arms around my neck and your legs around my waist." When he bends, I move forward to do as he says. I am careful not to choke him with my arms before I lift one leg and then the other. His hands grasp my thighs to make sure I'm on before he stands to his full height. My breath rushes out of me. I haven't had a piggyback ride since Cora gave me one when we were children. "Hold on, *bacca*. I'm going to scale the tree, but I won't let you fall." When I nod, he moves to the base of the tree and looks up. "Here we go."

I stop breathing when he holds out his hands, now tipped with claws, and digs them into the bark. He tests his hold, making sure his claws are embedded deep enough before he starts to climb. The ground quickly grows farther away, and it takes everything in me not to look down. My stomach drops at the feeling of being so high and the memory of what it felt like to fall down such a distance. I don't remember much of the impact, but I remember the fall. I remember looking up to see Cora screaming after me. I remember her horror.

I shove the memories away and focus on Weyland's movements. I can feel his muscles flex and relax between my thighs and I become consumed with that. Watching him scale the tree without much of a struggle is sexier than I expect, so by the time we reach the top, I'm wholly focused on him. Each movement and every sound goes right to my core, creating a welcome distraction from the sheer height we're at.

Weyland finds a branch that's above the other trees but is so large, it'll be easy to sit and stand on.

"You can let go now, *bacca*," he instructs.

"Are you sure?" I ask, biting my lip. My arms and legs are still locked around him, and fear makes my words breathy.

"I would never let you fall, Kai," he assures me. "I've got you."

Taking a deep breath, I slowly unlock my legs and let them slide down. His hands remain on my thighs, making sure I'm steady before I loosen my fingers. He ducks and spins, putting me in front of him before I can release him completely.

"That's it," he murmurs. "I've got you."

His attentiveness has me sucking in air—not out of fear but arousal. It's been so long since my body has reacted as it should. It takes me a few seconds to gather my senses enough to meet his gaze. When I do, those brilliant eyes flash as if he knows. When his fingers clench on my side where he steadies me, I realize he probably does.

Kaito's words come back to me in this moment, and I flush bright red at the realization. Lycans have a great sense of smell.

"Oh, um . . . ," I start, but Weyland, ever the gentleman, gently guides me back toward the trunk where the branch is the widest.

"Do not be embarrassed, *bacca*," he murmurs. "Your scent is intoxicating."

If it's possible to flush brighter than I already am, I do. His voice has dropped an octave and there's a huskiness to it that wasn't there before, but he doesn't push. Instead, he settles down on the large branch, sitting with his back against the trunk so that he looks out over the land. When he offers me his hand, I immediately take it and kneel, settling between his legs. It makes me feel safer to be caged in by him, and I lean back against his chest, sighing at the feeling of safety I've only felt with my monsters.

The land is dark right now but dawn is close. I can feel it in the air, this proverbial holding of breath around us. It's as if the forest itself waits anxiously for the sun to rise. In the Dead Lands, it's muted, but as it crests the horizon, I realize it's not so muted now that the wall has come down. Usually, we're beneath the trees where the sunlight is filtered. Here, though, so high in the sky, it's far less muted. It touches the Dead Lands first, chasing away the darkness that makes it scary. As it spreads, I realize this particular tree has a view of every land. The Shadow Lands light up second, revealing the place I grew up in, and when the Gilded Lands light up and the castle comes into view, there's a pang in my chest but the fear is gone. The king is dead. Although he still lives in my nightmares and his scars still stain my skin, he can't hurt me again. Cora made sure of that, and now my monsters chase away my nightmares.

"It's beautiful," I whisper, taking it all in. "Three worlds no longer separated."

Weyland nods. "There are those who prefer it how it was, but I, for one, am thankful the wall came down. Had it not, I never would have found you," he says against my ear. "You gave me a reason to fight, Kai, and for that, I will always be grateful."

"You did the same for me," I tell him. "All four of you. I'm . . . I feel stronger now. I'm not completely healed, but I'm getting there because of you, Kaito, Rook, and Dade."

His arms tighten around me, holding me close. "We only wish to see you happy, *bacca*."

I rest my fingers against his forearm before tilting my head back and around to look into his eyes. His hand quickly comes up to support the back of my head. "I think if I can be truly happy and whole," I say, making sure he's looking at me, "it will be with the four of you."

His eyes flash again, and I can tell he's restraining himself for my benefit. I reach up and cup his jaw, running my fingers along the scruff there. "What's wrong, wolfie?" I ask, partly teasing and partly not wanting to cause him stress.

For a moment, memories of me teasing another man flit across my memory. It was so easy and fun, but I have changed since then.

He grits his teeth and tilts his head back. "Every instinct in me wants me to claim you." The corded muscle on his neck stands out as a muscle ticks in his jaw. "The desperation to kiss you chokes me," he rasps, his touch respectful on my body despite his words. "I can't . . . I shouldn't . . ."

His struggle does something to me. I want him. I do. There are lingering fears in my mind. I slipped into the darkness when I tried with Kaito, but I've made progress since then. My body is starting to come alive again, so surely that means I'm healing.

"Weyland," I whisper, "look at me."

He takes a few seconds to gather his wits, but he tilts his head down, his bright eyes meeting mine. His pupils are large and desperation flickers there. I know, despite how he feels, that if I don't want to do anything, we won't. He would never push, so this has to be my decision.

"If you want to kiss me," I whisper, still cupping his jawline, "you can."

I think he stops breathing. "But—"

"I want to kiss you," I say, making sure he's looking into my eyes and seeing the truth there. There's still a sense of unease and a little bit of fear, but I'm not lying. I want to kiss Weyland. I want to do more than that, but a kiss is a good place to start. Perhaps as I heal, I'll be able to offer more of myself, but there's no telling how long it will take me to mend. "I want you to kiss me," I repeat when he watches me carefully.

"You're certain?" he asks. He turns me so I'm facing him, then he drapes my legs over his so we're facing each other in a much more intimate position than we were. Desire sparks through me, sliding down to my core and bringing it back to life for a moment. "We don't have to."

"I'm certain." I cup his jaw between my hands, looking up at him. "Kiss me."

He takes a deep breath, as if collecting himself. I didn't know if I could ever get to this, if I could give them this part of me. They never pushed, never insisted, and now all he cares about is me and how I'm handling it, but I can see his desire flashing in his eyes. Every part of him is tense, as if he's holding himself back and reminding himself to be careful.

"Okay," he murmurs, leaning his forehead against mine. "Okay."

Carefully, oh so carefully, he closes the distance between us, his lips pressing the barest of kisses on mine. It's featherlight, a trial, and the moment he pulls back, I want more.

"A better kiss," I tell him. "A real one."

He hesitates, but then he leans down again. His hand comes up to gently caress the back of my neck so as not to harm me. He makes sure I'm okay with the hold before he presses his lips against mine again. This time, we sort of linger there for a second until I sigh and open my lips, inviting him in and asking for more.

Weyland groans and sweeps inside, tasting me. He uses his hand on the back of my head to help direct me for the kiss. My arms come up to wrap around his neck, my fingers tangling in his hair as I try to get closer. His other hand grips my waist and pulls me closer until my core is pressed against his arousal. I gasp against his lips and he pauses, thinking I'm panicked. Instead, I take the opportunity to sweep my tongue inside, to claim him as he claimed me. His breaths grow rapid with desire, and he breaks the kiss to trail his lips down my neck, winding my body tight.

"Oh!" I gasp, leaning my head back. Tingles start in my toes and travel upward, lighting my body up from the inside out and dragging me from the darkness. The world grows bright around us and—

"Kai," Weyland rasps. It's the sound of disbelief that has me popping my eyes open and trying to figure out what he's worried about.

At first, I can't make sense of what I'm seeing. There's so much light, I think the sun must be right above us, but then I make sense of the light. It's not coming from the sun at all.

It's coming from me.

"What . . . ?" I stare at my skin in surprise. The light I felt was literal. It arcs along my skin like lightning, giving off a glow that turns me into some sort of beacon. "Weyland, what's happening?"

The light reflects in his eyes as he stares at me in wonder. He doesn't remove his hands despite the bright light, but it doesn't appear to hurt him either. "Magic," he whispers. "Kai, this is magic."

I shake my head. "No. That's impossible. I'm human."

I'm reminded about Cora, though, and her connection with her monsters and the magic she utilized. However, that doesn't make sense for me. For Cora, yes, but not for me. I'm too . . . too . . .

"*Bacca*," Weyland whispers, leaning in to press a kiss to my forehead. "We should tell the others and see what they know." He hesitates. "I don't know much about magic but the others might."

"But what does it do?" I ask, staring at my hand in wonder. "What if it's from you?"

Weyland meets my eyes. "We both know it's coming from you, *bacca*, and that's okay. Wrap your arms and legs around me and I'll get us down."

He hesitates, his head swooping down to kiss my lips. "Thank you, *bacca*."

My heart squeezes. Magic?

But I'm human.

CHAPTER
TWENTY-NINE

KAI

The trip down the tree was almost scarier than the trip up it, but I held on tight. When we reached the ground, Weyland didn't let me down. Instead, he told me to hold on, his hands tightening on my thighs ever so slightly, and began to run. I made a sound of protest because I'm heavy, but he snorted and said that I'm not heavy at all.

We made it back to the cabin in record time. It's a stark reminder that they hold themselves back so much for me. We'd taken an hour to reach that tree, but we made it back in ten minutes. I appreciate that they give me space to move at my own pace, but it still makes me sad that they have to hold back everything about themselves just to be with me.

Maybe one day, they won't have to.

Kaito, Dade, and Rook are all settled in the cabin when Weyland bursts inside. They spring to their feet at the look on his face, but when they see the expression on mine, they calm. I don't look afraid, only confused.

"Something has transpired," Weyland announces, lowering me to my feet and steadying me before leading me over to the cushions and helping me sit despite his rushed words and excitement. "Something big."

Rook's brows rise. "The date did not go well?"

Weyland's face pinches. "On the contrary, it was amazing. Why would you think otherwise?"

Rook laughs, and I can tell he enjoys teasing Weyland. Apparently, the boogeyman has a sense of humor. "Do explain, lycan."

Weyland glances at me and I straighten, realizing he wants me to explain. "Oh, um . . . Well, the date was going well . . ."

Rook stalks a few steps closer, his black eyes swallowing me whole and leaving me vibrating. "Yes, little oblivion?"

Dade and Kaito are listening intently, their eyes on me. Having so much attention focused on me makes me shift on my feet, and I start to wring my fingers together. "We . . . We, um . . ." I grow hot with my blush and press my cool hands against my cheeks. "We might have . . . kissed."

Kaito takes a step closer. "Are you okay?"

The last time I tried to kiss someone—him—it hadn't gone well.

"Yes," I murmur. "Yes, I didn't . . . I'm okay."

Dade watches me closely. "What happened during the kiss to cause the confusion?"

I bite my lip, unsure how to explain it, so I just describe how it felt. "At first, it felt like tingles, as if my body were waking up, but then it felt like . . . lightning beneath my skin."

"That turned into literal lightning across her flesh," Weyland adds. "She began to glow, and the arcs danced across her skin."

Rook's eyes focus on me intently, as if he can see through me. "You wield magic, little oblivion?"

I grimace. "Wield is a strong word."

"What does the lightning do?" Dade asks, frowning.

"I don't know," I reply honestly. "It faded, and as far as we can tell, it didn't change anything around us. Perhaps it was a fluke."

Rook shakes his head. "No, not a fluke." He comes closer and touches my chin with his claws, tilting my head up. "An awakening. You're becoming who you were meant to be, little oblivion."

I swallow as I stare up into his dark eyes. "What if that scares me?"

He smiles and leans closer, until his breath fans across my cheeks. There's temptation in his eyes to kiss me again and see if he can wake up the lightning, but he holds himself back. When Rook decides to kiss me, I know it won't be as gentle as Weyland's. I'll have to be ready to be folded into the darkness and fight the nightmares within it.

"We all fear the shedding, Kai," he murmurs. "That moment where we shed our skin like a snake, but on the other side is who you were meant to be." He leans closer, his lips just above mine. I can taste the shadows between us, and I can feel them stroke my flesh. "You will not be alone there."

I look deep into his eyes and take in his expression, this monster who has become as important as the others. "You promise?"

He smiles, revealing sharp teeth. "With every fiber of my being, little oblivion," he says softly. "You will never be alone again."

CHAPTER
THIRTY

KAI

We are out gathering mushrooms when we hear voices and horns.

The sound of a successful hunt echoes through the trees, one I heard many times in the Shadow Lands, only that sound doesn't belong here. Neither do the humans making it. Without hesitation, Rook wraps his shadows around us, concealing us as we crouch together on the verge of the meadow, our foraging basket forgotten.

After my date with Weyland and my display of magic, I needed some normalcy, so when we finished our chores, we set out to forage. My mind still whirs with what happened and Rook's implication that my magic will grow—not to mention my lips still tingle from Weyland's kiss. My skin aches as if he has brought it back to life, and now, every time I look at one of them, I can't stop my eyes from falling to their lips as I imagine them kissing me, touching me, and making me feel alive again.

My mind clears, however, when I see the hunting party emerge from the trees. Five human men laugh and joke, their clothes speckled with blood, as they wander toward us, completely unconcerned. It's only when they are halfway across the meadow that I see what they are carrying between them. Skewered on a huge wooden pole is a creature.

No, a monster.

It has two arms, two legs, a tail, and scaled skin. Its eyes are open and unseeing, its blood dripping to the ground as they walk.

My mouth parts on a gasp that Rook covers as I watch them drop the monster to the ground without ceremony, letting his body smack and roll. One even kicks him, defiling him in death, proving yet again who the real monsters are.

I hoped we were wrong, that it was one rogue party hunting monsters that we killed and stopped, but the evidence is before us. Humans are crossing into the Dead Lands and killing monsters.

Monsters like those that surround me, protect me, and care for me.

Monsters that might have family, children, and loved ones.

My sadness and worry turn to anger that I can't seem to contain no matter how much I try. I'm so very tired of innocents suffering and dying at the hands of men. Before I know it, I've risen to my feet with a strength I wasn't aware I had.

"Kai," Kaito hisses, reaching for me to pull me back down into the shadows, but I am done hiding.

It's time someone stood up for those who can't.

I stride from the shadows Rook provides, hearing them scrambling after me, and when I stop before the humans, the shadows fall away like a curtain. I feel the heat of my monsters at my back and it gives me strength. "What are you doing?" I demand.

All five of the human men spin, their eyes widening as they take in the monsters and then me. I see one reaching for a crossbow, but Dade plucks it from his hands and snaps it like a twig. "I wouldn't do that if I were you," he warns the men.

"I said, what are you doing?" My voice is stronger when I repeat myself. I tilt my chin up, determined to make a point.

The man in the middle, a huge man with a scar through his lip, watches me with dark eyes. "You're human," he comments, his thick voice accented strangely. I simply arch a brow and wait.

"I would answer her if I were you," Weyland says, and when I glance to my side, I see him playing with his claws. The humans shift uncomfortably, sharing glances as they try to figure out how they can escape.

"Hunting," the big man replies gruffly when it's clear we're not leaving. "What about you? Did you get lost . . . or did they steal you?" It's my turn to remain silent and his eyes narrow. "Come with us. We can protect you from them."

"Stop messing with the monsters," I say instead, ignoring his words.

"Is that a plea?" Another male chuckles, amused despite the monsters behind me.

"No, it's a warning." I cross my arms in annoyance. "How many of you are hunting here?"

"Enough," the big man answers, something in his expression giving me pause. Is he telling me so I'll trust them?

Do they think I'm a hostage here and speaking for the monsters because I'm commanded to?

Either way, I don't care.

"Stop messing with monsters or they will mess with you back," I say. "You don't want the monsters to fight back. Go now and tell your people."

One of the others steps forward aggressively. "Listen here—"

The big man places his arm across him, holding him back from whatever mistake he'd been about to make.

"It's time to go," he states calmly, his eyes shrewd, and with a nod at me, he starts to back them away.

"But our prize," one whines.

"Leave it," he orders as they reach for the dead monster. We watch them back away until we can't see them anymore, and then Dade and Weyland trail them to make sure they don't double back. I glance at the dead monster, sadness and anger dueling within me.

"We bury him," I tell Rook and Kaito. "We need to bury him."

I can feel them sharing looks behind me but I don't care. I know I just put a target on my back, but for once, I am not afraid.

I'm so tired of being afraid, so I'm choosing not to be.

I'm choosing to be brave like them so that one day, I can be someone who deserves them.

THIRTY-ONE

As we dig the grave in the meadow, I watch Kai carefully as she collects wildflowers. She is too calm. I do not like it. She stood toe to toe with those humans without flinching, without fear dancing in her eyes, and although I am very proud of her, I worry what that means for her and for us.

Now that they know a human female lives amongst us, will they seek her out? Is she in danger? I share a look with the others, all of us silently agreeing to keep a closer eye on our surroundings. Kai has been close to hunters twice. There will not be a third time.

Once the hole is dug, we carefully lay the monster in the ground and cover it up. With the dirt back in place, Kai heads our way, holding a bundle of flowers in her hand. We watch on in confusion as she lays them over the dirt.

"In our land, we laid flowers down as a remembrance, as sacrifice and apology. I offer that to you so you may find the peace in the next life you never did in this one. The flowers will mark your resting place; you will not be forgotten." She lays her hand next to them and bows her head. "I'm sorry."

The silence is heavy. Even the birds stop chirping, the only sound the swaying of the trees in the wind. When Kai lifts her head, her eyes are glassy. I reach over and help her stand before she brushes the lingering dirt from her palms.

"Let's go home." Without waiting for a reply, she turns and starts walking back to the trees, knowing we will follow.

Kai is too quiet after this morning. I don't like it. She was so happy before, so filled with life and hope, and now it's as if it's all drained from her again. I need to remind her that she can be happy here. I need to remind her why she should smile because despite the horrors of this morning, there is a lot to be happy about.

I need to remind her that she has us.

Taking her hand, I ignore the looks from the others and lead her outside. She comes willingly, not speaking until we are inside the shelter of the trees. "Kaito?" One word. My name. A question.

"I want to show you something," is all I tell her, my hand tightening on hers. She grips mine and nods, falling into step beside me.

We walk for a while in comfortable silence. The place I take her is deep within our land, so I know it will take a while for us to reach it, but it's important for her to see it and understand.

"There is old magic within this land," I tell her, and her head swings around. She tugs me to a stop, and I glance down at her, my heart warming like it does whenever I'm with her. "If you are to understand the magic inside you, then you must understand that," I tell her. "We are going to a place I found by mistake many moons ago."

"Okay," she whispers, searching my gaze. "But what's wrong?"

"What do you mean?" I frown.

"You are quiet, serious too. It's not like you. Was I wrong to confront the hunters?" she asks softly, worry in her eyes.

Gripping her sides, I tug her close, wrapping her in my arms. "No, you did good. I'm so proud of you, Kai."

154

She relaxes in my hold, and we stay like that for a while until I pull away. "Shall we carry on?"

"Sure," she whispers, but her eyes drop to my lips and linger.

Desire slams through me, and I'm suddenly very aware that her soft, warm body is pressed against every inch of mine. My hands hold her shapely hips and I flex my fingers.

"Kaito," she whispers.

"We should go," I respond, my voice hoarse, but I don't pull away and neither does she. She searches my eyes once more.

As her eyes drop to my lips again, want and jealousy pour through me.

She kissed Weyland without panicking. I worry if I kiss her again, she will panic once more like she did the first time we tried, and I don't think I could handle that so I turn away, but a gasp slips free of my lips as she grabs my arm, tugging me to face her, and with a soft smile, she presses her lips to mine, kissing me.

CHAPTER
THIRTY-TWO

KAI

The desire to kiss Kaito slammed into me so hard, I needed it to happen, and now here we are, our lips pressed together in the intimate act, his arms around me.

It's not enough.

It's nice, warm, and comforting, but we're out here in the middle of the forest. There's somewhere Kaito wants to take me, so there will be plenty of time for kissing, right?

The tingles beneath my skin have me breaking the kiss with a gasp to look down. I can't see the lightning right now—the kiss was too brief for that—but I can feel the beginnings of it. Kaito immediately leans in, his eyes searching my skin.

"I can't see it," he murmurs, his eyes wide as he trails his fingers over my arm. "But it's almost like there's static along your arm. I can sense the magic here."

Nodding, I look up into his eyes. "I think it will appear if we continue kissing."

Suddenly, we're both thinking of doing so again. It's obvious in his sharpened gaze, both of us wanting to lock ourselves together and kiss until we breathe each other's air and there's no way to tell where we begin and end in our joining. I don't know how much I'm ready for, but I know desire courses through my body. I know something low in my stomach yearns for Kaito in a way I haven't felt for so long. I want to kiss him and keep kissing him, but I also want to see whatever he wants to show me.

Kaito, as if sensing my conflict, smiles softly at me and threads his fingers with mine, breaking the tension. The gentle webbing between his fingers is soft against my skin, reminding me that these men I'm falling for aren't quite men at all, but it doesn't change anything about this moment. It doesn't change my desire for the four monsters who have saved me more than once, both from myself and other monsters. I'm slowly waking back up, and I'm starting to want a life filled with love and excitement.

They are reminding me why I should live.

"The place I want to take you to is in the Dead Lands," Kaito says. "Because of how far it is, it would be best if I carry you."

"Have I been slowing you down?" I ask, worried they have all watered themselves down for my benefit.

He tilts his head, studying me. "Sometimes it's best to move slowly to remind us what it's like for you. We do not change ourselves to meet your limitations. We walk slowly so that we may walk beside you, to be with you, and never take away your choices." He sighs. "But in this, it is very far, and if we're to make it back to the others in a timely manner so they don't come looking for us, then I should carry you."

I nod in understanding. When he gives me his back and kneels, I gently step forward and wrap my arms around his shoulders. He reaches back and hooks my thighs, wrapping them around his waist. I realize the mistake immediately as he adjusts my weight and begins to run. In this position, my core is pressed against his flexing muscles, against the heat of his body. I begin to burn, my fingers curling into each other to stop myself from caressing his body in a distracting way. My breathing changes as he runs, turning from deep, relaxing breaths to shallow gasps I try to hide against his back.

I'm so focused on the feeling of him between my thighs that it takes me far too long to understand just how fast we're moving. When I blink my eyes open in an attempt to push away my desire, I stare in surprise at just how fast the scenery is moving past us. I immediately slam my eyes shut again when it makes me feel dizzy.

If Kaito can run this fast on land, I wonder how fast he can move in the water.

"Almost there," Kaito murmurs, assuming my breathing is from anxiety rather than arousal.

When he begins to slow a few minutes later, I keep my eyes closed tightly until he comes to a complete stop. I can feel the deep breathing in his chest as he slows his heart rate. Clearly, he ran as fast as he possibly could and gave it his all, and everything about that thought reminds me how much I want him.

Kaito lowers my legs to the ground before turning to face me. My arms remain around his shoulders as I sway, but I keep my eyes closed as I catch my bearings. The feel of his flesh, smooth and slick, against mine is what I focus on to ground me.

"Open your eyes, Kai," he whispers.

I do as he says, opening my eyes achingly slowly. When I get a look at the scenery around us, they fly open the rest of the way in surprise, taking it all in.

"What is this place?" I murmur, staring in wonder.

There's a large, crystal-clear pool before us, and around it are the prettiest flowers and plants, adding to this whimsical, fantastical view. There's no waterfall, but there's a bubbling water source on the far side of the pool. Steam rises gently from the water—not enough to expect to boil inside, but enough to make me wary. There's a buzz in the air that I can't place, something that reminds me of . . .

"It's a natural spring," Kaito says. "It's fed by underground water that keeps it warm at all times. You'll never find yourself cold here." He gently tips my chin up. "This place is ancient. Old magic lives in the stone that forms the basin. The legends of this place speak of cleansing and awakening. From what I understand, those who swim within the waters are released from magical barriers. I don't know how true that is, since I've never swam here, but I figure it's worth a try."

His crooked grin makes me melt, my own answering smile splitting my lips. "Of course it's worth a try," I tease. "And if all else fails, swimming will surely release something."

It's only then, as I look into the distance, that I realize we're not far from the castle I've often seen from a distance in the Dead Lands. The old castle, with black, menacing spires, glitters like a well-lit beacon. No longer is it a sleeping giant, not when my sister calls it her home with her monsters. We're close enough that I can make out people on the balconies, and I wonder if one of them is Cora. The thought makes me miss her and for once, it doesn't send excruciating pain through my chest. Perhaps, one day, I'll be able to look her in the eye without flinching. Perhaps, I'll be able to hug her close and tell her I'm sorry for all the grief I've caused.

"What is it?" Kaito asks, leaning down to press his forehead against mine. "Did I choose our destination incorrectly?"

"No," I counter, shaking my head. "No, not at all. I just . . . I feel so much more alive right now."

Kaito straightens, his eyes bright as he studies me. "Alive?"

My smile is bright as I loop my arms around his shoulders again. "Alive," I repeat. Standing on my tiptoes, I lean up to his face. "Kiss me again, Kaito," I encourage. "Kiss me here in this place so full of magic, it saturates the air. Kiss me so that I can taste the wild sea on your lips."

Kaito doesn't need any extra prompting. He leans down and presses his lips to mine. At first, it starts just like the other, tentative and careful, a barely there meeting of lips that isn't quite enough. With a groan of arousal, I press myself tightly against him and deepen the kiss, parting my lips over his and tasting him completely. Kaito gasps, and his hands are suddenly harsh against my hips, pressing our bodies so tightly together, it makes me wish there weren't clothing creating a barrier between us. He takes control of the kiss, coaxing my lips open enough for his tongue to sweep inside. He's careful of his teeth, of deepening the kiss in case it all becomes too much, but it never does. Instead, I can feel the tingles beneath my skin that feel like lightning. My fingers buzz with the sensation and take hold of it. Everything inside me begs for it to release, for something to happen, and as we continue to kiss, the lightning comes from the inside out.

I can see the glow through my eyelids, but I don't stop, desperate for more. I feel less numb right now than I've felt since the king first took me. Right here, right now, with one of my monsters, I feel safe. I'm starting to feel less broken in his arms.

The glow brightens, and Kaito gasps as the lightning trails from my skin to his, accepting him as my own and caressing him the same way I do. Whatever this magic is, it's as much theirs as it is mine. I'm healing and living all because of my four monsters.

Carefully, with lightning dancing along my skin, I break the kiss and lean back with a smile. Kaito stares at me in wonder, his eyes wide and amazed.

"Beautiful," he whispers, watching the lightning dance between us. "So beautiful."

Taking his hand, I tug him toward the water behind us. "Come on, Kaito," I say with a smile. "Let's go for a swim."

THIRTY-THREE

CORA

I don't know what brings me to the balcony. One moment, I was inside, held in the arms of my monsters, and the next, I felt the overwhelming need to find the balcony and look out over the healing Dead Lands.

Strange, considering balconies and I have had a rocky relationship for the last year. They remind me too much of my sister, of her falling backwards over the banister and how I couldn't save her.

I avoid them as much as I can, otherwise I have to relive that loss time and time again, but on this occasion, I seek one out.

Despite the time, my grief hasn't lessened. We were never able to retrieve her body, and despite how foolish it makes me, I can't stop myself from feeling hope. I know it's futile. I know what my monsters have gently warned me of. It matters not. My heart wants Kai to live. It wants her to appear on my doorstep, whole, alive, and happy.

Unfortunately, the chances of that are as slim as the three realms suddenly getting along. Besides the uprisings in the Shadow Lands, many in the Gilded Lands despise having to share resources they were once given for nothing. It's been a whirlwind of change and it will take longer, but I'm prepared to face it all.

As long as my monsters remain at my side.

Grimus, Zetros, Bracken, Krug, Nero, and Razcorr.

They are all as important to me as the air I breathe.

Despite their love, they can't quite heal the loss of my sister. I've been able to dim it while I focus on healing the lands, but in moments like this, right here on this balcony, is when I miss her most.

I bow my head, sifting through my memories of Kai.

The two of us giggling in the darkness as we slipped from the house while our parents slept.

Her happiness when she finally met someone who wasn't a complete asshole.

The tears trailing from her eyes as I was forced through the wall.

The haunted, hollow shell of her as she apologized and tipped over the edge.

The first tears fall from my eyes and plop onto the concrete railing. They stain the black stone and tiny little spots of magic dance from there, as if my grief is somehow so full of magic, it leaks from my eyes. Every part of me yearns for my hope not to be misplaced, for something to somehow work out for the better.

Strong arms wrap around me from behind, but I don't flinch. I let them offer their warmth and strength as I cry for the sister I should have been able to save. My sadness reached them while they were sleeping, drawing them to me just as I would have been drawn to them. Wrapped in their arms, the pain becomes bearable, and once I'm able to focus on that, I'm able to focus on something else entirely —the soft buzz of old, burgeoning magic.

I whip up my head, staring out into the Dead Lands toward the bite of magic. Somehow, it feels familiar, as if I've felt such magic before and every part of me recognizes it. There's a soft, brief, pale yellow glow that's almost impossible to see before it's gone.

I lean in. "Did you see that?" I rasp. "Can you feel it?"

Nero presses his cheek to mine. "The magic?"

"Yes," I whisper. "Yes, the magic. It felt . . ."

"Powerful," Bracken says in his usual chipper voice.

I glance at him. "I was going to say familiar."

We fall into silence for a moment, but as I focus on it, nothing else comes. Sighing, I gesture toward the castle. "Whatever it was, it's gone now."

Raz tilts his head. "Would you like me to fly—"

I'm shaking my head before he can finish. "Whatever it is, it felt . . . new. We won't disturb whatever creature is learning to taste its magic again. If it comes to our door, then we shall address it."

After all, the Dead Lands are coming back to life. The monsters are learning how to live and taste magic again. It makes sense that they would start to harness what they once were.

Still, I can't help looking over my shoulder one last time, hope unfurling in my chest like the wings of a gargoyle.

It's a foolish hope, but still hope all the same.

CHAPTER
THIRTY-FOUR

KAI

Keeping hold of Kaito's hand, I move to the edge of the pool before I realize my mistake. He must sense it at the same time and squeezes my hand, so I look at him. "I'll turn away and get undressed first." He turns his back and for a moment, I find myself watching.

My cheeks heat as he quickly shucks his clothes, and my eyes widen at his round ass before he dives into the pool. I quickly glance away, not wanting to be caught.

"Okay," he calls. When I turn, he's resurfaced, his hair slicked back and eyes sparkling since he's in the water. With a grin, he turns in a circle to give me privacy. "I won't peek."

No, because he's better than I am.

I hesitantly tug at my top before shedding my clothes and stepping into the water. I groan at the first touch, already feeling the warmth unwinding my stress and muscles as I wade deeper until it's up to my shoulders. "Okay," I say, my voice high.

He turns and swims toward me, grinning. "Can you feel it?" He swims laps around me, his wide grin infectious, and I find myself

"The temperature?" I ask, tilting my head.

"The magic," he replies.

Closing my eyes, I focus on the feelings around me, sensing the magic in the water just like he said. My eyes pop open in wonder as he laughs and dives under, only to reappear farther in the pool. Unable to resist his playful side, I follow, swimming after him. Laughing, he swims away, letting me chase him. The magical water makes me more relaxed than I've ever been. I feel vibrant and whole and for a moment, I am, and it's all because of him.

When he dips under the water again and resurfaces behind me with a splash, I spin with a laugh. "Two can play at that game."

I dive under the water, swimming down into the darkness to scare him, but as the dark water closes around me and all the light disappears, old memories take hold.

Ones that took place within similar darkness.

Memories of roaming, harsh hands and cruel punishments close around me like a vise until I choke on water as I scream. Hands reach for me in the dark and yank me up and out until I desperately gasp in air.

There is a buzz, a voice, but my head is screaming too loud to hear it.

Finally, it penetrates the memories. "Kai, I'm here. You're okay. I'm here."

Kaito.

I blink away the lingering ghosts and focus on the blue orbs of my monster. With a slow blink, I realize I wanted to be saved. I wanted him to save me. I didn't want to sink down there like I expected.

As I'm staring into those loving, cerulean eyes, I realize the truth.

I don't want to die anymore.

I don't know when I stopped fighting to live, but now I am living to fight.

I don't want to die; I want to live.

With him, with them.

I want a future. I want their hands in the darkness. I want their promises. I want their mornings and goodnights. I want their meals and laughter. I want their songs and tears. I want them. I want this.

This . . . life.

It's a split-second epiphany but it feels like my whole world alters and shifts.

Remaking me into a new person.

The person they love and want.

A fighter.

"I've got you," he says, panic in his voice as he holds my naked body close under the water. He cuts through it and toward the edge of the pool, hoisting me up and partially out until I'm sitting on the side. I'm shivering, wet, and naked. "You're okay, you're okay," he rasps, his hands gliding over my body to search for any injuries.

When I cover them, he blinks and stops. "I'm okay," I croak. "Just a memory, I'm okay now."

He relaxes with a sigh, and it's the moment we both realize I'm naked and he's pressed between my legs.

Desire bursts to life from his touches and his closeness, chasing away the last of the ghosts haunting me.

His eyes widen and he tries to dive backwards, but I lock my legs around him.

I want to live, so I'm going to.

Leaning down, I cup his jaw and kiss him, claiming him as our bodies slide together.

I breathe in the life I find within his touch.

CHAPTER
THIRTY-FIVE

KAI

Groaning into my mouth, he forces my thighs wider as he moves between them, his wet body pressed tightly to mine as he takes over the kiss. His hands slide down my nude back, causing goosebumps to rise in his wake. Our tongues tangle as my legs tighten around him, until it's too much and not enough all at the same time.

Yanking my mouth away, I gasp for breath, my heart racing and body quaking with untapped desire. It's so strong, like a flame brought back to life after a long summer.

"I need . . . ," I begin. "I need more, please."

"I know what you need, Kai. I've got you. Trust me," he begs.

"Always."

"Good, and if it's too much, tell me to stop and I will," he replies, always making sure I'm okay.

I nod nervously, knowing exactly where this is going.

Even before the king, I wasn't a virgin. I never saw the need to keep myself pure like everyone else thought. I enjoyed my body and the pleasures found with others, but this is different. This is a rebirth, and I want to experience that first time with him.

My water monster. My sweet, loving savior.

His lips glide down my cheek, and my eyes flutter closed at the soft touch. I focus on the feelings he's creating as he slides them down my throat, licking my pulse until I'm gasping. My head tilts to give him better access as his hands stroke my sides. His soft, slow touches give me every opportunity to get used to them.

His sweetness almost makes me cry as his warm lips slide across my collarbone, taking the time to stop and kiss every scar. The love he pours into those kisses as he tries to heal the puckered skin moves me. "Kaito," I whimper.

"I've got you," he promises, his voice hushed against my body.

His hands stroke my sides, reassuring me as his lips slide across my breasts, making me gasp. My back arches as he sweeps his lips across my nipple before kissing across my other breast.

My hands come up to grip his shoulders and I beg, "Please."

I feel his lips tip up in a grin against my skin as he meets my gaze, and only then do his lips seal around my nipple. As he sucks my stiff peak, lightning arcs through me and a moan escapes my lips, loud and unchecked. My skin starts to glow once more as he slowly fans the flames of my want.

His teeth close around my tip, the sharp sting making my eyes widen even as my core clenches, coming back to life under his careful touch. Grinning, he turns his head and torments my other nipple until I claw at his shoulders. Only when I'm whining and rocking my hips, unable to stand the bolts of lightning under my skin, does he slide down.

His lips follow the path of my stomach, stopping to cherish each scar before he kneels in the water. It's a good thing he can breathe underwater because he's almost submerged by the time he's level with my center.

He spreads my thighs, and for a moment, shame fills me before I force it back, refusing to let it take root. I won't let it ruin this moment or any other. The king has claimed my past, but he won't claim my future.

"Keep your eyes on me the entire time, Kai," he murmurs. "On me, so you see who's touching you and giving you pleasure."

I nod, and he slides his lips up my thighs, teasing me as he ghosts them over my mound and back down my other thigh before repeating it. When he finally lays a chaste kiss over my core, I jerk at the first touch, and his hands hold me tighter as his lips slide up and down my pussy. I keep my eyes locked on him the entire time so nothing else can invade my thoughts.

I watch his blue gaze darken with desire and greed as his tongue darts out and tastes me, nearly making me come undone. His groan splits the air, and I shudder as my clit throbs in time with my racing heart, demanding attention.

"You taste so sweet, Kai," he praises, his tone filled with worship. "I want to live on your taste." As if to prove his words, his tongue drags along every inch of my core, tasting me as he groans before devouring me.

It's the only word that fits the way Kaito attacks me, licking and sucking my sensitive flesh until I'm shuddering and lifting my hips to beg for more. Pleasure blooms through me and it's so strong, it almost hurts.

One of his hands glides down my hip to join his mouth at my center, stroking my flesh as I cry out.

His finger circles my hole. "Okay?" he asks, and I nod, canting my hips for more.

He slowly pushes the digit inside me, reclaiming my stolen core. It's hard, and panic starts to invade my mind as old memories raise their ugly heads. I slam my eyes shut but it only makes the memories more potent, so I force my eyes open to see Kaito below me.

"Shh, I've got you," he tells me. "It's me, no one else. It will feel so good. Focus on me, Kai. Only me. I've got you." He keeps speaking until I relax, and then he slowly pulls his finger out and thrusts back in, mimicking sex as he adds another.

I wait for the panic to come but it doesn't, the lightning within my skin so bright, it chases off any lingering darkness.

"Good girl," he praises as he lowers his lips to my pussy and feasts. All the while, his fingers slowly fuck me, driving me toward spiraling pleasure I haven't felt in so long.

He's vicious in his attack, slow and caring but demanding all at the same time. His fingers stretch me deliciously, wiping out any other memory. His tongue catches every drop of my need before tormenting my clit into oblivion.

The pleasure blows through me as a scream catches in my throat, and as I shatter, so does the lightning.

It explodes through me and blows out like a storm, spreading across the land closest to us until I slump and it retreats inside me. The glow dims beneath my skin but never quite goes away, unlike before.

Kaito strokes me through it before slowly pulling his fingers free, and as I watch, he licks them clean before kissing up my body.

"You did so well, Kai," Kaito praises, kissing my face. "So good."

Lifting my arm, I hold it between us to show him the dim glow under my skin. "I guess the pool works," I comment idly, blushing. His slow smile only makes my blush deepen, until we're both staring at each other with some deep emotion passing between us.

I've crossed a line between us now and the truth is, I don't want to stop.

THIRTY-SIX

KAI

The trek back to the cabin is spent with lingering gazes and wandering hands. Kaito's tenderness surrounds me, and all I can think about is the way his lips felt on me, how he held me, and the way his eyes remained focused on me so I knew whom I was with the entire time. The darkness lost in the end.

I'm healing.

The king is no longer the only memory in my mind. It's fading now, and those horrible memories are being replaced with all the good ones I'm making instead. The darkness still tries to creep in sometimes, but I have better weapons to help me fight them now.

With my monsters at my side, perhaps the darkness can be banished completely.

When the cabin comes into view, I don't think anything of it. I'm simply happy to giggle with Kaito as he teases me and dances around me like a child. His happiness is as infectious as his smile, so I find myself laughing with him, genuinely enjoying myself as we walk up to the door, and then we step inside.

The first thing I notice is that Dade, Weyland, and Rook are all inside. Rook is standing by the fire, stirring something in the large pot. I hadn't realized he could cook so it surprises me a little, but the moment we step inside, he stops what he's doing and turns, meeting my eyes. He opens his mouth to say something, perhaps a greeting of some sort, but his mouth snaps shut before the words come out, his eyes blazing in the firelight.

Dade straightens and rolls his shoulders but otherwise, he is the picture of calm. His features are schooled so he's hiding whatever emotion he's feeling, just as Rook's are.

Weyland doesn't display any of the same decorum though. He takes a huge sniff of the air as we walk in and his expression morphs into jealousy so thick, it permeates the room. Dade shoots a glare at Weyland, but the wolf vibrates with jealousy. Despite that, he doesn't lash out. He doesn't do anything to make me uncomfortable. Instead, he grits his teeth and says, "I hope you had a good date."

I glance at Kaito before my eyes trail over to Dade and Rook. I don't know when it happened, but it's become easy to read the thoughts in all their eyes and have a silent conversation between us. It's as if, at some point, we've become far closer than I ever imagined, and I never even noticed until now. Patting Kaito's shoulder, I step a little closer to Weyland and hold out my hand for him. He stares at my fingers for a second, confused.

"Come outside with me," I request softly, my hand lingering between us.

He immediately stands and takes my hand, his large, warm fingers engulfing my own.

"Don't go too far," Dade warns. "There's been a lot of movement in the Dead Lands lately."

I nod at his warning and continue to pull Weyland outside. "We won't go much farther than the cabin. Promise."

Once outside and a few steps away, I turn to Weyland who stands stiffly. He's tense, his whole body a study in forced compliance as he tries his best not to react to whatever scent I bear.

"Are you okay?" I whisper, looking up at him through my lashes. I can feel his jealousy, but it doesn't feel aggressive. There's nothing directed at me, which is a relief. I would hate to hurt any of them, but I won't apologize for following my heart, not even to them. "I didn't mean to upset—"

"No," he growls, his voice coming out harsh. When he realizes how it sounds, he repeats the word softer and sighs. "No, it's nothing you did. I'm just . . ." He runs a hand through his hair. "I've imagined bringing you pleasure for so long that smelling your release on Kaito has me wanting, *bacca*. I'm not angry. I'm just jealous that the fish man got to taste you is all."

Reaching up to cup his jaw, I draw his gaze to mine, forcing him to look at me. "I didn't purposely choose which of you was the first to push my darkness aside enough for such intimacies, but I am healing, Weyland." I sigh. "I'm sorry if this is difficult. I never expected such . . ." I shake my head, unsure what to say. "I'm healing, and I want you."

His eyes widen at my words, as if he's surprised to hear them. Silly wolf. Hasn't he realized how I feel? Perhaps I haven't been as vocal as I should be.

I trail my hands from his jaw to his neck, stroking his skin before dipping my fingers beneath his shirt. The harsh breath that rattles from his lungs tells me he likes the touch and that he's eager for more.

The power I seem to hold over these monsters is addicting.

"I haven't felt desire in so long, it's almost new to be able to feel it engulf me," I murmur. "But I desire each of you. Every time I look at you, I want you. Each time I look at Kaito, Dade, and Rook, I want them. I'm not sure how much I can push, but don't think I don't want you equally as much as each of them, Weyland." My fingers stroke along his collarbones, pressing the collar of his shirt open. "Don't think I haven't imagined touching you the same way."

His eyes close as my fingers caress him. "*Bacca* . . ."

"Shhh," I murmur. "Just let me touch you."

For so long, I haven't been able to explore. I haven't been able to touch at my own will and determine where I want my hands to go.

It's been so long since I've had this freedom and I want more of it. When I am in control, the darkness stays blissfully away, and my fingers can trail slowly along Weyland's body without fear.

I know this must be some kind of torture for the wolf. His hands are clenched tightly at his sides and his eyes are shut tight as he settles into my touch. His shoulders are tense as he holds himself back and keeps himself in check.

I carefully pop the buttons free on his shirt, exposing his muscular chest to my view. The hard planes of his body are beautiful as I run my fingers along each ridge. They leap and jump beneath my fingertips, eager for more than a lingering touch, but I explore every inch of his chest. When I'm done, I move around him, trailing my fingers along the muscles on his back. Every part of Weyland was made with strength, just as his wolf form is. He's beautiful, the wildness in his soul leaking into the way he holds himself. Weyland's body was made for study, as if he were some art piece on display.

When I circle him again, he opens his eyes, the brightness there reflecting the light coming from the cabin windows. They flash like those of a wild animal in the dark, a predator lying just beneath the surface.

"One day," he rasps, his voice so thick with arousal, it makes my core clench. "One day, I'm going to explore you just the same, *bacca*. I'm going to caress every inch of you and follow with my lips until you're writhing with desire." He leans in, his breath brushing across my neck. "I will only take you when you beg me, when you're desperate for my cock."

My face flushes at his words, my fingers clenching on his sides. I sway, and the urge to ask him what he's waiting for lingers on the tip of my tongue. But tonight, I made progress with Kaito, and I don't want to undo the healing I've done by forcing things too quickly.

I lean back and meet his eyes, my lips pulling into a smile. "One day," I promise, lifting his hand to place a kiss against his palm. His eyes widen at the touch, at the intimacy of it. "One day, we'll do such things without the darkness dancing at my heels."

Weyland cups my jaw, the sweetness I know him for flickering in his eyes despite his words. I know he'll never push me. I know he'll never insist on things before I'm ready. He leans in and gently kisses my forehead.

His smile is sweetness and desire all wrapped into one. "One day, you'll lead the darkness itself, *bacca*, and then it can never hold you hostage again."

Because he believes I can, I believe it too.

THIRTY-SEVEN

A few days later, when Dade asks if I'd like to go foraging with him, I jump at the chance. The dread unicorn is an interesting creature, but in his uniqueness, he's also incredibly beautiful. If I hadn't seen him in his unicorn form before, I would have a hard time believing the monster before me could turn into something equally as beautiful as he is in this form.

While I've been healing and learning to open up again, Dade has learned what it's like to wear his human form again. No one would ever mistake him for a human in this form, though, and he's had to adjust. It must be strange to have hands after having hooves for so long. I watched him fumble with a mug for a few seconds as he tried to remember how his fingers worked. I've also seen him drop item after item for the same reason, but it's been months now and he no longer fumbles. He's as smooth as the others, and one would never know he had to relearn these things.

Now, as we step out of the cabin and I put on the jacket Kaito made me, Dade looks at me with a grin.

"Would you like to walk, or would you like to ride?" he asks, his red eyes flickering with excitement.

I frown. "What would we ride?"

With a wink, he shifts, his body morphing into the warhorse I'd first seen him as. He shakes out his mane and prances in place. *You ride me*, he replies within my mind.

"I ride you?" I squeak, staring at him with wide eyes. "Won't I fall off?"

Amusement flickers in the dread unicorn's eyes. *I would never let you fall.*

I hesitate for a few seconds. Fear dances in my mind. There's no saddle, and I've never had the opportunity to learn how to ride horses. In the Shadow Lands, horses were reserved for those who were higher rank or for the Gilded Lands. Common people weren't allowed to ride the beasts for whatever reason. Once I was in the Gilded Lands, I wasn't allowed to leave the castle, let alone learn to ride a horse. Even if I had that experience, Dade is much larger than any horse I've ever seen. I don't even know how I'm going to climb upon him.

Do not worry, he purrs in my mind. Carefully, the giant dread unicorn kneels before me and lowers himself to the ground. I watch in wonder as he settles, looking at me expectantly. *Climb on.*

Biting my lip, I look between his back and his eyes. "You're sure?"

His eyes twinkle. *I've never been more certain of something in my life, Kai. Besides*, he says, snorting at me, *it's been too long since I ran in this form.*

I touch my fingers to his smooth fur, the oil-slick colors dancing from the light of the cabin. His skin moves beneath my fingers, as if he wants nothing more than for me to touch him. I trace his large form, stroking his mane.

Use that to pull yourself up, he instructs. *Throw one leg over once you're high enough.*

I assume it won't hurt him if he's telling me to use it, but I'm still gentle as I do as he says. I heft myself up onto his back, my fingers threading into his mane to steady myself against him.

Now hold on, he says as he starts to stand. It jostles me as he launches to his feet, but I hang on tightly. A fall from this height would hurt, and I have no desire to embarrass myself. *Remember, I won't let you fall.*

"I trust you," I tell him, and the words are as true as any others. I trust Dade just as I do them all. I've never been so trusting in all my life. The only other person I've trusted as much as my monsters is Cora.

Good.

One word and then Dade takes off into the trees. I squeak and lean down to get a good hold of him, afraid of falling after everything I said. I clamp my eyes shut when the trees whip by in a blur. Dade is so fast, I can't make out anything we pass as we run, my human eyes too weak to follow. After a few minutes, I start to relax. We enter the plains where trees don't grow and for the first time, I sit up fully on his back and take it all in. In the distance, I can see the castle. I realize we must be running fast, closing the distance quickly.

I laugh at the speed, at the feeling of flying, and suddenly yearn to feel it completely. I clamp my thighs around him and slowly release my grip. When I don't immediately fall off, I open my arms wide. The wind whips past us, my hair blowing behind me as we run. I keep my eyes open to take it all in. As the weightlessness hits me, I start to laugh, hearing pure joy in the sound as we fly across the plains together. The laughter bubbles up and out, taking over and reminding me exactly why I want to live. I whoop and shout in excitement, and Dade throws his head back with a deep whinny as if shouting his own enjoyment.

We fly together, and my heart swells just a little more for the monsters I call mine.

When Dade begins to slow, we're surrounded by trees again, coming full circle back into the forest. He transforms without warning, his strong arms catching me before I can tumble from his back. The grin he flashes down at me makes my insides flip as I wrap my arms around his shoulders.

"That was amazing," I tell him, still laughing at the feeling of it.

His eyes sparkle in amusement. "I'm glad it pleased you."

Our eyes lock while I'm high on the feeling of freedom after the run. The way he's looking at me reminds me just how much I've come to care for these monsters. Fear ruled my life before, but I'm learning to live again. I reach up and cup his jaw. He knows loss like I do, and I like to think we're both bringing each other back to life.

"Thank you," I murmur, stroking his jaw. "Thank you for learning to live with me."

His eyes flash with a strong emotion that's there and gone before I can properly name it. When he leans down, I don't pull away. He hesitates before our lips can touch, allowing me the option to pull back.

I don't.

Instead, I lean up and close the distance, pressing my lips against his. He's softer than I expected, moving slow and unsteady as if he has to remember the action. Once memory takes hold, his lips move against mine, caressing but not deepening. It's a sweet kiss, a gentle one, and it tangles my insides up and makes me yearn for more of his touch. The lightning wakes beneath my skin, buzzing with excitement, desperate for release, but before anything else can happen —*bang!*

The sound is followed by laughter and whoops of excitement.

I freeze, my hands on Dade. He moves first, breaking the kiss and setting me gently on the ground, immediately ducking to hide his tall form. He keeps me behind him to protect me, scanning the forest in front of us. We duck farther down when they appear, hiding behind bushes to avoid detection. Rook isn't with us to hide us with his shadows, but Dade knows what he's doing. I press my hand against his back, terror flickering in my heart. Going from so much excitement to fear is almost exhausting, but I keep myself steady for Dade's benefit. I won't be the damsel in distress and distract him. I can help.

This hunting party is larger than any we've seen. There has to be at least two dozen men, many of them with their backs to us. My eyes trace over the ones in the middle carrying cages of dead monsters. Dade tenses, clearly wanting to act.

"Did you see the expression on that last one?" A man laughs. "I expected the monsters to be scarier. They are far easier to hunt than I was told."

"Stick with us and you'll get to kill all the monsters you want," another answers with a grin. "We've killed thirty-nine. No one else has gotten close to us."

My heart squeezes painfully. Thirty-nine? They've killed so many and for what?

Dade vibrates with anger at the admission, and before I can stop him, he's standing from our hiding place, his hard eyes on the group of men. I can tell he's imagining killing them.

Too many eyes turn to him, and too many weapons point at him. Although I have no doubt he can handle himself, some instinct has me standing up after him, horror in my heart.

"Dade, no!" I cry.

Silence falls across the group as they see not only this dread unicorn in human form, but a small human woman with him, and then one man steps through the others. Familiar eyes focus on mine, eyes I once looked into with love. Merryl stares at me in surprise and horror, his hand reaching out to stall the nearest man's weapon.

The world closes in on me as my past stands before us, and he looks at me as if he never expected to see me again. How could he?

He takes a stumbling step forward that has Dade tensing further, uncertain of what's going on.

I swallow as he opens and closes his mouth before he speaks our familiarity into the universe.

"Kai?" he rasps. "Kai, is that you?"

THIRTY-EIGHT

Dade's head jerks to me, his eyes wide and confused.

"Kai, it is. It is you," Merryl whispers, making Dade whip back to face him and let out a monstrous growl as he steps toward me, away from the hunters, his need to protect too strong to ignore.

Merryl glances at Dade but then focuses back on me, too stunned to concentrate on anything else. I'm silent, unsure what to say or do. It's like looking into a mirror of my past. He looks the exact same, yet I have changed so much. I used to think this man was my future. I loved him. I cherished him. I gave him my everything.

We were supposed to have a happy life together, yet here we stand, with a field between us and a lifetime of hurt.

I'm hurt, I realize, staring into his familiar eyes. Hurt and angry.

He didn't try to stop the king. He didn't try to save me. I know it would have been pointless, but the truth is he never even tried to save me, protect me, or get me back. Despite me being his "one true love" and future wife, he never fought for me. He let me be taken away and tortured and tormented without lifting a finger, and now here he stands, looking at me like everything is perfect and right again.

Nothing will ever be right again, not after what I went through.

My body was defiled, my soul was scarred, and my heart turned cold, yet here he stands, well and happy, fed and clothed. He thrives while I died inside, crying every night for him, wishing on a star that he would come and rescue me and we would ride away together into our happily ever after.

Fairy tales are for children, though, and I am not a child.

I don't want a hero. I want a monster.

It's then that I comprehend whom he's with—hunters.

He is with the humans who are trapping and killing monsters— monsters like the ones I care for, who saved me . . . monsters like me.

"Kai, come here." He holds out his hand, oblivious to the anger darkening my expression. "I'll protect you."

"Why? You never did before," I mutter.

Dade steps before me, and Merryl's hand drops. I peek around Dade, my hand going to his back. There are so many of them watching.

"You know this chick, Merryl?" one burly man asks.

"Yeah, sh-he's my . . . mine," he stutters, his eyes wide as he tries to make sense of everything.

"She's your nothing," Dade snarls, making all the hunters jerk.

I can almost see Dade stomping his feet in anger and roaring his claim on me, and my body heats at the realization. He protects and owns me, and he's not afraid to show it or stand up to a greater force.

"Move, monster, before I make you," Merryl snarls, fury in his tone alongside hatred. I have never experienced either from him before. He was always so calm, so kind. It's why I liked him. He was nothing like my father.

I guess we have both changed after all.

"You won't get anywhere near her, not even over my dead body," Dade snarls, backing me up to the forest.

"Then over your dead body it is!" someone cheers.

"Dade," I whisper worriedly.

These are monster hunters, and we are monsters. I can't lose him, not when I just found him.

Before he can respond, though, there's a howl. It's echoed by growls and calls from within the trees, and I watch in awe as monsters pour from the shadows within. With a loud battle cry, they charge the hunters.

There are so many monsters, all working together to attack.

Grabbing Dade's hand, I tug until he looks at me. "We must go," I tell him.

He glances back but sees the monsters have it handled, so with a sharp nod, he holds my hand tighter and we slip into the woods, escaping the hunters and my past.

CHAPTER
THIRTY-NINE
DADE

I don't speak. I can't. We run as fast as we can, and I make sure to zigzag and look behind us in case they are following. Kai is quiet at my side, her hand in mine, but she feels so far away.

I remember the look in that hunter's eyes—the recognition and familiarity.

It was hard not to. He knew her, and more than that, he loved her.

My Kai. *He loved her.*

I swallow my anger and jealousy and speed up, desperate to put as much distance between us and that human. I don't stop until we are in the cabin, the door slammed shut. I press my face to the wood, breathing heavily, and try to calm my racing heart. I feel her step back, still silent.

"Kai, what is it?" Kaito demands.

"An attack?" Weyland questions.

"Little oblivion?" Rook murmurs.

"Dade?" she asks softly, and her voice is what unleashes me.

Turning, I meet her eyes. "Do you still love him?" My tone is cruel, accusatory, and she flinches. I want to take it back, but I don't

I stare her down, ignoring the others. I need to know. In my eyes, Kai is already mine. I can stand her loving these other monsters, but I can't stand her loving a hunter.

The small voice in my head tells me it's because she would leave us for him—her own kind, who would hunt and kill us for simply being born. I lost my family once, and I can't lose another.

"Well?" I demand when she just stares at me.

Her eyes are wide and glassy, her shoulders slumped. She's the picture of anxiety, but I can't seem to stop myself. I have to know.

"Well?" I yell, and she flinches again, her eyes dropping to the floor. Her flinch, that sign of fear, makes my chest hurt, especially because I caused it, but I'm afraid, too. I'm afraid of losing her.

"I did once," she admits softly, and all the air whooshes out of me as I hit the door, barely able to hold myself up.

She loved him. She loved him, and he still wants her.

She'll leave me like everyone else.

I feel her gaze on me, and she suddenly blows out a breath, the anxiety in her stance disappearing. "I loved him once, but I was a different person then." I meet her gaze, my heart breaking. "I was just Kai from the Shadow Lands. I loved him, yet when the king took me . . ." She shakes her head. "He never came for me. He never even tried to help me." She laughs bitterly, tugging at her hair as I step forward, drawn by her pain.

"I don't know what he would have done against a king, so I can't even blame him, right? But he didn't try. He didn't once try to stop him. He never came looking for me. It's selfish but deep down, I wish he had done something. So yes, Dade, I loved that man once in another lifetime, but any love I had for him died with the girl in that castle. I was given a second chance here with you. I chose you. All of you. I will always choose you."

My heart stutters and speeds up. She chooses us?

"I would never let you go," I admit, my voice raw. "I would fight for you until my last breath."

"I know you would." She smiles brightly as she looks at the

others. "All of you would. It took me finding monsters to find my place, but it is my place, Dade. No matter what happens, we will face it together." She holds out her hand, hope in her eyes.

I don't hesitate. I lay my own in hers, curling my bigger one around her fingers.

I tug her closer, and she giggles as she hits my chest. I wrap her in my arms, holding her tightly. "I would have fought for you," I whisper, and she nuzzles her head against my skin.

"We all would have," Kaito adds, coming over and wrapping himself around her from behind.

Weyland and Rook quickly join us, and we embrace her until she's held in all of our arms.

We are four monsters who would carve out their souls before they ever let the little human in our midst be hurt again.

She's right. He's her past, and he'll remain there, but the four of us are her future.

CHAPTER
FORTY

KAI

My mind often wanders to Cora. In moments of relaxation or silence, my memories of her resurface—good memories, bad memories, memories of our time together before we both became someone else. My sister, a queen, is bridging the gap between monster and man, and I am something different from before. I don't know what I am anymore, but clearly, I'm not as powerless as I thought. It's strange that it took me being surrounded by monsters to realize that.

Now, I play with my power. It's still weak, as if it directly correlates with the speed of healing. Perhaps, the stronger I become against my darkness, the stronger my powers will be. Right now, I don't know much about them other than the fact that the lightning comes to life in moments of passion. I don't exactly know what the power can do, so I start to focus on trying to bring it out. When Rook suggested meditation, I went with it. That's how I find myself sitting outside in the grass with my eyes closed.

The grass beneath me is soft and lush, cushioning me as I sit cross-legged with my back straight. My hands rest on my knees as I focus on my breathing—breathe in for six seconds, breathe out for three, repeat.

Rook sits opposite me, his shadows trailing along the grass around him. He's mediating too, though what he practices, I don't know. I'm just happy he decided to do it with me.

"When you feel at ease," he murmurs, his voice gentle so as not to startle me. "I want you to focus on your power. Study it, feel it, and coax it to come out."

I nod despite neither one of us having our eyes open. Rook's shadows dance around me, caressing me as they move. They make it damn difficult to focus on anything else. After a few minutes of trying to ignore them, I simply accept the touch and try to focus on my power instead.

"Good girl," Rook purrs. His pride echoes in his voice, and it makes something inside me swell. I straighten further, my pulse fluttering.

The lightning awakens beneath my skin, but I don't crack my eyes open. Instead, I focus on the feeling of it, on the way it dances beneath my skin and manifests on the outside of it. I do as Rook asks. I coax it to react, to manifest as I wish it to. I push it over to Rook to dance it over his skin, but it doesn't listen. In my ease, the lightning latches onto something stronger than my desire—my love for Cora.

The thoughts that plague me are prevalent in my mind. I miss her, but there's still guilt when I think of her. I still can't stomach the look on her face as I'd fallen from the castle. The memory is no longer shrouded by the shadows in my mind, so I see it as clearly as if I were standing before her again. She'd held no anger toward me, and she didn't blame me, but the pain I've caused her . . .

I crack my eyes open and stare at the strange-looking glass my lightning formed between Rook and me. The pictures dance across it, blurry at first before my memories sharpen and appear for the both of us to watch. Cora stands before me, her monsters by her side. Her hand is outstretched as she asks me to take it, and I feel my pain at the realization I'm no longer the woman I was, that I was too broken to stay with her. Then, there is the moment I stepped back and tumbled over the edge.

Rook's shadows sharpen as they caress me, stroking along my skin. "How can you not be angry?" he asks, his voice thick with emotion at the memories that begin to flash. The recollections the king is in are muted, the memories beginning to blur because I don't want to see them again, but I also don't want Rook to witness that. Despite the blur, he can garner enough from them. "How can you not want to rip that world to shreds?"

I smile at him, at the way he absorbs my past and doesn't judge me for it. "That's an easy answer," I murmur. "Because Cora is a part of that world, and I would never want to do anything to hurt her."

Even though I've hurt her the most.

Rook looks up from the portal into my past and meets my eyes. "You underestimate yourself, little oblivion. If you wanted to make him pay—"

"He has," I interrupt. "The man who broke me died by my sister's hands, but if he were still alive, I would make the monsters look harmless."

Rook's shadows stroke along my body. "Did you get a taste for blood while you were licking your wounds, little oblivion?" he purrs. "Did the darkness forge you into a dagger?"

I meet his eyes. "Maybe it did. Maybe I'm no longer Kai Black of the Shadow Lands. Maybe I'm something else."

His shadows stroke along my jaw, enveloping me. "You're still Kai Black," he murmurs. "You're still Cora's sister."

"And if I'm not?" I ask, looking down. "If I'm a monster now?"

His shadows tug my chin back up, forcing my eyes to his. "It doesn't matter," he says, his voice steady. "You're still ours, and if you think a sister who loves you enough to take your place in a strangled Dead Lands would ever turn you away, then you're not looking close enough, little oblivion."

The pulse in my neck flutters as his shadows swirl around me, driving me mad. The memories on the glass created by my lightning grow sharper, brighter, as they show memories of Cora and me in the Shadow Lands, of us giggling and sneaking out. Merryl flashes across it, but the image of him only makes me angry so it flicker away before being replaced by Cora's laughing face and the memories of her mischievousness.

I see the moment she looked back at me as the wall closed around her.

I thought that would be the last time I'd ever see my sister. No hunt ever survived, but it doesn't surprise me that Cora would be the one who did. They threw her to the monsters, and she came back leading them. The monsters at her side loved her. Even in my brokenness, I'd seen the clear adoration on their faces as they looked at her. They would happily walk into fire to save her. Together, they brought down the wall, joined all three lands back together, and overthrew the king. Cora was always the strong one. She was always the best of us.

"You share her fierce eyes," Rook comments, his gaze on the glass between us. The memory of Cora stepping through the wall repeats over and over again. The next time I saw her was in the Gilded Lands in an alley, when I was already broken.

I find myself falling into the darker memories again, the images blurring. When Rook's shadows circle me once more, I finally realize what I'm doing. I blink, and the glass begins to fade away, my lightning still dancing in the air between us. It doesn't disappear, simply changes direction to focus on Rook. My gaze lingers on his as the lightning begins to dance along his skin. I watch his muscles jump beneath it, his dark eyes reflecting the light back to me.

"I can see the darkness in your eyes, little oblivion," Rook rasps, his attention completely on me. "I can feel your urge to push away affection."

I take a deep, stuttering breath. "Sometimes, being offered tenderness in the darkness feels like proof that you've been ruined." My voice is a whisper, as if I don't dare to speak the words any louder. All this time, I've felt undeserving of their affections, and while I'm overcoming that, there's still this guilt in my soul—guilt that they have to take care of me and that I wasn't whole to begin with.

"Not ruined," Rook says, leaning closer. "Forged." His smile is broken by his sharp teeth. "And what a marvelous weapon you'll be when you stand up to your demons."

When his breath suddenly fans across my cheeks, I can barely convince myself to fill my lungs with air. "A weapon or a trinket?"

"A weapon," he assures me. "You've always been stronger than you think you are, little oblivion. I saw it in your memories. I see you now." His clawed hand comes up to caress my jaw. "And you'll shake the world with your reckoning."

I search his eyes. Though they are dark and deep, I see his honesty there. He's open before me, bare, and I can't stop myself. As the shadows swirl around us, I reach up to cup his face.

His eyes widen a fraction as I lean in and press my lips to his.

FORTY-ONE

Kissing Kaito is like kissing the ocean, like a gentle storm swallowing you and welcoming you home. Kissing Weyland is more like kissing the wild, like tangling with some feral creature held carefully in check. With Dade, it's the same feeling as when I rode him, like my arms are open wide and I'm flying.

It feels like none of that with Rook.

Rook doesn't move at first, as if he's afraid to while my lips are pressed so softly against his. I need him. I need a piece of him to tuck into my heart and hold the darkness at bay. My monsters are healing me every single day and doing more for me than I realize. I'm awake now, more awake than I've ever been. I used to think I loved Merryl before the king took me. I thought that was love, but now I realize it was only the better option at the time. This feeling, this all-encompassing passion that's awakening in me for my monsters, is what love is supposed to be. This love drunk desire to be near them, to talk to them, to hold them close is what everyone searches for.

For the first time, I wonder what would have happened if the king hadn't taken me. Would I have leapt off the castle for Kaito to find me? Would I be sitting here now with Rook, absorbed in the coolness of his shadows and the warmth of his body? Did I have to be broken to be whole again?

I'm starting to learn that those who are the most broken are the most beautiful.

When Rook's surprise disappears and his lips begin to move, it washes away all my thoughts. His hand circles my head and grips my hair, and he deepens the kiss as he takes control. I keep my eyes open just in case my own shadows try to come barreling in, but Rook's shadows seem to be the only ones able to slip inside.

Kissing Rook is like sinking into a pool of oil and welcoming those thick shadows into my soul as they wrap around me like a blanket. It's the comfort of darkness, of my demons welcoming me home. As I kiss him, I let my mind drift. I let my fear and anxiety float away. There's only Rook and me sitting in the midst of his shadows, our tongues tangling and my pussy throbbing. When his hand trails up my leg, pushing my dress up, I let him, knowing without a doubt who I'm here with. There's no mistaking him for anyone else, not when his shadows hold me so carefully.

He breaks the kiss and drags his teeth along my jaw and down my neck. He kisses the pulse point there, making it flutter at the touch. He could tear my throat out, this boogeyman who scares other monsters, but he holds himself with a gentleness no human man could rival. It takes power to be so deadly and so gentle at the same time.

"Little oblivion," he purrs against my skin. "I want nothing more than to make you scream your pleasure for all of the Dead Lands to hear." His lips continue to kiss their way along my skin, and my hand finds its way into his hair to hold him to me. "But you are not ready for this."

I tense and look down at him as he trails his lips across my shoulder. "I am."

"I should not be your first among us," he continues, his cool fingers trailing up my inner thigh. "I am no easy lover, but Kaito is, and Weyland will be. It should be one of them."

Annoyance flares through me alongside my desire. I know they always wish to protect me, but I know my own mind, my own body.

"Don't I get a choice?" I ask, my fingers digging into his scalp in punishment. "Shouldn't I be the one who decides?"

"Yes," he says, leaning back just enough to look into my eyes. "But I won't just love you, little oblivion. I will rip you to shreds and stitch you back together again. I will unlock your memories, and your shadows will pour out to dance with mine. I will destroy you, then I will remake you, and I will expect nothing less." He presses a kiss against my forehead. "You are strong and growing stronger every day. I want nothing more than to be selfish and sate myself with your body as I've imagined doing since I first saw you wrapped in your darkness, but you are not ready for me yet, and I won't undo all your healing by pushing the matter."

I stare at him before huffing. "Well . . . I suppose I understand." I don't want to take three steps back by pushing myself too far. I've yet to make love with any of them, and if Rook claims he shouldn't be the first, then I should trust him. Still, I'm disappointed. My shoulders droop at the realization. "Okay," I murmur. "I believe you."

He chuckles. "Despite that, I would never leave you wanting, little oblivion."

Frowning at him, I tilt my head. "But you just said—"

"I said I will not claim you." He leans in and nuzzles my neck. "That doesn't mean I can't bring you pleasure." His shadows wrap around me and press where I want his lips to be, starting to stroke me. "I won't leave you to mourn the loss, little oblivion, but I will leave you yearning."

The next brush of his shadows along my skin makes me arch my back as they stroke and push at my clothing, slipping beneath the edges. Rook's strong arms encircle me and lay me down on the grass. He hovers over me, his eyes hungrily drinking me in as I begin to writhe beneath him. When his shadows curl around my nipples and tug, they harden until it's almost painful, and I'm desperate for more. My fingers clench the grass, afraid to touch him in case he decides this is too much.

"Open your eyes, little oblivion," he instructs, and when I do, he grins. "I want to see the way your pupils widen at your pleasure. I want to see how the irises darken as you come apart in my shadows."

It takes everything inside me to keep them open, to focus on him. His shadows curl around me so completely, I don't worry about the memories slamming back in. Still, I stay focused on him as the shadows stroke my skin. When the first shadows trail along my thighs, I forget to breathe. When they trace along my core, I forget to think.

"Rook," I pant as the shadows spread my thighs apart, holding me hostage without holding me at all. I can stop this at any moment, but I don't want to. I'm desperate for him, for his touch, and if I can't have that, then his shadows are the next best thing.

"Kai," he murmurs, his arousal written across his face. "Is this okay?"

I nod frantically as his shadows stroke along my entrance as he waits for permission. "Please," is the only word I can get out between my pants.

He doesn't touch me, and yet he does. He covers me in his essence, in his shadows, and I welcome him inside. It's a muted version of him, but I understand that I'm not ready for everything he has to offer—not yet, but I will be.

Slowly, the shadow at my entrance presses inside. It widens as it strokes, perfectly phallic-shaped, as he pauses to make sure I'm okay. When I begin to writhe beneath him, desperate for more, his shadows start to move. They stroke inside me, gentle as can be, while others twist around my nipples, tugging and caressing. They cover every inch of me.

It's been so long that my orgasm rises embarrassingly fast. I gasp, trying to hold on, my eyes clamping shut as the feeling rushes over me. My skin tingles, my body vibrates, and I can't—

"Open your eyes, little oblivion," he growls.

The shadows on my nipples verge on the edge of pain with the command, and I open my eyes again. Our gazes meet, and everything inside me shatters. I cry out, my back arching off the ground as the wave crashes over me. I tear at the grass, my legs shaking with the intense feeling as Rook purrs above me.

"There it is," he growls, his hand coming up to stroke my waist. "Beautiful. So beautiful." He leans down and inhales, as if my own darkness is intoxicating to him. Perhaps it is.

I collapse against the ground, my body aching from my orgasm, but he was right.

The moment I can think again, I yearn for him, for more, for everything.

He grins and presses another kiss against my lips. When he pulls away, I can still taste the shadows.

"Damn you." I laugh and hug him close, amused by his tactics.

He freezes for a second, as if surprised by my embrace, and then he wraps his arms around me.

"Do you want to go see her?" he asks against my hair. "Your sister?"

My heart flutters as my arms tighten around him. Fear trickles back in—fear of her pain, fear of facing the guilt. "Not yet," I whisper. "Not yet."

Shadows, I can't face her yet.

FORTY-TWO

KAI

L ife is good. I'm happy.

I'm growing closer to my men every day. They touch me now, unafraid to reach for me, and I don't flinch. I enjoy their caresses and attention, and under it all is that fiery desire we are all trying to resist. Why, I don't know, but I do know one day it, will snap.

I should have known nothing can stay good forever, though, because where there is happiness, there is pain. That is something I know all too well.

I feel it this morning when I wake up. Something is amiss in the air, a sense of wrongness. It's clear my guys feel it as well. They are on edge, their eyes sharp. They do not let me out of their sight, even when I bathe. I can't put my finger on why I'm on edge, but when I scan the forest, the hair on the back of my neck rises.

"Let's head back," I murmur, dressing quickly after my bath and taking Kaito's hand. He escorts me back, the others already outside watching, as if they feel it too.

Once back in the cabin, I find my eyes wandering to the door as I stir the stew we are cooking for breakfast. My body is on alert, an old survival instinct that I learned to trust. I used to lie in my dark room in the castle and would always know the king was coming. I trusted it when I still lived in my father's house and his fits of rage would strike. It kept me alive more than once, and I know well enough to trust it now.

Something is wrong. Something is coming.

We are in danger.

"Something is wrong," I tell them sternly as I turn from the stew, and I don't know if it's my tone or the way I stand with my eyes on the wooden door, but they instantly surround me. Weyland snarls, Kaito holds me, Dade stomps in agitation, and Rook's shadows dance protectively around us.

"I feel it too," Weyland agrees. "Something is in the air." He lifts his head, inhaling deeply.

"Anything?" Dade demands, trusting my and Weyland's instincts, working as a team.

When Weyland's eyes open wide, I know I was right. "Human hunters," he snarls, turning to us. "Surrounding us. Move now!"

I don't know how they snuck up on us, nor do we have time to debate it. If Weyland says we need to move, then we need to move, and fast.

"How many?" Rook asks as his shadows increase until we are obscured by them. Kaito's hand finds mine, holding tight as he tugs me next to him protectively.

"Ten at least," Weyland snarls. "I can smell their hate."

We sensed them too late to act. The door explodes inwards, chips of broken wood flying at us like daggers. Rook snarls, waving his hand, and they stop midair before turning slowly and flying outwards through the now gaping doorway. There's a scream and a thud before everything goes quiet.

Too quiet.

My hand tingles in Kaito's grip as my power awakens. Electricity seems to fill me, moving below my skin as if preparing for the attack.

I could have used this a long time ago, but now is not the time to dwell on the past.

We are being hunted, and I no longer want to be prey.

"Stay here," Rook commands as he moves through the shadows.

"No," I hiss, reaching for him, but he's already out of my grasp and slipping out the door. My eyes widen in worry, my heart hammering.

"I'll help him," Weyland promises, kissing my cheek before hurrying out after Rook.

Dade moves to my other side, sandwiching me between him and Kaito to protect me. I almost leap from my skin when a roar sounds outside—Weyland. Despite Kaito's grasp, I rush through the door, ignoring their calls to come back. As I break through the doorway and get a good look at the scene before me, my heart stops.

Weyland's head is tipped back in a roar of anger and pain. One of his feet is caught in a metal bear trap we used to use around the village, and blood gushes from the wound where the teeth sink in. It had clearly been hidden, a trap set for a wolf. Covering my mouth in horror, I stumble toward him to help, thinking there must be something I can do. When he kicks the trap off with a feral growl and throws himself at the hunters heading his way with spears, I stumble to a stop, unsure how to help now that he's free.

I can see his injury, but it doesn't seem to slow him down as he barrels into them, Rook hurrying to his side to offer support. Shadows wrap around the hunters as he moves and swallows their screams.

"Kai!" My name makes me whirl. I hadn't realized I had gone so far from the cabin in my panic, and I gasp when I see Kaito and Dade fighting their own hunters while trying to get to me.

Torn between my men, I hesitate, and it's my downfall.

Arms wrap around me from behind, locking me into an unwanted embrace. "Shh, I've got you. Let's go."

The familiar voice startles me, which is why I don't react at first as

209

I'm dragged toward the trees. When my brain kicks in and I realize what's happening, I start to struggle, screaming and kicking out at the man who holds me. My powers surge through me, my anger fueling them. "Damn it, Kai! It's me! I've got you. Let me save you from these monsters. I swear you'll be safe. I'm here to rescue you. It's me."

Merryl. The man who hadn't rescued me when it mattered. The man who thinks to rescue me now when I don't need it.

I struggle until my elbow connects with his side and he grunts, his hold weakening enough for me to slip from his arms and whirl to face him.

"It's me." He holds out his hand as if placating a wild animal. "Come on. Come with me."

A scream of agony rips through the air and I turn, searching. Kaito is staring down at his hands and his stomach, where a spear sticks from the muscle there. The hunter yanks it free, and blood spurts from the wound. Kaito's hands cover it as he falls to his knees in shock.

Panic tears through me at the sight and, ignoring Merryl's outstretched hand, I race toward Kaito. "Rook!" I scream without looking, but luckily, he hears me and understands. His shadows race to Kaito, wrapping around him protectively and obscuring him from the hunters while Dade quickly grabs the one who stabbed Kaito and snaps his neck, effortlessly tossing him aside.

I race across the familiar ground faster than I've ever been able to move before. My dress flares behind me as my skin glows with my powers. A hunter rushes toward me, but I lift my hand, my powers flaring brightly from within. He flies backward, his eyes wide in shock, before I plunge into the welcoming shadows and drop to my knees before Kaito.

"Kai," he groans as he starts to fall.

I catch him, wrapping my arms around his shoulders and lowering him onto my lap. Panic fills my heart as I cover the wound on his stomach with my hands, feeling his warm blood pump through our joined fingers.

"So beautiful," he rasps as he stares up at me with wonder.

"Shh, I've got you. You're going to be okay." I don't really know if he will be, but I do know I can't lose Kaito.

He saved me, but more than that, he brought me back to life.

He's mine.

Tears fill my eyes as the shadows fade away when Rook and Weyland rush over, the hunters dead where they were fighting. Any who are left race toward Merryl where he stands, staring at me. I meet his gaze briefly before dismissing him. Instead, I drop my eyes to Kaito to find he's pale.

He's blinking too fast now, and his heart is thundering so loudly, it echoes in my ears.

My head lifts, my eyes glassy with tears as I meet Merryl's gaze one last time while his men rush back into the forest with panicked yells. I know there's anger reflected in mine, and there's surprise in his. My hands are coated in Kaito's blood as I try to staunch the flow, and for a moment, as I meet the eyes of the man I once loved, I see his hatred there. I see his hatred for the monsters. I see his hatred for what I've become.

Uncaring of Merryl's feelings, I press harder against the wound.

The sight of the red blood seeping between my fingers has ghosts rearing their ugly heads until my vision blurs and fades, the image of me pressing my hands to my own wounds taking over until I'm panting.

Anger and pain twirl inside me.

My head tips back with a pained scream, and I release it all.

CHAPTER
FORTY-THREE

KAI

My ragged scream echoes into the Dead Lands, pure pain and anger.

"Kai." The voice drags me from my fury and agony. Dropping my head, I meet Kaito's astonished, wide eyes. "You're glowing."

I follow his gaze, my eyes dropping to my body to see he's right. I am glowing, but not from happiness or desire—from pain and worry. My powers feel it, and I glow from within like a lightning storm.

My men circle us, their backs to us to protect us while they keep their eyes on the forest as if the hunters would dare attack again, but my entire focus is on Kaito. He's losing too much blood. "Why did you let him stab you?" I sob.

"Sorry." He grins around a pained wince. "Next time, I'll politely ask them not to."

A cough racks his body as he groans, his blood soaking into the earth below.

He's dying. It's a death wound. I can tell it is. His organs practi-

Kaito is going to die.

The man who saved me, who looked after me and tended to me, who held me through my nightmares. The man who kissed me so sweetly despite his fears. The man who loves me with everything in him . . .

The man I am in love with is dying in my arms.

No, he can't die. He was never supposed to. I was supposed to be the one who died. Doesn't that mean something? He saved a life, and he deserves his own in return. No, I can't let him die.

I *will* not.

"You don't get to leave me," I whisper out loud, my voice cracking as the sky seems to darken with my pain. "You don't. I just found you. It's not fair. You hear me? It's not fucking fair. I get to be happy. We get to be happy. We deserve it. You do not get to leave me."

He covers my hand, smiling weakly. "Shh, my love. I'm not going anywhere. I wouldn't dare."

"Promise me. Promise me you won't leave me," I sob.

Tears fall from his eyes, flowing into the ground. "I promise, Kai, whatever happens, I will never leave you alone. I will always be with you, always in your heart, even if my body leaves this earth. My soul will stay here with you where you loved me."

Shaking my head, I press harder against the wound. "No, not good enough. We're staying here at our cabin and growing old together. We'll forage and play and we'll be happy."

"It's okay," he whispers shakily, his strength failing him, but he still pushes through. "You won't be alone, Kai, and that's enough for me. It's okay, my love. It's okay to love them even when I'm gone. Be happy for me, okay? Please, just be happy. That's all I want. I was so alone, so empty before you. You say I saved you, but the truth is, Kai, you saved me. You saved me, my love. I'm so thankful for the time we had together, no matter how short. Don't be pained. Do not let it hurt you. Love and live."

"No," I sob, pressing my lips to his cooling ones. "I can't live

without you. I won't. We have a full life before us. I demand it."
Lifting my eyes to the sky, I scream, "Do you hear me? I demand it!
Have you not taken enough from me? Haven't I given enough? You
don't get him; he's mine! I'm keeping him." I break into sobs. "Please,
please don't take him from me. Please, please, I'll do anything. Don't
take him from me."

Reaching up with a shaking hand, he cups the back of my head
and pulls me down. "Kiss me, Kai. Kiss me so I go into the next world
with your taste on my lips."

Crying, I press my lips to his, doing as he asks despite my anger
at the unfairness of it all.

"I love you," I whisper. "I love you so much. I can't let you go. I
can't."

How much can one person endure?

Why does everyone else get to be happy while all I know is pain
and loss?

Why do good people have to die while the wicked live?

Why can't I live a peaceful, happy life? Why does it hurt too
much to be alive?

"I can't," I repeat. "I won't."

I beg the wind, I plead with this world, and I hand over my soul.

For the first time, something listens, only it isn't another person
—it's that power under my skin I have yet to explore.

It crawls through me and flows down my arms, the glow brightening so fast, I can barely stand to look at it, so I keep my eyes
focused on Kaito beneath me. I gasp as I feel the power push into
Kaito as it searches. He jerks with a groan, his eyes widening, and I
pull away and glance down. My hands glow so brightly, they almost
blind me, my eyes watering from the effort it takes to focus on them.

"Kaito," I whisper, an old instinct guiding me as my powers flow
through me and into him.

I'm *healing* him.

His color returns, the blood stops running, and under my hands, I
feel the wound begin to stitch itself together and finally close. When

the glow lessens and finally stops, I lift my bloodstained hands to see his perfectly unmarred stomach. All that remains is a thin, glowing scar.

Lifting my eyes to Kaito's astonished gaze, my heart stills.

I healed him.

"Kai." He grabs me, lurching up and pressing his lips to mine. I taste his desperation and love, and I have no doubt he tastes my tears and hope, and when we break apart, he presses his forehead to mine. "You saved me."

"It's only fair," I croak, happiness filling my heart.

He wraps me up in his arms, holding me.

Here, on the bloodstained Dead Lands, held by my monster, I start to believe in this world again.

In right and wrong.

In happiness and hope.

In myself.

CHAPTER
FORTY-FOUR

KAI

"We need to leave," Dade growls later. He's pacing inside the door of the cabin, his eyes constantly looking out the windows in case the hunters return. "We can't stay here."

Rook nods from his own position at the back of the cabin, making sure none appear from the back. They fall into the roles easily, their eyes hard and bodies almost vibrating. "The warhorse is correct. They know our location. Next time they come, they'll bring more hunters with them."

I don't answer, not right away. My eyes are on Kaito where he sits at the table, his head in his hands. Every so often, his eyes meet mine and linger, and we're reminded again that he almost died. He *would* have died had my power not chosen to wake up. I hold my hand out in front of me, staring at it. Right now, it looks normal, like a very human hand, but whatever power I've been blessed with, whatever power that has decided to awaken now of all times, makes me look decidedly less human. Human but not. Monster but not. What exactly am I if I can heal a mortal wound?

What does that make me?

I'm not sure, but I can't be anything but grateful that it saved Kaito.

Even as I watch the new shapes dance across the arm of my skin. The ink appears like magic not moments after healing him and it moves across my arm as if with a mind of its own.

A tattoo.

"Where can we go that's safe?" Weyland asks. He runs a hand through his hair in agitation. There are scratches and small wounds on his skin that he refused to let me heal for fear I'd use too much of my power. It's true I was exhausted after healing Kaito, but now, I'm only rife with anxiety.

"There are places in the Dead Lands," Kaito offers slowly.

"Not all monsters will welcome Kai in their territories," Dade points out. "She could be in danger from them. Plus, the hunters have been hunting there for months now. They likely know many places we would go."

"What about the Shadow Lands? Or the Gilded Lands?" Kaito suggests. "Surely, they wouldn't think to look for us there."

"Too dangerous," Rook replies. "We stand out too much." He gestures to himself, to his body, as if to prove his point. "No. The Dead Lands is our best chance."

I listen to them go back and forth for hours, trying to discern where the best place to run is. At first, I offer nothing. What do I know about hiding? What do I know about the hunters? All I know is that I brought this upon them. Because of me, Merryl will return and hurt them. Because of me, they are in danger.

When Kaito slams his fists against the table, I realize I've zoned out. It startles me back to awareness, and I blink at them when I see them arguing.

"We must decide! Talking is doing nothing!" Kaito snarls. "Kai is in danger here!"

"Yes! But no one has any ideas," Weyland retorts. "You haven't been helpful either—"

"I say we just go. We leave," Dade offers. "We'll figure out where later."

"A journey without direction is a death sentence," Rook counters. "We need a plan—"

I clear my throat, and all four of them turn to me, their eyes blazing with the heat of the moment. Until now, I allowed them to discuss what's best for me, but I'm no longer the Kai who was afraid of her own shadow. This is my life. I won't move through it without purpose or care. It's time I took control of it and chose the direction I want my future to go rather than allow others to.

"I think I might have an idea," I murmur. When they continue to look at me expectantly, I say, "My sister, she would protect us."

Kaito straightens, his eyes wide. "Are you certain you're ready for that, Kai?"

No, I think. *No, I'm not, but* . . . "We need her help, and it has to happen at some point." I don't mention that I could likely avoid it for years, so afraid of seeing her pain and confronting the guilt that eats me alive. Cora once gave everything for me, and I'd been too broken to stay by her side. Some part of me understands it had to happen the way it did for me to meet my monsters, but it doesn't make it hurt any less. How can I ever look her in the eye after everything that's happened? How can I look the queen in the eye and know that I failed my sister?

Rook is watching me closely, his eyes seeing more than they should. He can see into the shadows themselves, into the darkness that I carry. I know he can, but he doesn't bring up any of the thoughts he learns from that darkness. Instead, he tilts his head. "Are you sure you want to do this, little oblivion?"

"What choice do we have?" I ask him with a sigh. "We're being hunted. Cora needs to know just how bad the monster hunters have gotten, and we need help. It's either go to her or wander around the Dead Lands with no true plan."

"Yes, but your pain is more important," Dade offers. "We wouldn't like to cause more pain."

It's not more important. I know that. I nearly watched Kaito die beneath my hands. I watched him bleed from a mortal wound that no creature could survive. My guilt is not more important than that. My fear has no place in the face of such danger. I'd march into any situation to save my monsters and keep any of them from going through that again. There's never a guarantee that my power will wake up on command the next time. There's no guarantee that there will be time to save them. So, no.

"It's not pain," I whisper. "It's fear, and I'm so tired of being afraid." I reach over the table and take Kaito's hand. His webbed fingers thread with mine, offering comfort when just a few hours ago, he was dying. "My sister will help us, or at the very least, help with the hunters. It's the only option we have."

Rook's eyes should be terrifying, but I meet his gaze, unflinching. I've grown since I left the king's castle. I'm still afraid, yes, but I'm no longer just afraid of the world. I'm more afraid of losing my monsters, of them dying and leaving me on this earth without them. I can't live without them. I refuse to.

Weyland nods. "Then we should leave straightaway. I'll pack up the food we have."

"I'll grab essentials," Kaito adds. "Dade, you keep watch in case they return."

Rook and I remain at the table, his eyes still on me. When the others get to work gathering things, he doesn't move. I can see the tension in his shoulders brought on by concern for my well-being.

"Are you so certain of this idea, little oblivion?" he asks softly. "We can make other plans."

I tilt my chin up. "I will no longer live only in fear," I tell him. "Cora is my sister. I . . . I owe her everything that I am."

"I can see the uncertainty in your eyes," he murmurs. "It lingers there with your strength."

I glance down at the woodgrain of the table, running my fingers along the texture there. "The last time I saw Cora, I was throwing myself from a castle, too broken to see any other option. My guilt eats me alive. My fear that she'll hate me sticks in my throat, even though I know Cora could never hate me. I let her step through that wall for me," I rasp, "and when she returned to save me yet again, I couldn't even do her the honor of sticking around. I'm a terrible sister, but Cora was always a great one."

Rook watches me choke out the words, and then he reaches for my hand. The coolness of his shadows dances along my skin, raising awareness without meaning to. Rook simply exists to exist. Every part of him is a reminder of darkness and light. It's a strange combination, seeing something so deadly be so gentle when he takes my hand.

"I am willing to bet that Cora would never call you a terrible sister, little oblivion."

I choke down the sob that threatens to rip from my throat. "You're right. She never would, but that doesn't mean I'm not exactly that."

"You are not a terrible person or a terrible sister, little oblivion," he states. "You were just hurting. Sometimes, we must suffer such things to rise again, and here you are, ready to face the fear in your veins and the pain in your heart. This is who you were meant to be. When you see your sister again, she will see that."

"I hope you're right," I tell him, but despite his reassurance, that fear still fills my chest and tries to drag me down.

I'm not the same Kai who leapt from a tower though. I'm not the same woman who was terrified to live. I'm not helpless and broken.

I'm something else now, and I'm not alone.

Standing from my chair, I go to help the others pack what we need, if only to stop my mind from focusing on my racing heart.

It's time to go home.

FORTY-FIVE

KAI

It only takes us another hour to finish packing. Each of my monsters wears a pack that can be adjusted if needed for their other form. Dade walks as a man for now, but I don't doubt he'll shift into his warhorse form at some point, and Weyland may prefer to wear his wolf skin once we're deep in the Dead Lands. Either way, we made sure that the packs could be worn regardless. They refused to allow me to carry one, claiming that I'm already tired from my use of power earlier. I tried to argue, but it had been useless when I swayed on my feet. Now, we stand before the cabin, my eyes lingering on what has been my home for months and months now. It feels like a betrayal to leave it, but we can't stay here, not while Merryl still hunts us.

Still, looking at the cabin feels like some great goodbye. I can't help the emotion that lodges in my throat as I stare at the now dark windows and the closed door. Will we ever return? Will we be able to?

This is where I chose to fight to live again.

Where I faced my nightmares.

Where I fell in love.

I walk forward and press my hand against the wooden door. When I lean my forehead against it, I feel them circle me. Their hands touch me, offering comfort and strength. They understand that this has been our home, our safe haven, and now we must leave it to the forest. We may never return. We may never be this happy again.

"We'll be back," Kaito promises, his hand smoothing down my back.

It's not about the cabin. It is, but it isn't. It's about the happy memories I have of this place, the laughter we shared within these walls. I hadn't even been able to smile in the beginning, but these four walls witnessed my return. They'd been my shelter when I needed it, but the wood and nails are not what made it a home.

My monsters did.

"Even if we don't," I murmur, "that's okay. We have each other. That's what is most important." I press away from the door and smile up at Kaito. When he takes my hand and squeezes, I square my shoulders and turn toward the forest. "Let's go."

As we leave, I look back once, taking in the darkness of the cabin, and smile. Whether we return or not, it'll always have a special place in my heart. I fell in love there not once, but four times. I grew stronger there.

Within those walls, I was born again.

GROWING up in the Shadow Lands, the thorns separating us from the monsters, I always thought the Dead Lands were . . . well, dead, but my time in the cabin and exploring the surrounding areas with my monsters has shown a completely different world. The forest has started to come to life in a way that reminds me that beauty is everywhere. Trees stand covered in fresh colors, their leaves sprouting and giving new life. Flowers bloom everywhere—in the trees, along the ground, in the bushes—as if breathing life for the first time.

Everything pulses with life, and as we walk slowly through the trees, I can feel its heartbeat. The same lightning that flows through my veins lives in this world, trickling along the leaves and weaving through the ground. When I stroke my fingers along them, that pulse answers like I ask a question, and it makes something lighter in my chest. This is where I'm meant to be. This is who I'm meant to be.

When I start to slow, my exhaustion catching up with me, Dade transforms, and Kaito sets me upon his back to ride. The first time I rode him was a wild ride. Now, he only goes as fast as the others move. This isn't a race, and we have to move carefully in case we come into contact with more hunters. We don't know how many there are. We don't know if Merryl's party is the only one or if there are other hunting parties killing their way through the Dead Lands, so we tread carefully.

Cora's castle is a few days' journey at our current pace. I appreciate that we aren't just rushing directly there because it gives me more time to prepare myself. The more I think about her reaction to seeing me alive, the more my stomach churns with anxiety. Will she hate me? Will she be afraid? Will she send me away?

I'm so lost in my thoughts, my fingers intertwined with Dade's mane to keep from falling off, that I don't recognize the danger right away—not until Dade freezes beside the others. I glance around, concerned, and then jerk upright when I see the creature before us.

Long and sinuous, the snake woman takes us all in, her eyes trailing over Kaito, Dade, and Weyland. She pauses on Rook, fear flickering in her gaze, but when she catches sight of me on Dade's back, her fear is replaced by surprise.

What's more, I recognize this monster. This is the snake woman we freed from the first hunting party. She seems to recognize us in turn, her shoulders tensing. She likely doesn't see me as a threat, but my four monsters are.

"We mean you no harm," I offer, holding up my hands. "We're only passing through."

Her long, beautiful tail shifts behind her as if the urge to flee is so strong, she can't help but move. "You are the ones who saved me."

Kaito glances up at me and then back at the naga. "Yes," he answers for me. "The hunters are getting bolder, so we are going for help."

She tilts her head. "Who would help us? We are but monsters to all."

"The queen," I reply, tilting my chin up. "The new queen."

The naga studies me carefully, weighing our words. Once she seems to take in everything, she bows her head slightly. "I am so hungry, but I will allow you to pass without a fight. Today, you. Tomorrow, me. A life for a life." When she backs away, Dade starts to move again. I don't think the naga would stand a chance against my monsters, but hunger is the great motivator. I've seen humans do terrible things out of hunger. Monsters would be no different.

"The hunters will follow," I tell her as we pass. "You should move farther inland."

She bows her head to me as I pass. "I will take your advice, little monster tamer. Thank you."

From then on, many of the monsters we pass don't give us any trouble. Most run away at the sight of us, terrified they will become our next meal. Some see me in the midst of monsters and decide that it's better to remain indifferent rather than become an enemy. A rare few interact and ask questions.

It isn't until we get closer to resting for the night that we meet our first conflict.

Rook senses it first and freezes, his hand shooting out to stop the others from moving, but they are not fast enough to hide from the creature that steps out from the bushes. Kaito jerks back in surprise, but the others stare at it like they've seen it before. I side with Kaito. The creature is grotesque. It's humanoid, standing on two legs like I do, and he's clearly male, his physique built like that of a warrior. His skin is a mottled gray and black broken up by streaks of red. His face, however, lacks the most humanity. Though he has two large black eyes, there's a multitude of other, smaller eyes smattered across his forehead, and his mouth is circled by large fangs. Everything about him makes me think of spiders, and I shudder where I sit on Dade.

"What—" I start, but Rook's hand on my thigh stops me.

"No sudden movements," he warns. "Draw no attention to yourself."

The spider creature tilts his head at the sound of Rook's voice and takes a step closer.

We won't leave here without a fight, Dade says inside my mind. *This is a fae male from the Arachna Clan. Dangerous. Lethal. Deadly.*

My fingers tighten in his mane, the lightning beneath my skin dancing with my nervous energy, and that's a mistake. The lightning lights up my skin, making me glow, and the fae's many eyes focus hungrily on me. Whatever power I possess, he wants it. Strands of drool begin to drip from his fangs as he starts to chortle and takes a step closer.

"What a pretty power," he purrs, and his voice makes my skin crawl. It feels like thousands of tiny spiders crawling along my skin, and I shiver. "I'd like to taste your power, pretty human."

"She is spoken for," Rook warns. "I suggest you continue on your way."

Weyland shakes his head. "His clan isn't known for peace."

We should be thankful there is only one. We would not stand a chance against the whole clan, Dade whispers in my mind.

"Do they often travel alone?" I ask him in a soft voice.

No, he replies, and I understand the weight in that word. The others won't be far behind. We can't linger.

"Don't let him bite you," Rook snarls just before he leaps forward. The fae immediately goes on alert and steps out of the way of my shadow monster, moving with a speed I don't expect. When large spider legs burst from his spine and help him move, I shriek and cling to Dade tightly as he avoids the fae.

"Come here, pretty power," the fae coos. "Let me taste you."

Weyland shifts so fast, I can't even follow the transition. He leaps into the shadows to help Rook while Dade and Kaito stay with me. I watch in horror as the spider tries and fails to come after me, his large spider legs giving him speed and agility that my monsters don't have. When he disappears, we all turn, frantic to find where he's at.

Rook snarls, "Watch your backs."

The sound of fast-moving legs draws our attention, but it's a trick we don't expect. The web comes from nowhere, latching onto my arm and jerking me off Dade's back. I scream in terror as I slam against the ground, losing my breath from the impact, before being tugged toward the trees. Kaito shouts and leaps after me, slicing the web with his nails and trying to drag me backwards to the others, but the fae appears from above with a hiss.

"Pretty power," he coos as he drags me toward him. He's far stronger than Kaito, who calls for the others in desperation. My arm pops as I'm tugged between them, my fear freezing me as the fae moves over me on his spider legs so he's looking down at me. His fangs spread, and I turn my face away in horror.

"Rook!" I scream as I feel his hot breath. My lightning shoots along my skin, and the fae's eyes widen in surprise.

"Powerful human," he purrs. "So potent I can taste it in the air. Just a taste."

His fangs open, and I scream, waiting for the feeling of being bit by this creature. My monsters attack him, but he doesn't react to the wounds they inflict.

My lightning zaps out and touches the spider, but he only shivers in ecstasy. "Just a taste," he repeats. "And then I'll save the rest for later."

He leans in, shivering, and then his eyes widen. I feel it a second later—the first pinprick of pain along my stomach. The fae looks down in surprise, and I follow his gaze to see what stopped him. Dade stands over us, his breathing ragged and hard. His large, sharp horn pierces the fae, going through his back and out of his stomach where it continues to pierce my stomach the smallest amount. We'd been too close to judge the true distance. The fae slumps, but before he can fall on top of me, Rook and Weyland haul him off, the squelch of Dade's horn coming out of him making me cringe. Kaito immediately rushes to me, checking me over. His hand traces over the bit of blood on my stomach from Dade.

"Did he bite you?" he asks frantically. "Kai, did he bite you?"

I realize he has to repeat himself because I'm still in shock, my eyes wide in horror and my heart threatening to burst from my chest.

"No," I say. "No, he didn't bite me."

Kaito relaxes. "Oh, thank the Dead Lands."

"Did I hurt you?" Dade asks, rushing forward once they make sure the fae is dead.

"I'm fine," I assure him, pushing my hair out of my eyes. "I'm going to have nightmares about that fae for the rest of my life, but I'm okay."

"We need to move right now," Rook growls. "Someone, pick her up. We run from here."

The next hour is spent running at their full speed to put as much distance as possible between us and the dead fae. Apparently, the Arachna Clan doesn't take well to one of their own being killed. Even Rook seems shaken, which tells me all I need to know.

If these are creatures that scare the boogeyman of the Dead Lands, then I don't want anything to do with them.

They run until they are exhausted, and only then do we rest. I try to convince myself we're not being followed and that we're safe now, but I can't wipe away the feeling of spiders running along my skin no matter how hard I try.

FORTY-SIX

KAI

Even after eating the meal Kaito prepares, I am restless. The fire burns close by, the orange light flickering around us and keeping me warm. A huge boulder shelters us from the forest and only allows a small walkway to the cave we have taken shelter in. Dade stands there now, protecting us, and I turn away from the sliver of darkness I see beyond, not wanting to see that fae ever again.

My skin still crawls like I can feel it touching me, those leering eyes and fangs descending toward me. Shivering, I wrap myself tighter in the blanket one of them produced for me, and as they plan the next day's journey, I force my eyes to close. I'm still exhausted from healing Kaito, and after today's attack, I know I need to sleep.

My hand drifts to my stomach under the blanket, covering the thin cut there. We checked it as soon as we found shelter. It wasn't deep, just bleeding a lot. Dade feels horrible, and I can feel his guilt no matter how much I thank him for saving me. This small wound is nothing compared to what would have happened had he not. Weyland carefully bandaged the cut. They had all been silent while he wrapped it, as if my injury was on their shoulders. No matter how much I tell them otherwise, they still seem to carry that guilt.

Leaving my hand on the bandage, I squeeze my eyes shut, forcing myself to think of only good things as I fight my brain to calm down and sleep. Minutes or maybe hours later, I feel a hand stroke my head softly. "Sleep, *bacca*. No one can hurt you here."

As if I needed to hear that, I finally slip into the waiting oblivion.

Pincers dig into the soft skin of my sides as my eyes snap open. My body is freezing, my heart pounding as I stare into the face of the spider fae. Its lips twist in a cruel, mocking grin, showcasing its sharp teeth. All the better to eat me with. Its eyes blink as one as the spider legs tug me closer.

"Just a taste." It cackles as I scream, writhing in its grip.

It's just a dream, just a dream, *I tell myself.* Wake up!

It's no use. I'm dragged closer and closer toward that waiting mouth, my screams echoing around the forest, until inky smoke wraps around his mouth. Familiar darkness obscures everything until I can't see through it, and I feel myself relax. I drop to the ground as the dream changes, and when the smoke parts, I know I have Rook to thank as he emerges from it.

Eyes hard and wanting, he doesn't stop until he reaches me. He tilts my chin up, his mouth crashing onto mine, kissing me furiously. He drains every last drop of fear from me and replaces it with burning desire.

His smoke wraps around us until I can only feel him. His lips drag down my chin and across my neck as he leaves open-mouthed kisses along my pulse. My head tilts back of its own accord, my eyes shutting as I accept the darkness. His hands stroke my body, teasing me and bringing me back to life.

My core clenches, and heat roars through me from a need so strong, I cry out.

"Shh, I have you, little oblivion," he promises as tendrils of shadow snake under my clothes and stroke my skin, sliding across my breasts tauntingly before moving down my stomach and my mound. I part my legs without thought, and his chuckle makes me shiver.

"So eager, little oblivion. If I woke you now, would you be wet?"

"Rook, please," I beg, reaching for him, but all I find is smoke.

My hands fist in it as I gasp. Those smoky tendrils slip inside me, burrowing deep, and as my mouth parts on a scream, more slide inside my lips and down my throat until I'm impaled on his shadows.

"Wake up, little oblivion," he croons, the voice dark in my ear. "I have had enough of your dreams. I want the real thing."

Shaking, I tilt my hips, needing more.

"Wake up," he commands, and when I snap upright, his voice comes from above me. My eyes widen as I see him kneeling at my side, a grin tugging at his lips. His eyes are completely black, and his shadows crawl across my blanket and under it, stroking my skin like he was in my dream.

My skin is coated in sweat, and as I clench my thighs together, I can feel my own wetness on them. Desire hums through me, my every nerve ending alive as I peer up at Rook, and I can't for the life of me figure out why I haven't had him yet.

I could have died today.

We all could have yesterday.

I'm tired of waiting, of holding back, so I reach for him. I feel the others watching, no doubt scenting my desire. They probably even felt it, yet I can't take my eyes from Rook as he waits, letting me close the distance, and when I kick off the blanket and get to my knees, I press my lips to his like he did in my dream.

His plump mouth parts on a groan, and I sweep my tongue inside as I press closer until I'm plastered against his body, his every hard muscle warming my soft curves.

My eyes snap open when another warm body presses against my back. A hand comes around and grips my chin, roughly tugging my head back until my eyes meet Dade's. Rook doesn't seem bothered. His lips brush down my neck, his hands sliding beneath my clothes as Dade leans down and kisses me.

They stoke the flames within me as I'm held between them, kneeling next to the fire on top of my blankets.

"Do you want us, little oblivion?" Rook croons as he sweeps his lips back up, and Dade tilts my head down, letting Rook kiss me again.

The juxtaposition between Dade's soft kiss and Rook's possessive one has me panting. My core clenches desperately, needing to be filled.

"Say yes," Dade begs in my ear. "Say yes and you'll have us. We can feel your desire, Kai. Let us show you more pleasure than you could ever imagine."

"Say yes," Rook whispers against my lips.

Opening my eyes, I glance between them, my teeth digging into my lower lip, but the insistent throb of my clit and the desire in my veins make my decision. I can't fathom why I wouldn't want what they are offering, even if I'm nervous. "Yes," I whisper, my voice rough with my arousal.

It's all the permission they need. Working together, they strip me of my clothes until I'm naked and shivering between them. My nipples pebble in the cool air, my thighs sliding apart as I kneel.

"I will keep watch," Kaito calls.

"Me too, since we rested," Weyland adds. I hesitate when I glance over at him, but when he winks and I sense no jealousy, just desire, I relax back into my unicorn and shadow master.

I'm not sure how this is going to work, but I let them take control as they move me around however they want. Rook's head descends lower, his lips kissing along my nipples, as I feel Dade's hand slide down my side and around my belly.

His long fingers move between my thighs and stroke my center.

Moaning, I widen my legs as I lean back into Dade, who rewards me by sliding those thick fingers inside me, stretching me deliciously. The pleasure has me rolling my hips as Rook sucks one of my nipples into his mouth, his smoky tendrils sliding across my skin and playing with the other.

Dade's fingers thrust in and out of me, and I feel another tendril of smoke slide down and focus on my throbbing bundle of nerves. The shadow tendril slides across it, circling it until I cry out, my hips grinding down. I'm already on the verge of finding release, and they have barely touched me.

"Let go, little oblivion," Rook murmurs against my skin.

"We'll catch you," Dade promises darkly in my ear.

Like their words control me, my body lights up with pleasure under their masterful touch. The cresting wave of my pleasure grows bigger and bigger until I scream out my release when it slams through me. My core clenches on Dade's fingers, holding him tight inside me as my legs shake, my heart hammering so hard, it might burst out of my chest.

They kiss and stroke me through it until I slump against them, panting and limp with lazy pleasure.

"We've got you," Dade promises as he catches me in his arms and turns me. His lips rub against mine as I sigh in ecstasy. When my eyelids flutter open, he grins at me, his eyes moving down my body and heating.

Dade stills, his dark eyes on mine as he leans down and kisses the small wound, as if he can make it better.

"I'll take that pretty mouth first," Rook says. "When I get inside her, she will know about it."

It's a threat, and I shiver at his tone.

"Fine by me." Dade grins as he kisses me again. "That means I get you, my little mate."

I don't know what they are talking about at first, not until they manhandle me and I'm on all fours. My ass is in the air, my head level with Rook's waist, and I watch as he frees his cock. My eyes widen at the size of him. No wonder he's not going to fuck me.

He's massive.

There is no way he would even fit inside me.

He strokes his length, and I swallow greedily, that part of me waking up once more. No ghosts, no bad memories—just desire. I always did like playing, and sucking cocks was one of my favorite things. I love to watch them shatter for me. With Merryl—I cut that thought off right there and raise my eyes to Rook.

"Next time, I'll be inside that pretty human pussy," he promises.

"But for now, take your unicorn like a good girl and taste your shadows."

I feel Dade's hand sliding across my hips and tugging me back until I'm almost lifted from my knees. My eyes slide shut on a moan when his warm, wet tongue drags along my center.

"Next time, I want to feast on her," he growls behind me, "but she needs us too much right now."

It's true. I'm practically humping his face, desperate to feel them inside me, and when he slides his tongue into my channel, I nearly detonate again.

Rook's hand grips my chin, forcing me to look up at him as I feel Dade's huge cock press against my pussy. My eyes widen in want and fear, and Rook drinks in my expression as Dade starts to push into me, letting me feel every hard inch of his cock.

I gasp, reaching back to tug at his hands.

He's bigger than I've ever had, and as he stretches me, it almost hurts. His fingers rub at my bundle of nerves until I relax and moan in pleasure, and he slides all the way inside me.

"Fuck," he groans, his hips pressed to my ass. "She's tight and so hot."

"Open your mouth, little oblivion," Rook orders, digging his fingers into my jaw to force me. "I want in that pretty mouth while he claims your pussy."

I have no choice but to open wide, and he slides his huge cock along my tongue, marking me with his precum, as Dade slowly pulls out of me and thrusts in, forcing me forward so I choke on Rook's length and salty taste.

Rook's hand slides up, gripping my hair and tugging me off him as my eyes water before pushing me back down, forcing me to take his length. Hollowing my cheeks, I dig my nails into the blanket and hold on as he ruts into my mouth. I force my throat open to take him, taking quick, sharp breaths each time he pulls out. My eyes water at the size of him, at the press of him down my throat.

Dade speeds up, the slap of his skin against mine loud in our little cave as I whimper between them, pushing back and swallowing, needing it all.

The touch of their skin and hands makes me wild.

There is nothing but love and desire here, with no room for anything else. Emotions flow through us like water, claiming us until we are feral beasts joining together.

Dade's fingers almost cut into my hips as he yanks me off and on his cock. His snarls fill the small space as he tilts me back once more until his length powers inside me, rubbing at a spot that has me crying out around Rook's cock.

I suck Rook harder, even as my eyes water and my jaw aches. Those dark eyes hold me captive, his lips parted on a moan as he drives to the back of my throat and watches me gag. "So beautiful, little oblivion. So ours," he praises.

"Look at how well you are taking us," Dade adds, his voice thick with desire. "You were made for us."

"She was, our perfect little human. You were born to be ours, to be fucked like this between us." Rook slams all the way down my throat as I gasp, clawing at the bedding. "You were made to be fucked, Kai, made to be filled with pleasure. Made to be ours. Never forget that."

I scream as I feel Rook's shadows slide down my back before forcing themselves between my splayed ass cheeks and working inside my tight muscle there as Dade speeds up. He pounds into me, his hands clawing at my hips as he growls.

I shatter around them.

I cry out around Rook's cock and clench on Dade's until they both bellow. Dade fills me, hard and deep, as I feel him explode. His release fills me as he pants, the warmth spreading and then dripping down my thighs. Rook's shadows explode in the cavern, blocking out all the light as he spills down my throat.

I have no choice but to swallow, choking on it as he pulls back, spilling across my lips and cheeks as he falls back with a groan.

I lick my lips clean of his taste as I fall forward on top of him, exhausted. Dade pulls from me carefully, dragging his lips down my back as he tugs me down onto the blanket, wrapping our sweaty bodies together.

"My Kai," he murmurs in my ear. It's clear he wants to say more, but he settles for kissing my neck.

Rook crawls closer, holding me between them.

"Shit," I hear Weyland say.

"I shouldn't have volunteered to keep watch." Kaito chuckles, but it sounds pained rather than jealous.

Grinning, I snuggle deeper between my unicorn and shadow monster, content and satisfied, and I fall into a dreamless sleep.

FORTY-SEVEN

KAI

The next few days are grueling. We all decided we needed to push as hard as we could after we found hunters' tracks the morning we woke up in our cave. We need to get to the castle before more innocent lives are lost. It means when we rest for a few hours, we all slump together in an exhausted heap, too tired for anything else.

Luckily, we don't run into any more spider fae, and the monsters we pass seem to be fleeing into the mountains as well and too scared to pay us much attention.

The deeper we go into the Dead Lands, the more ruin I find. It's as if it's still healing. The trees bloom, but they are darker, and the grass is almost black. Everything is in shades of gray.

On our third day, I see it.

Lifting my head from Weyland's shoulder as I ride on his back, I gawk. Sitting upon the mountain is the black castle, its huge spires stretching into the gray sky and piercing the clouds like a sword. The blackness glints with the low sunlight, reflected back by the obsidian color. It looks like a beacon, a haven for monsters, and it's also the

I tighten my legs and arms as we pause in the trees, the wind blowing around us. "Are you ready, *bacca*?"

"No, but I never will be." I sigh. "Let's go." I force my voice to be firm despite the emotions swirling inside me. I don't want them to think I can't handle this, even if I'm not sure I can.

Silently, we make our way through the trees, heading up to the castle. The closer we get, the more magnificent and terrifying it seems. The black seems to absorb all light around it, and the towers and spires have deadly spikes along them, and I swear I see something large fly from the top of one. When I try to focus on it, it's gone.

We walk slowly across a worn stone bridge toward the huge, sprawling castle. It makes me feel small in the face of it.

When we finally reach the open doors of the castle, I slide from Weyland's back, refusing to be carried to my sister. I don't want her to see me as weak anymore, so I stand on my own two feet, my monsters spread around me. My hair is braided back and dirty from the journey, but my heart is filled with determination and anxiety.

I blow out a low breath and gather my courage, then I step inside the black castle.

Lanterns glow on the walls as we step inside, their flames filling the space with warmth. The opulent I has me looking around in wonder. Paintings line the walls, as do great, intricate tapestries depicting battles and celebrations.

Unlike the castle in the Gilded Lands, it feels warm and loved. It might be over the top, but the darkness makes me smile. It's perfect for Cora.

Somehow, we seem to know which direction to go, and we find ourselves in a large room, the obsidian color continued throughout, but I don't focus onIdecor here—I focus on my sister.

Cora sits upon a throne at the end of the room, perched on a huge monster's lap. Massive windows above them let in very little light. She laughs, still not having seen us, and the sound fills the space with warmth and joy. She's oblivious as I rush forward, leaving my monsters at the entrance, before I skid to a stop in front of her throne.

My heart beats triple time, my hands clenched into fists at my sides as her head jerks around, as does the huge monster's, who's wearing a matching crown. His eyes are alight with danger and fury, but I look at her.

It's Cora I worry about.

Her blonde hair glows with power, flowing across her shoulders and down her black dress, which clings to her skin. Her face has filled out, no longer looking gaunt and starved. Her eyes glitter with love and happiness, even as they widen, her plump lips parting.

"Hi, Cora," I croak. "Long time no see." The words don't seem like enough, and I feel foolish when they fall from my lips, but I can barely speak, let alone think of better ones.

She doesn't move for a moment, and I swallow hard, thinking I made a mistake after all. I'm about to start rambling, desperate for her to say something, but she flings herself toward me. I hold up my hand for my monsters, stopping them from rushing between us, and when she wraps me in her arms, I shudder. My own arms come up and hold her tight, and I bury my head in her shoulder as tears fill my eyes and start to flow down my face. I feel her own wetting my shoulder before she pulls back, her eyes glassy with pain.

She grips my cheeks hard as she looks me over. "It's you. You're really here. You're alive. Kai, you're alive."

I crack a smile. "I am. I missed you, sister."

The fear in my heart eases.

I'm home.

FORTY-EIGHT

KAI

"How? When?" Cora's questions fall from her lips faster than I can follow them as she pulls back to peer at me as if to reassure herself that I'm real. We're both crying, our tears making our voices thick with the emotions that fill the room. Behind her, the horned monster stands, his eyes hard on my monsters.

"I'll explain everything," I promise. I turn and check on my monsters where they stand stiffly behind me, their eyes on the king. "They are with me," I explain. "They are safe."

Weyland, Kaito, and Dade all bow their heads toward the monster king. Rook doesn't bother, his own eyes hard and unwavering. Luckily, the king doesn't seem upset by the sign of rebellion.

"Grim," Cora chides, glancing over her shoulder. "Ease up. This is my sister, and these monsters are her . . ."

"Mates," I state, lifting my chin. "They are my mates."

Cora's smile is bright. "Then they are family." She loops her arm through mine, just like she used to when we were children in the Shadow Lands, and starts to lead me away from the throne room.

There is no hesitation or anger, just acceptance and love, and my tears fall harder.

"Come. We have much to discuss." Her eyes trace over my body, no doubt taking note of the differences. The last time Cora saw me, I was starved, gaunt, and damaged. Although scars still litter my skin, I appear far healthier than I'd been thanks to my monsters—not to mention the new, inky drawing on my skin and the color of my hair.

"No weapons," Grim commands of my monsters.

Rook laughs and holds up his hand. "I am a weapon, Your Majesty. Do you expect me to stay outside?"

"Yes," the king answers at the same time as Cora says, "Of course not! You're welcome in our home."

Rook grins at the king and then purposely looks toward Cora, bowing to her instead. The move seems to make the king feel better. He straightens and nods, an understanding passing between them.

"Nero and Raz will be here shortly," he tells Cora. "The others will be alerted."

"No need," a large, stone-colored man declares from the side. I hadn't even noticed him, mistaking him for a statue. His large wings are folded against his back, and his expression is unreadable. "They've already been notified."

I recognize him, not because we'd had a proper introduction, but because he was the one who dove after me over the side of the tower. He'd been too late. He didn't know me, but he knew how important I was to Cora, so he risked his life to save me. Now, seeing me standing before him, he takes in my appearance, and I see something ease in him despite there being no emotion on his face.

I realize he blamed himself.

The guilt comes back tenfold as Cora drags me from the throne room and into a beautiful courtyard. Here, everything blooms brightly rather than the washed-out gray of the forest outside. Flowers shine vibrantly in every color, and the trees drip with fruit I don't recognize. What we would have given to have trees like this in the Shadow Lands as children, and now they have a home here in

Cora's castle. The grass is green and brilliant, and the scent of all the blooming trees fills my nostrils and relaxes me. It puts me at ease despite the talk I know Cora and I must have. Though I'm glad she's happy to see me, there will still be hard conversations ahead. I know that, she knows that, but for now, in this moment, we're two sisters who have been reunited.

Grim, the monster king, follows our party. The gargoyle trails along with him, studying my monsters. Weyland and Kaito watch him carefully, but Rook and Dade are focused on me and the space between me and the king. Do they suspect maliciousness from him?

Cora settles on a stone bench and pulls me down with her. Her dress shifts around her legs, and it makes me hyperaware of the fact that I'm still dirty from our journey. I'm wearing baggy pants and a shirt meant for Kaito's slender frame rather than my own curves. It was the best we could do, and I'd grown comfortable in them, but sitting beside Cora with her glittering black crown and her pristine dress makes me aware that I'm underdressed for a queen's company.

I have changed, but so has she.

Gone is the tired, determined Shadow Lands girl, and in her place is a queen.

We stare at each other in silence, my heart beating loudly in my ears. We don't speak for several long minutes, as if we're both burning each other's image into our brains. The last memory we have of each other isn't a pleasant one, and I hope we can replace that with new ones. Still, I owe her an explanation. It's been months since we last saw each other, and I'm only now coming to see her.

"How did you—" Cora begins as I say, "I'm sure you're—"

We both cut off and laugh. It feels like old times and it puts me at ease, so I sigh and take her hand. "I know you're wondering how I'm alive."

She nods eagerly. "We searched for you." She gestures toward the gargoyle. "Raz searched along the river, trying to find any trace. When he came back empty-handed, I hoped . . . well, I hoped you made it."

Even after what I'd done, she looked for me. She hoped I'd come back. What a fool I've been to fear this meeting.

I glance over at Kaito. "When I fell from that tower, I wanted to die. I expected to. I was a broken, hollow shell of the woman I'd once been. He'd broken me, Cora." I look at my sister, the woman who sacrificed herself to save me, knowing she deserves the truth. "Kaito saved me and nursed me back to health. Weyland showed up soon after. It took a long time to be able to exist again. When Dade and Rook appeared, I was still damaged, and I'm still fighting, but . . ."

Cora watches me carefully, her eyes tracing my face before shifting over to my monsters. They are tense, as if not quite sure what to do. "You saved my sister," she tells them. "For that, you have my deepest gratitude. Please, treat this castle as your home. You are welcome here despite what the grumpy minotaur would have you think." She leans close to me and whispers, "He's always grumpy. You'll get used to it."

"I heard that," the king grumbles.

"You were meant to," Cora sings with a smile, but when she focuses on me again, her smile fades. "Do you still feel it?"

I shift uncomfortably. "Feel what?"

"The urge to die?"

I can see the pain in her eyes as she asks that question. She mourned me, had already gone through grief, and now here I sit. I'd fallen from that tower by my own hand, and I can see the fear in her eyes that I'll do so again. Slowly, I look over at my monsters, taking them in. Love fills my heart, and I know the answer to Cora's question without a doubt.

"Not anymore," I admit with a slow smile. "Not anymore."

FORTY-NINE

KAI

"Why are you in this castle?" I ask as we walk through the halls. We'd grown tired of the courtyard, and I needed to move. I'm so filled with anxious energy and excitement that I can't seem to sit still. My monsters follow behind us, along with three of Cora's. The king, Raz, and a naga she calls Nero. He slithered up a few minutes ago with a wink to me and a, "I knew you were alive," thrown my way. I've liked him ever since.

"We originally planned to build a home in the Shadow Lands," Cora admits, "right in the center of the three realms, but we were met with . . . Well, not everyone was happy about the wall coming down. My monsters thought it would be better for us to remain here until things become more stable." She sighs and glances over at me. I can see the strain around her eyes despite her attempts to hide it. "I thought bringing down the thorns and connecting the magic would save us, but I guess happily ever after is never that easy."

I bite my lip as she talks, thinking over her words. "The violence you were met with, were they speaking out against the monsters specifically?"

Cora glances at me with furrowed brows. "How did you know?"

"That's actually why we came to see you," I begin. "There have been groups of humans traveling through the Dead Lands, capturing and killing monsters. We've stopped a few of them, but there are so many—"

"Wait. They are hunting monsters?" Grim asks, storming forward. "Did you say they are hunting them?"

I nod. "They are."

"And they are doing a pretty good job of it," Weyland adds with a frown. "They attacked our cabin and came after Kai."

"Why would they come after you?" Cora asks, frowning. "No one should even know you're alive, let alone come after you specifically."

I grimace. "Well, about that . . ."

Cora stops us. "What is it?"

I glance over at Rook, who nods his head, offering comfort. "Merryl is leading them."

Cora's brows shoot up. "Merryl? Your ex-fiancé who couldn't be bothered to save you?"

Anger fills me at that statement, anger that's reflected in Cora's eyes. "One and the same."

We start walking again.

"Well, that's a problem." She looks over at Grim. "We'll discuss what to do about this once the others arrive, but for now . . ." Cora sighs, and I know she's about to bring up everything else. "I should apologize, Kai."

This time, it's me who stops us. "For what?"

"For not showing up to save you fast enough. I should have been there—"

"Cora," I rasp, turning her to face me so she can fully hear my words. Cora has a way of taking the world on her shoulders, and I need her to understand. "You have nothing to apologize for. I . . ."

I realize that I need to tell her everything, that I can't leave anything out. "When you stepped through that wall and the gilded king came for me, I blamed you for a while," I admit, looking down at our joined hands. She flinches at my words, so I rush to explain. "I thought that somehow, you taking my place led to me being in his clutches, but that was silly and selfish of me. Neither one of us could have predicted what happened, and ultimately, you saved me, but it was my duty to save myself and I failed. It wasn't up to you. You did the best you could, and I appreciate that you came for me when you did. Neither one of us could have changed my fate, and I wouldn't want you to."

I smile, pulling her into a hug. "If things didn't happen the way they did, I never would have met my monsters. I never would have made my way back to you. You were just a girl, Cora, yet you protected me all my life. It should have been the other way around."

She sniffs, and I know she's crying. Her arms wrap tighter around me, holding me in a death grip, as if she's afraid I'll disappear.

"I was lost in the shadows," I whisper into her hair, "but I'm not anymore, and I'm going to stand at your side, Cora. We have to stop this. We have to save the monsters."

She leans back, her tear-filled eyes searching mine. "You're stronger now," she murmurs. "I can see the steel in your gaze."

I smile. "I am, and I'm prepared to fight for this happiness we've found."

We smile at each other, happy despite the rising war.

"Look at them," I hear Nero say. "Do you see it?"

"What?" Weyland asks.

"The strength," Nero murmurs. "The strength between sisters. The power."

Grim hums. "They'll shake the world."

I grin, squeezing Cora's hand gently, and she repeats the action.

"Yes," I say, standing taller. "We will."

FIFTY

DADE

K ai and her sister are inseparable. They have so much to catch up on, and I relax throughout the day as nothing but smiles replace her tears. Their bond is evident and strong, so when Cora takes Kai away to bathe and dress, I stay behind, trusting they are safe in the castle. Cora's mates seem to believe the same, and even though they are only in the next chamber, it reassures me that both our mates are fine.

Cora's mates seem nice enough, though the grumpy minotaur keeps glaring at Rook who is sitting next to me. The fire burns in the chamber, the flames lighting up the stone walls. Kaito lingers near the door, waiting for Kai but wanting to be part of it. Weyland is walking around, looking at everything, while the naga, Nero, follows him. There is a grinning dark fey watching us as he plays with a knife —Bracken, the gargoyle, Razcorr, informed us. There is a man who is a kraken who introduced himself as Zetros as well.

Bracken grins. "Quite the collection of monsters."

Grim, the minotaur, sighs like he is used to the fey and simply tolerates him.

251

"Ignore him," Zetros calls as he slides to the floor near me, stretching out. "He's always an ass."

"Where is Krug?" Razcorr calls, peering around.

"Krug?" Rook inquires.

"Cora's orc," the gargoyle explains.

"Probably creeping around, waiting for her," Bracken grumbles.

When I glance back, I can see Kaito has slipped away while we were all talking, no doubt to check on Kai. None of us like being away from her for long, but especially him. She is always at his side. I expect jealousy to flare in me, but only gratitude does that he is with her. We've all grown used to each other, our very own family. After not having one for so long, it's nice.

"Cora's sister, Kai . . ." Grim leans forward, his eyes hard and worried. "She is truly okay? Cora has been so worried and heartbroken."

Even the fey sobers at that, nodding. Clearly, Cora has been very worried about Kai. I know Kai was worried she would blame her or be angry, but from what I can see, she is overjoyed she is back.

"She is." I nod. "She wasn't for a while, but she's healing, and she's fighting the darkness inside now—one we all carry."

Rook nods, wrapping tendrils of shadows around his fingers, and Grim shoots him a glare.

"She dispels mine," I add, sharing with them. "Until her, there was only darkness, pain, and loneliness, then she came into our lives. We are nothing without her."

"It's the same with us," Grim says, his words sharp but loving. "Cora is our light."

"Grim is a monster of few words." Zetros laughs, nudging me. "But he isn't wrong. Our Cora saved us all in a way. Me especially."

I tilt my head, and he smiles sadly. "I was imprisoned for a very long time, and it messed with my head. Cora washed my soul clean. She accepted my scars and kissed them better, so yes, I know what you mean about being saved."

"I think Kaito was a prisoner," Weyland offers, and we all turn around to see him. "He confessed some things to me once, but from what I understood, the king created him and kept him locked away until he escaped."

"I will speak with him," Zetros offers, "to see if I can help in any way."

"No wonder they get along so well," Rook murmurs, his shadows sliding across my skin, but I'm used to it by now. Grim glares at him the entire time though.

"True, they were both prisoners." I nod, finally understanding. Although we all have a bond, the one between Kaito and Kai seems deep, and now I know why.

"If it's true and humans are hunting monsters," Grim finally says as we lapse into silence, "then a war is brewing."

"It is," Rook replies. "I feel the death that awaits in the shadows. This will only end with a battle—a battle for this land's soul."

"Then we must prepare. We must be strong enough," Razcorr adds as he and Weyland tread closer.

"No matter what, Cora and Kai are to be protected." Grim looks us all over as he sits up taller, every inch the king, even without the crown or throne.

We all nod. "Agreed."

"They won't like it." Rook smiles. "They are fighters."

"They are all that matters. If we lose them, we die," Grim snarls.

"Oh, I can't wait for the bloodshed," Bracken murmurs, and we all turn to him before sharing a look.

"We'll discuss it with our mates," Grim states as we lapse into silence once more.

A bond stretches between us, the monsters who love two great women.

Two women we can't afford to lose.

Suddenly, there's a bang that echoes through the castle. We all turn as the door opens, an annoyed Kaito standing there with a hulking orc at his side. "Found the orc," he mutters as we all burst into laughter.

FIFTY-ONE

KAI

I sink deeper into the water, watching the fragrant ripples close above my head. The bathing chamber is bigger than our old house, with a black tub large enough for me and my monsters. Cora hustled me in here and filled it for me with a wordless look. I open my eyes and see dirt and blood slide off my body until I feel somewhat clean. The door opens, and Cora bustles in from the chamber beyond with some garments draped over her arm.

When she sees me, she stops and swallows hard.

I tilt my head back, wondering what's with her expression. I have been waiting all day for her anger or resentment, and I haven't gotten it. She has been kind, loving, and glad to have me back. All my worry and anxiety were for nothing.

It's like old times again, except now we're in a castle.

She blinks, turns away, and clears her throat, and I swear I see tears sliding down her cheeks, which makes my heart clench in pain. "You look beautiful," she says as she moves closer and sinks gracefully to the floor, resting her chin on the side of the tub.

Leaning over, I wipe her cheeks clean, and she presses her face into my palm, sighing as she closes her eyes.

I lean my head onto the tub's side, watching her. My gaze roves over my sister's face. She has grown, that's for sure. Gone is the Shadow Land's girl, and in her place is a true queen.

"Let me help you." She grabs the soap, and I relax as she washes my hair for me. When she's done, I stand and step from the bath. I dry off with a towel before she helps me into a simple, floor-length gown.

The devastating emerald green shines against my skin, the fabric soft and silky. The top is covered in lace detail, and the billowing sleeves are almost sheer. "Perfect." She smiles. "I knew there was a reason I bought this one."

Nodding, I tug at the dress, feeling the softness as I follow her into the bedchamber beyond. She pushes me onto a waiting stool, and I let her brush my hair like she did when we were kids until she steps back and nods.

"Perfect, but then again, you always were."

"Thank you," I tell her honestly as I stand.

She watches as I explore the room, taking everything in. It's intricate and ornate, far nicer than anything we had as children. There's a balcony beyond, but I stay far away, not wanting to make her nervous. That trauma won't disappear anytime soon.

The bed calls to me. It's giant and looks soft, and I can't resist.

I flop back onto the luxurious bed, eager to feel the softness, and I'm not surprised when Cora lies next to me. Our hands find each other's over the quilt and clasp as we stare at the ceiling, the soft breeze from the open doorway fluttering around us.

"I thought I'd lost you forever," she admits. "It felt like I'd lost a piece of my soul."

I turn my head to meet her tear-filled eyes, sad that those tears are because of me.

"I know you felt like you had no way out. I'm not angry, Kai. I just . . . I missed you so much. Every day, I wanted to find you to tell you something. I'd wake every morning and for a moment, I'd forget you were gone, and then the pain would rush back."

"Cora, I'm sorry," I rasp.

Squeezing my hand, she moves closer. "It's in the past now. You're back. That's all that matters, and we are together again."

"Like old times," I tease, making her laugh, the sound more familiar than my own voice, and another piece of me heals.

How many nights did we lie like this together on that dirty, hard floor? She must be thinking the same thing because she smiles softly.

"A bit of a better bed though." She giggles.

"A bit." I grin, turning to my side to see her better.

She has grown up well, becoming beautiful, regal, kind, and strong, but then again, I always knew she would. Cora was always destined for great things. It was in her soul. I knew it from the moment she came into this world, stern-faced and prepared, not screaming like normal babies.

"Are you happy?" I ask her.

She blinks and searches my gaze before her smile grows. "More than I've ever been."

"Good, that's good."

"Are you?" she asks after a pregnant pause.

"I am," I admit. "It's been hard, and some days are worse than others, but when I think about it, I'm truly happy to be alive and with my monsters."

She wiggles her eyebrows. "Your monsters, eh?"

"You're one to speak." I laugh, pushing her away.

"I have many holes. What can I say?"

"Cora!" I shout, kicking her away as she laughs.

"What? Don't tell me you haven't tried sharing." She wiggles her eyebrows. "There was this one time—"

"Stop!" I cover my ears, even as I laugh.

"Okay, okay." She pulls my hands away as she collapses against me, grinning. I hold her tighter, unable to stop a giggle from escaping my lips.

"I like your hair, by the way. It's badass," she says as she props her head on my arm and looks at me.

257

"Thanks." I look down at her dress. "I like your dress and crown."

"I don't. I'd rather be in pants." She winks just as a knock comes at the door.

We both turn as a slightly panicked, stern voice calls, "Please hurry. I'm running out of ways to deal with all these monsters."

Grim.

Cora giggles and grabs my hand. "Come on. Let's rescue my minotaur before he kills them simply to shut them up."

Smiling, I lace my fingers with hers and follow her.

It's just like old times.

FIFTY-TWO

Happiness overflows my heart and soul, and I can barely contain it. It's not only because Kai is alive and well, but also because she found her own bright spot of joy. After Grim knocks on the door, we walk out of the room and settle in the courtyard. Someone decided to prepare some food while Kai and I were in the bathing room. I suspect it was Nero, because the naga has taken to cooking in a way I never expected. I certainly won't complain since I get to eat all his tasty meals.

"Are you hungry?" I ask Kai, gesturing toward the table. "Nero is an excellent chef."

Nero grins from where he hangs from a fruit tree, his large, iridescent body draped through the branches like a garland. Seeing him grin from his position reminds me of when he dragged me up one of the fruit trees with him. He'd taken the sweet fruit and squeezed the juice over my body before licking it off. The memory makes me flush, and Nero's grin widens like he knows what I'm thinking.

"My mate flatters me only because the very first meals I cooked were atrocious," Nero adds, flashing a softer grin toward my sister. "She's grateful I'm no longer trying to kill us."

Kai giggles, and the sound makes something in my heart flare. I never thought I would hear that sound again. The Kai who leapt from the king's tower had lost the ability to laugh, but this Kai is stronger and happier. I've never been more grateful for the stubborn persistence of monsters. I suspect they helped her heal in a way I never could have, and I'll be forever grateful for the four monsters who take up residence between us in the courtyard.

"So, you never mentioned how everyone met," I say, grabbing a handful of food and settling onto a bench. "I can tell our story if you'd like."

"I don't think there's a monster alive who doesn't know your story," Weyland comments with a boyish grin. The werewolf is interesting and would be scary in his appearance if not for the genuinely sweet expressions he wears. Of course, I have no doubt he can go feral at a moment's notice, but it's easy to see why Kai would fall in love with him. Rook, in contrast, mostly just terrifies me. The only reason I can stomach being near him is because of the clear adoration he has for my sister. Grim described him as the boogeyman, and I understand why. Rook seems like the sort of monster you whisper about, not the one you fall in love with, but here he is.

Kai smiles at her monsters and shrugs. "There's not much to tell. Each one of them found me. Kaito was first, and he nursed me back to health. Weyland appeared a little while after I grew strong enough to explore. Dade came in the midst of a battle. And Rook . . ." She glances at the shadow monster and smiles. "Rook found me in the shadows."

I tilt my head. "As if fate guided them home."

"Fate indeed," Rook murmurs, and his voice feels like the cool shadows that leak around his feet.

Grim grumbles something under his breath, and I turn toward him with a raised brow. "Care to share, minotaur?" I ask teasingly.

"We should discuss the hunting parties and come up with a plan to deal with them," he declares, his heated eyes on me. I see a promise for pleasure and a need to act in his gaze. Yes, there's still a threat we must face, but at least we won't ever face such struggles alone.

Never again.

"Grim is right." I sigh, focusing on Kai. "You said Merryl is leading them?"

Kai nods. "We ran into him once, and he tried to take me, thinking I needed to be saved. I don't think he understood that I was with them by choice, not until he came to our cabin and attacked. He tried to steal me and nearly killed Kaito in the process."

I crinkle my nose up. "Why is he so interested in fighting now? The spineless bastard didn't help when . . . well, you know."

I see anger flicker in Kai's eyes—it's not directed at me, but at a man who promised to love and protect her. In the end, he'd done nothing of the sort, so he doesn't get to play the hero now.

"Yes, well, apparently he's more of a fool than I thought."

Dade snorts under his breath, clearly in agreement. When we glance at him, he nods. "A fool indeed."

Zetros speaks up from his place at the table. "So what do we do about this human and his hunting parties?"

Krug sniffs. "They are well organized and strategic for humans, using their strengths. When we face them, they'll be prepared."

"But they can't hope to take on ten monsters and two powerful sisters," Weyland points out. "Kai's and Cora's powers can—"

"Wait," I say, interrupting him. "What do you mean Kai's powers?"

Kai flushes. "Ah, yes. About that . . ." She holds up her hand and closes her eyes. For a few seconds, nothing happens, but then I see a spark, and then another, before tiny lightning streaks begin to dance along her palm and up her arm. Her skin glows with it.

I reach out and touch Grim's hand in surprise and excitement. I thought I was a fluke, but two sisters with power? That means it's in our blood.

My smile fades at that realization. If we carry it in our blood, then it came from one of our parents. It couldn't have been my father because he would have used it if given the advantage, which leaves our mother.

How sad to be so suppressed and never know the power in your veins.

"Do you know what it can do?" I ask curiously. I move closer, and her lightning leaps from her to me so suddenly, I startle. It's cool to the touch, with a slight buzz around it as it twists along my skin. It doesn't hurt. In fact, it feels calming and safe.

"I know it can heal," Kai admits. "Kaito was dying, and I saved him."

Kaito proudly points to a scar on his chest like it's a badge of honor. "A fatal wound. Kai stitched it back together with her lightning."

Grim nods as if he isn't shocked. "Complimenting powers. The healer and the sword."

"It's as if we're meant to be one unit," I murmur, meeting Kai's eyes. After all these years of struggle and pain, the answer was inside us the whole time.

I reach for her, and she takes my hand without hesitation. We share a smile between us—the same smile we used to share while hiding under the covers and telling each other scary stories as children. It's a promise between two sisters to always be there for one another until the very end.

"Merryl may be a fool," I say, "but perhaps he could be reasoned with if he understood the consequences of starting a war between monsters and humans. I hoped we could settle the three realms, but if he's the leader of the rebellion, then perhaps it's best to try negotiating first."

"Negotiating?" Rook asks, narrowing his eyes. "This human kills monsters for sport."

Grim sniffs. "When Cora says negotiating, she means we offer him an option and he either takes it or doesn't. There will be no gifting him anything."

Rook settles back and nods. "Better."

"So we send a message," Kai says. "We ask to meet him on neutral ground in the Shadow Lands, and then we try to make him see reason."

"And if he doesn't?" I ask, watching my sister closely. "If he claims the monsters should all be put down?"

Kai's eyes harden, and I see the warrior she's become. "Then we put him down," she growls.

Clearly, there's no love lost between my sister and her ex-fiancé, but I don't blame her. If I were in her position, I would have slaughtered the asshole a long time ago for refusing to help me.

It doesn't matter now, though, because she doesn't need him.

Kai has us now—her sister and her monsters.

Her family.

CHAPTER
FIFTY-THREE
KAI

With our plan made and the message sent, it's simply a matter of waiting for a response from the man I once thought I loved, which means there's no more planning until then.

"Now what?" Bracken asks. The dark fey is reclined across a bench, tossing a citrus fruit in the air over and over again, like a cat playing with yarn. Somehow, I feel like the fey is more akin to some great beast than a house cat. He sits up after his question and wiggles his eyebrows. "An orgy?"

Cora snorts and throws some of her fruit at him. He catches it with a grin and pops the fruit into his mouth.

"You'll have to forgive Bracken." She laughs. "He doesn't have the best manners."

Bracken stands and steps around my sister, his fingers stroking along her hips. "You like my chaos, Goldie."

Cora smiles. "Maybe I do. Maybe I don't."

His eyes heat at the challenge, and he snaps his teeth at her. "Later," he promises and puts another small fruit into his mouth.

The yawn slips from my lips before I can stop it, and Cora smiles

"Perhaps some rest is in order. I'm sure you're all weary after your long journey. You have full use of the room I showed you to. If you require more bedding for anyone who prefers the floor, there should be plenty in the cabinet."

"Your kindness is appreciated," Kaito replies with all the grace of royalty.

Cora comes up and wraps her arms around me in another tight hug. "I'm so glad you're back," she whispers, and in that whisper, I hear her fear of losing me again.

"I'm never going anywhere ever again," I promise as I return the hug just as tightly. "Wherever you go, I go."

She sighs. "Make sure you don't go somewhere I can't follow," she rasps and releases me. I nod in answer, and her shoulders relax, as if she's been carrying that tension with her since the tower. "Good. We'll let you retire for the evening then. Let me know if there's anything you need."

"Unless it's an emergency, it can wait until morning," Grim grumbles, his expression full of heat for his queen.

I laugh. "I'm sure we'll be fine. Thank you."

Weyland grabs a large platter of meat as we move to leave, and I raise my brows at him. "What?" he asks. "I'm starving."

Together, the five of us retire to the room Cora had shown me, and I take in the large bed. Though it's sizable, I doubt we can all fit in it comfortably. At least there's a couch in the room as well—one of them can sleep there if the need arises.

When the door closes behind me, I turn, expecting to find all four of my monsters behind me. Instead, I find only Kaito and Weyland.

"Where are Dade and Rook?" I ask, frowning.

"Giving us some privacy," Kaito answers, and although he's always kind, there's a fierceness in his large eyes that makes my heart skip a beat.

"Privacy for what?" I rasp. I have to lick my lips when they are suddenly dry, and their eyes follow the action.

"Whatever you wish," Weyland replies. "If you would like to

266

sleep, then we'll do that," he replies sweetly, but there's a challenge in his eyes—one I feel burning through me.

I meet his gaze. "I don't want to sleep," I whisper. "I'm not tired at all."

Kaito smiles so brightly, it's blinding. "Very good, Kai."

When Kaito strides toward me, I hold still, not quite sure how to start this. My mouth waters for him, for Weyland, as they both watch me hungrily. I've yet to have sex with mos of them, and now my two sweet monsters are offering just that. My body hums with excitement, and I have to clamp my thighs together to keep from lunging toward them.

Kaito stalks around me like a predator and I'm easy prey, while Weyland watches as he does so, content to stand by while Kaito winds me up.

Kaito stops behind me and leans down, his breath fanning across my shoulders. When he presses his lips there, I shiver. His claws trail softly down my arm, over my elbow, then my forearm, before tracing the lines on my palm. I tilt my head to the side to give him access, trusting him completely. He gently tugs at the strap of the dress, pulling it down my arm and letting it hang at my waist, revealing a single breast to Weyland's eyes. The wolf makes a sound of longing, but he doesn't come closer.

Not yet.

When the strap on my other arm follows, fully revealing my chest to them, my nipples pebble at the attention and cool air. Kaito's hands come around to cup them, and I find myself leaning back against his chest as he strokes me.

"Kai," he whispers along my skin as he worships me. "So beautiful."

Weyland seizes the opportunity to stalk forward, his eyes on me as he moves closer. His warmth covers my front as he stops before me. I don't know what I expect him to do, but when he drops to his knees, I gasp in surprise.

With heated eyes, Weyland grabs the hem of my dress and slowly raises it, giving me ample opportunity to say no. I don't. With a grin, he hooks one of my knees over his shoulder. My dress cascades around my hips, leaving me bare for him as he leans in and swipes his tongue up my slit. My legs threaten to buckle, but they support me, keeping me on my feet.

I moan, leaning back harder against Kaito. His claws cup my chin and turn my head to the side. When he claims my lips, I moan into his mouth, desperate for more. He breaks the kiss, and I mewl in protest, making him smile.

"If, at any time, it becomes overwhelming, tell us to stop," Kaito instructs. "No matter what we're doing, we'll stop. Understand?"

I nod my head frantically. Of course I'm not stopping now, but I appreciate the sentiment. Before, I wasn't strong enough for a kiss and Kaito remembers. Now, my healing has brought me here, and I'm eager to taste my monsters.

"More," I say. "I need more."

Weyland chuckles against my core, sending vibrations through my body. "As you wish," he growls.

He stands suddenly and lifts me over his shoulder, carting me to the large bed in the center of the room. He sets me on the comforter on my knees and presses me down so I fall forward. When I feel him lift my dress, I tense, expecting his cock, but instead, he dives back into my pussy with his tongue, winding me up until I'm groaning in pleasure.

Kaito climbs onto the bed from the other side, crawling toward me. He kneels before me, cupping my chin and forcing me to look up into his face. "You have the prettiest lips," he says. "I've imagined sliding between them and feeling your throat constrict around me. I've imagined your hair twisted between my claws while you look up at me."

With my eyes on his, I open my lips, eager to taste him. He groans as if he's in agony and yanks the cloth from his hips that hides him from my gaze. My eyes widen at the strangeness and size of his cock. It's the same color as the rest of him, and the spots that trail over his body are along the shaft. The head is more elongated, and small ridges line along the underside. When he leans forward and traces the tip along my lips, I dart my tongue out to taste. He moans as I lick him before taking the head completely into my mouth and sucking.

His hold tightens on my jaw as he starts to pump slowly and carefully inside.

Abruptly, Weyland's tongue leaves my core, and I wiggle my ass in protest, but his claws come down to stroke my backside. "Patience, little mate," he purrs, and then I feel him pressing against me.

I can't see him, but I can certainly feel him as he teases my pussy, coating his cock with my wetness. When he begins to ease inside, I press back, eager to be claimed and feel completely filled by them. He slowly works himself inside with small thrusts that drive me mad with need. When I feel stretched, he continues, filling me until he's fully seated against my ass.

"Look at you being filled by us," Kaito growls. "You're so beautiful like this."

They both pick up speed at the same time. Weyland's warmth surrounds me as he leans down and circles me, his arms wrapping around my waist as he begins to pump faster, his cock pressing against the sensitive flesh inside me. I cry out around Kaito's cock, my body tightening with pleasure so fast, I can't control it.

"My mate," Weyland growls in my ear. "Our mate."

He starts to thrust harder, his breath fanning across the back of my neck as Kaito fills my mouth. I'm a bundle of sensation, my fingers tightening on the comforter until I'm keening between them. My body explodes, my core clenching around Weyland's cock, and he growls in pleasure as I milk him.

"Fuck." Kaito groans. "You look so perfect like this, Kai."

He pops his cock free and traces it around my lips, letting me scream out my pleasure as Weyland continues to pump inside me, his thrusts becoming more feral, more desperate.

"Do you want him to fill you?" Kaito asks. "Do you want his cum dripping from your cunt when I fill it?"

My eyes widen. "God, yes!" I cry, digging my nails into the sheets. "Please."

"Because you asked so prettily," Weyland growls in my ear. He slams inside me and groans, and I feel his warmth start to fill me, spilling from my pussy and dripping down my inner thighs.

Kaito smiles down at me with wickedness in his eyes. When Weyland pulls from my body, Kaito lifts me and falls backward, settling me on top of him. He spreads my thighs around his hips, his cock dancing between us. Weyland's cum drips from my pussy and onto Kaito, but he doesn't seem to care. He grabs the base of his cock and positions it so I can rise on my knees and sink down onto him. I throw my head back at the sensation of his elongated head and the feeling of the ridges hitting the sensitive flesh inside.

It seems to curve at the perfect angle inside me and is driving me wild with need.

Weyland appears behind me, his chest pressing against my back. "Now move," he instructs, his claws going beneath my ass and lifting, moving me like a puppet. I shudder and gasp as he helps me fuck Kaito, grinding against my back as his teeth scrape along my shoulder. Kaito's hands cup my breasts and knead, his groans filling the room as I ride him. With their attention, I shudder and crash into another orgasm, crying out in pleasure as my own juice runs down his cock. When Weyland's teeth drag along my neck again, I tilt it to the side, giving him access and permission. I feel him pause behind me, and then his teeth sink into my flesh.

My lightning explodes out of me, the power I carry reacting to the intense pleasure of Weyland and Kaito claiming me at the same time. It dances along my skin, but it doesn't hurt either of them as it traces along their bodies. Kaito's hips lift from the bed in pleasure as the lightning claims him, his hands going to my hips. He immediately starts to fuck up into me hard, fast, and brutal, as my power adds another level of pleasure. Weyland's teeth release my shoulder, and he licks the mark, his cock begging for more behind me. I reach back and stroke him as Kaito fucks me, my cries so loud, no one in the castle could miss them.

"Come with me," I cry, my head back in pleasure as my body tightens and I explode. I drag them along with me. Kaito groans and jerks beneath me, while Weyland spills into my hand behind me, his body pressed against mine. We all grind against each other as we explode, my lightning only heightening everything until it fades, leaving behind a glow on my skin. We collapse together as we try to catch our breath.

"Wow," I murmur, my chest rising and falling rapidly. Sex has never been quite so . . . explosive.

Weyland chuckles behind me. "You're so beautiful like this," he whispers.

"Glowing?" I ask, smiling as I look over my shoulder.

"No," he answers, tracing his claws along the mark on my shoulder. "Ours."

I flush and press a kiss to his nose before doing the same to Kaito, feeling spent, happy, and comfortable. I've never felt so safe. "I love you," I tell them both, "so very much."

They repeat the words, easing me into a sense of comfort I've never experienced, and I slide into sleep so fast, I don't even have a chance to tell them how safe they make me feel.

But they know.

FIFTY-FOUR

KAI

My eyes slam open as pleasure explodes through me. The force is so strong, I cry out, my mind muddled and confused as my body twists in the sheets.

When I fell asleep, I was between Weyland and Kaito, but I can feel them all surrounding me, my powers and instincts always tuned to them, telling me they are here and awake.

My back arches in ecstasy as I scream, caught between confusion and pleasure.

When I slump, my thighs slick with my own release, I force my eyes open and glance down, my frown only growing when I realize no one is touching me.

Well, not really. I watch a dark tendril slide from my pussy and up my body. As my mouth opens to speak, it thrusts inside, choking me as it forces itself deeper. Somehow, it tastes of me and the darky smokiness of Rook.

My eyes water as I blink, and Rook leans into me casually, grinning above me. "You look so pretty choking on me," he purrs, his hand possessively stroking down my body. "So sweet curled up beside me, rubbing these tempting curves against me until I couldn't resist. You needed me even in your sleep, so as your mate, I provided." His tendrils pull back, letting me draw in desperate breaths. When my voice comes, it's hoarse from pleasure and his touch.

"Rook," I start, but before I can even decide what to say, his lips crash onto mine.

I lose myself in him as he swallows my groan. His hand grips my chin as his shadows trail across my body, tweaking my nipples and sliding lower, where they slip inside me. He forces my pussy wide with his shadows, exposing me completely. They rip my legs open, spreading me, before they slide up and into my ass.

I cry into his lips at the new touch and try to pull away, but he holds me in place, dominating my mouth as the boogeyman of the Dead Lands claims my body in every sense of the word until I shatter again. He continues kissing me, swallowing my pleasure before I rip my mouth away, panting and shuddering.

My body is overly sensitive, like a live wire, and my skin is glowing. Lightning crackles from my skin and hits everything in its path. It seemingly burns and singes the wood despite not hurting them, but I can't seem to stop.

"It's too much," I exclaim, squeezing my eyes shut. "I can't stop it —" My voice is panicked and tight.

"Shh, we have you."

Dade.

His grounding hands slide across my body, absorbing my lightning, and when I open my eyes, Rook has wrapped his shadows around us, protecting the room and the world beyond from me. My lightning bounces off it and them, seeking an outlet.

My human form is simply too weak to hold all this power in, one that is seemingly awake and waiting for . . . something.

It continues to grow, tripling inside me until I feel like I might burst.

More hands join Dade's, sliding along my body and taking it into themselves, lessening that growing power inside me until I can suck in a shaky breath.

"What's happening?" I ask.

"I think you called your power when you came," Rook murmurs, watching me, not the least bit scared. "It seems you've been holding it back subconsciously, fearing it. You are more powerful than you know, little mate, and it wants out."

"It's okay," Kaito says. "We have you. Let it go. Let it out."

"But the castle—"

"Everything will be fine," Weyland promises.

"Trust us," Dade demands.

I try, I really do, but my body is still tense with the need to hold this back. I'm worried about what might happen. Cora is here, her mates—

"Let go," Rook commands, his voice cruel. "Now!"

I do, letting the power slip through my fingers like a rope I have released. It unravels inside me, deeper than I ever thought.

Their hands hold me, even as I lift into the air from the force of the power surrounding us. Some absorbs into them, forming tiny electric threads between them and me until we are a circle and I am the center. My eyes shine so brightly, even I can see them, and my skin glows like the moon.

"Beautiful," Kaito whispers as all that power explodes.

I DON'T KNOW how long the darkness consumes me, but it's a familiar, comforting inkiness, and when I finally emerge, I feel rested and healed.

My men surround me as I sit up, my chest heaving. Frowning, I glance over them, my eyes widening when I see the wet stains on their clothes. Did my power make them come?

Not only that, but above each of their hearts is a tiny, jagged, glowing lightning bolt that seems to pulse in time with their hearts.

My hands cover my mouth as I look them over. "Are you okay?" I ask softly, afraid I hurt them.

"Never better," Weyland replies, lifting his hand and forming an okay symbol before letting it flop back.

"Just give me a minute, and I'll be fine," Dade says.

"Just a minute," Rook rasps, his shadows swirling around him as if he has lost all control.

Kaito tries to lift his head but drops it, and I gasp worriedly.

"I'm so sorry. I'll never let that happen again." Tears fill my eyes as I watch them, wondering how badly I hurt them. "I'm sorry, let me heal—"

"Stop making our mate worry," Dade grumbles, forcing himself to sit up, and when he sees my tears, he kicks the others. "Now."

They all jerk upright and crowd closer. Weyland cups my face as I sniffle. "Shh, we are okay. You didn't hurt us. It's the opposite, my love."

"I don't know what that means," I sob.

Rook chuckles even as Dade elbows him.

Kaito takes my hand kindly. "You gave us more pleasure than we have ever felt, that's all. It is simply taking us a moment to recover."

"Oh," I whisper, my heart skipping a beat as my tears start to dry. "I didn't hurt you?"

"No, never," Rook promises, kissing my cheek. "In fact, feel free to do that anytime. I've never come so hard. It was like your mouth, hand, and cunt were wrapped around my cock at the same time." Dade elbows him again as I giggle.

Weyland shakes his head, smiling as he kisses away my tears. "You have to trust us."

"I do." I sigh, leaning into their embraces. "I do," I repeat firmly.

I do, I just worry what this means.

What did I unleash?

Only time will tell.

FIFTY-FIVE

"S o you were busy this morning, huh?" Cora says with a grin, and I choke on my water. Rook pats my back as I sputter, and she giggles. "Nice electric show we had."

Oh shadows, kill me now.

I was hoping she hadn't noticed, but of course she did.

After cleaning up and dressing, we found Cora and her monsters waiting for us in a large dining room, the table filled with more food than I could have ever imagined. It's nice eating together. It feels right, like home, even in this sprawling castle, simply because my mates and sister are here.

Right now, though, I wish they weren't here so I could sink into the floor as Cora wiggles her eyebrows at me knowingly.

"Don't tease," Grim says. "After all, she didn't mention if she saw you screaming in the skies with Razcorr."

Cora shrugs. "I'm not ashamed. I had a great time."

Groaning, I cover my heated cheeks. "Can we please change the subject?"

"I was thinking I could show you the grounds today and make you comfortable, if you want?" Cora suggests. "If you will be here fo a while, we could prepare a wing for you and get you some clothes." She looks hopeful, and it fills me with joy.

It comes crashing down, however, when Cora's mate Krug steps into the room. His expression is cold and hard, and we all instantly quiet down. "They have responded. They will meet us there when the moon fills the sky this evening."

Everyone is silent as we stare at him.

Merryl and the humans are meeting us tonight.

We have to reason with them and end this. Nothing else matters.

It is a stark reminder that monsters are dying while we play house.

We have no time to waste.

I'M NERVOUS, but you wouldn't know it by looking at me.

Cora produced an amazing gown spun from Nero's scales that will protect me. It shines brightly and is painted a deep black to show my glowing skin. She also braided my hair into an elaborate updo that looks like a crown. Physically, I look every bit the monster lover. I look like a dark wraith standing between my men, my sister, and her mates as we form a line across the dark grass that blows in the light wind.

The moon is high above us, shining brightly in the darkened sky.

The woods around us are quiet, as if the monsters sensed what's happening tonight and fled. We spent all day preparing for what may happen and journeying to the neutral territory at the very edge of the Shadow Lands to meet, yet I'm still nervous.

What will Merryl do?

I know humans are unpredictable, especially when threatened.

Part of me hopes they will back down, while another part of me feels like they never will and all that will come from this is death and bloodshed—blood that will spill across this neutral ground and spark a war neither side can afford to fight.

I can scarcely believe it has come to this. The man I knew and loved would never hurt anyone, yet I have changed and so has he. Now, he hunts monsters, the very beings I love and have become, and the ones my sister has become queen of.

He threatens everything, so we have to end this tonight before more horror and pain descend on these lands. We have a chance for a better start, and under Cora's rule, everyone can be free and equal.

Some don't want freedom though. Some crave chains and pain, power and imbalance.

Some thrive on it.

We may be monsters shielded by shadows and cloaked in darkness with fangs and fur, but it's the humans who step out of the trees who are monstrous at heart. They are killers and hunters.

Merryl stands at the front of their group. For a moment, I see the boy I fell in love with before his face hardens. At his side are over thirty humans, who are all looking at us in disgust. Their bodies are covered in weapons and traps, and they are streaked with dirt and blood that I can smell from here.

They don't stop until they stand in the clearing with a yawning gap between us that I feel will never be bridged. My powers flood my senses, as if detecting my nervousness or knowing something I don't.

For a moment, silence fills the clearing before a burly man at Merryl's side steps forward. He's older, with a scarred face, dark, angry eyes, and a shaved head. I'm assuming he is a farm worker from his muscles. "You wanted to meet, false queen?" he asks. "Well, we are here." He bows mockingly as Cora frowns at him.

"You forget I come from the Shadow Lands."

"You did before you let monsters defile you and turn you into one of them," he sneers, and Cora's mates snarl, stepping closer, but she holds up her hand, stopping them.

"You seem angry. Maybe you should go get defiled. It might calm you down a bit," she replies coolly, wearing a mocking grin on her face. "But yes, I asked to meet—"

279

"Kai, come with us now," Merryl snaps, and every head turns to him. His eyes are on me as he ignores everything else, and he holds out his hand. I feel every gaze swinging between me and him. "Last chance," he warns, his voice thick.

I step forward, and he sighs with relief, but I stop just before him, ignoring his extended hand. "No," I tell him. "This is where I belong."

I watch his hand curl into a fist and drop. "With those beasts?" he spits.

"With them," I murmur with a nod. "Please, Merryl, stop this. You aren't a bad guy, but this is wrong—"

I gasp when his hand snaps out, gripping my arm. "I tried to give you a choice, but if you want to paint me as the bad guy, then so be it. I'll be your captor, just like the king. Maybe he was right."

My eyes widen as horror winds through me, and then I feel the ground hum with movement. I snap my head around to see more hunters pouring from the trees, all draped in weapons and encircling Cora and our monsters.

It's an ambush.

Merryl's hand tightens on my arm, making me look back at him even as shadows race across the ground and up my legs. My mates growl as they split their attention between the threat behind them and the one touching their mate, but my entire focus is on Merryl and the hate I see in his eyes.

I see his need for violence so he can control me, own me, just like every man before him.

"You think they are beasts? Then what am I?" I snarl, and I let go, releasing the powers that are crying to be let out and join the fight, sensing the threat to myself and my mates.

My skin begins to glow and my eyes light up. Even my hair illuminates as I watch Merryl's stand on edge from where he touches me before he cries out in pain and lets go.

My power does not attack my mates, but it does attack him, sensing the threat.

Eyes wide, he stumbles back, looking at me in horror.

"What have they done? They've ruined you. You're a monster," he whispers.

We are both oblivious to everything else going on around us. I'm caught in this moment, one I knew we were destined to experience, even from the beginning.

Love changes to hate, and desire morphs to disgust.

"You are corrupt. You are no better than them. Look at you! Look at what they've done to you, Kai! You should have come with me and trusted me to protect you—"

"You never protected me! You never could. You are weak, Merryl. When the king came for me, you did nothing. Yet here you are, pretending this is all for me. They didn't ruin me; the king did. No, these monsters, these beasts as you call them, saved me." I step closer, feeling my power mix with Rook's shadows as they hold back the other hunters.

"You have to stop this, Merryl. This is my last warning to you. I know somewhere deep inside, you are still the man I loved—a gentle man. You must see this is wrong."

He watches me, swallowing hard. "That's where you're wrong, Kai. We have both changed," he whispers. "If you are with them, then you are against us. We won't stop. It is too late. Don't you see?"

Frowning in confusion, I follow his eyes and gasp in horror.

Flames burn through the woods, eating the land and trees in the Dead Lands as they burn a path to us.

The Dead Lands burn, and so do we.

CHAPTER
FIFTY-SIX

KAI

The fire spreads rapidly, consuming the land at a pace it shouldn't. The Dead Lands have only just begun to come back to life, the green within the trees a symbol of hope in the darkness, but the new growth is still young, and so the dryness of the Dead Lands aids the fire's spread. I stare in horror as we're surrounded on all sides and screams rip through the air from the monsters in the forest. We came to this neutral ground to seek peace, and instead, the humans took all attempts of peace off the table.

They are destroying our home.

"Come," Rook growls as he lifts me into his arms. "We must go."

"The Dead Lands!" I cry. "The monsters!"

I'm not dressed for running, but even if I'd been able to, I would stumble under the sight of the forest. This place that has become my home means more to me than the Shadow Lands ever could. I healed here, loved here, and found my sister again. This place is home, and they lit it on fire like it means nothing.

Anger fills me, anger that drags my power from my heart with my bitterness. Our choices are always stolen from us. They were stolen from us in the Shadow Lands, and they were stolen from us now. Beside me, Cora screams for her home. This should not be happening. This never should have been possible.

I'm thrown over Rook's shoulder, and he bursts into a sprint. Beside him, Grim runs with Cora over his shoulder. We're both dressed as queens, not in clothing suitable for fighting—a mistake we will never make again. We wanted to appear nonthreatening, like we were there to bring peace, and they betrayed the grounds of neutrality. For that and burning this realm, they will pay.

I reach for Cora in my anguish, my arm outstretched despite our mad dash toward the Shadow Lands to escape the flames that consume our home. She clasps her fingers in mine, and my power burns brighter. Lightning flashes from me as she glows, and together, we begin to scream.

"Get to the Gilded Lands! Take shelter! Follow us for sanctuary!"

Cora is not only the queen of the monsters; she's the queen of everything. I understand why she never wanted to live in the Gilded Castle. I don't wish to ever return myself, but we must. The monsters from the Dead Lands won't have anywhere to go, and the Shadow Lands still fear them, but the castle in the Gilded Lands will be plenty large enough to house the fleeing monsters.

As we scream, our power lighting the way while we run, monsters join our ranks. They sprint alongside my and my sister's mates. We stay connected, our hands intertwined as we lead them to safety. Rook carries me without effort, his shadows dancing around us as Kaito, Dade, and Weyland follow. They make sure we remain safe against the human hunters who likely lie in wait. What easy targets they must think we make. We may be monsters, but we will never be the demons they are.

Merryl will pay for what he's done. Gone is the man in my memories, and he's been replaced by the hateful, terrible man I saw just before the fire. He never saved me then, and he dooms me now.

The fire rages around us, feeding on not only the dry brush but the magic in the air. The flames change colors as the magic begins to bleed. The blue, green, purple, and black flames grow hotter with the magic, singeing my hair as we run. Another burst of magic booms out of me, keeping the flames at bay without conscious effort. Cora does the same. Her gargoyle flies overhead, a beacon for the monsters capable of flight. They fill the air as we scramble through the trees.

The old wall, now crumbling and dead, appears, and we scramble over it with the flames on our heels. The moment we touch the Shadow Lands, Rook and Grim set Cora and me down.

With our hands still clasped, we face the wall and the flames that surge forward.

"We have to stop the fire," Cora rasps, looking over at me. "Can you help me?"

I nod. There was never a question.

Cora begins to glow, her power brightening. I close my eyes and feel her draw on my own power as she uses it to feed her magic. We sway beneath the weight, but strong hands clasp my shoulders, and I can only assume they do the same to hers as well.

Our monsters. Our mates.

When I open my eyes again, a familiar wall has been built. The flames beat against the other side, making the vines red-hot, but they do not cross. It's another wall, but this time, all the monsters are on this side with us.

I look over at Cora and see tears flowing down her cheeks from a pain I recognize.

"We will knock it down again," I promise. "It won't stand forever."

Cora nods and wipes her face. "Yes, but at what cost?" She meets my eyes. "War is coming, Kai, and I can't stop it."

I squeeze her hand despite my exhaustion. "We may not stop it from coming, but we will end it."

We turn and take in the humans gathering to stare at us. Some are afraid, and some are curious, but among them are those who are angry.

"We should go to the castle," Cora murmurs, her worried eyes dancing to me. "Will you be okay?"

That castle was once my prison.

Strong hands still remain on my shoulders, and I straighten, tilting my chin up. "I will be," I promise. "I will be."

THE CASTLE HAS TURNED into a home for wayward monsters. Oh, how the old king would turn in his grave. Those who made it out of the flames and those who are still making their way through the fire and over the wall are all welcomed to the castle with open arms. Many of those who arrive have never had a bed, so we offer whatever they are comfortable with. Many of them have taken up residence in the now overgrown courtyard, hiding among the flowers struggling to grow among the weeds. A few times, I have been startled by one rushing out, only to realize they were children—a sight I had yet to see. Just like human children, they laugh and play despite the scary ordeal we all went through, and it gives me some semblance of peace.

I haven't been able to step inside the castle yet, preferring to help those outside and resting in the courtyard. I offer what I can, making sure everyone is comfortable before they go inside, but I will eventually have to face my past.

When the monsters stop trickling in, I stand before the large entrance with a heavy heart. The last time I was here, I was a prisoner. Now, it's meant to be a safe haven. It's a strange juxtaposition to hate a place so much and yet be thankful for it.

This is your home now. You will make me very happy here.

Get on the floor. I want you on your knees.

Your sister isn't going to save you now.

The words echo in my mind like a distant memory. They are less harsh now, less brutal, but they are there all the same. I don't think they'll ever disappear, as they have become a part of me, but over time, as I continue to heal, perhaps they'll fade more.

A strong hand slips into mine, and the touch of shadows dances across my lips, grounding me. I glance up at Rook with a smile despite the memories.

"Come, little oblivion," he purrs. "The darkness will quiver in the face of my own."

Holding onto his hand tightly, I step inside the castle for the first time since I threw myself off it.

CHAPTER

FIFTY-SEVEN

KAI

I spent hours anguishing about which room to pick. Cora and
her monsters claimed the highest towers were ideal for protection, but those towers were where the king resided and where I
had . . . where he hurt me over and over again. Bile gathers in my
throat when I think about staying in those rooms, so I tell Cora I
can't stay there. I expect her to be annoyed, or at least for her
monsters to be, but they all look at me in understanding. Somehow,
that only makes it more real. In the end, I select a room as far away
from the king's as possible, on the opposite side of the castle and a
few floors down. I convince Grimus that we can watch the other side
for threats, and he admits it's smart, even if we're less protected here.
When Rook reminds the minotaur that we won't be without protection and we are strong, he relents, and we settle in.

Somehow, the echoes of my past still reach me.

Despite my monsters holding me close that night, they can't fully
chase away the nightmares. When I awake for the second time from
a brutal nightmare of the king punishing me, shadows surrounding
me to keep the worst at bay, I give up on getting any sleep. There is
too much to worry about.

Rook offers to get up with me, but I reassure him that I'll be fine. Still, as I meander through the castle, his shadows remain at my heels, following in case I should need him. My heart grows fluttery at his support and care, and I welcome the shadows as I pad across the cold, stone floors on bare feet.

I'm not sure where I'm going until I find myself there. These chambers used to belong to the king. I know them well. I suffered in them. I'm not surprised my feet carried me here, but I am surprised to find they weren't the only ones to do so.

On the balcony I once leapt from is a figure. She glows, so I know who she is immediately. I step toward her slowly, knowing she can sense me and I won't startle her. Cora is radiant in this low light, her beauty only highlighted by the wind in her hair and the fluttering hem of her dress.

When I appear beside her, no words are exchanged at first. She simply reaches for my hand, and we stand side by side in the tower I once fell from. The Dead Lands still burn in the distance, the fires untamed with the magic it feeds on. The orange and red illuminate the kingdom in a ghastly light, but despite that brightness, that isn't what catches my eye. It's the lights from the Shadow Lands, outside of the town boundaries, where small fires and tents are set up.

"The hunters are amassing their army," Cora says in explanation.

My heart throbs painfully in my chest. "Are there many?"

"Enough to fight a war," she admits. "Many joined because of their hatred. Most joined out of fear of repercussions if they didn't."

"That means we have a chance to convince them not to fight," I reason. "We can ask—"

"Fear is a heavy motivator, Kai. You know that better than most," she whispers with a painful glance at me. "Fear is stronger than hope, and all we have had for so long is fear. They are preparing for a war, and that's what they'll have. I hoped to avoid this, but . . ."

"You couldn't have known the outcome, Cora," I tell her gently. "You freed the lands, but there will always be those who cling to their cage when they know nothing else."

She sighs. "A lot of people, a lot of monsters, will die," she rasps. When I hear a sob catch in her throat and see tears trickle from her eyes, I tug her close and wrap my arm around her. "I wanted to change our future," she whispers, "but we are only repeating history."

She turns into me, letting her tears out, and I cry with her. She needs me, and everything in me says that Kaito saved me for a reason, that I healed for a reason.

I was meant to be here for Cora.

For the first time in our lives, I am the one who stands taller, weathering the pain for her as she breaks.

"Let it all out," I coo. "Let it out, Cora, and when you're ready, we'll make it better together."

"Promise?" she croaks into my shoulder.

"Promise," I answer.

My eyes catch on the flames in the Dead Lands, on the magic there. They dance, sparkle, and burn.

Oh, how they burn.

War is strange.

We all know it's coming, we can feel it on the crisp early morning air, yet I find myself smiling at Cora's mates' antics. I eat, although I don't taste the food I force myself to consume, and I shower and dress like it's a normal day, but it isn't.

Anticipation hangs heavily in the air. We all know the hunters will strike soon. They will gather their forces and march on us, determined to end the monsters once and for all and claim the kingdom. Under their reign, magic will die, half-breeds will be punished, and all the beauty and differences which make our land unique, if scarred, will be ash.

Our histories will be rewritten, and our future hangs in the balance.

Standing before the mirror in the room we claimed, I eye myself as these thoughts trouble me. Cora is preparing, as should I, but I am just staring.

My skin glows, reminding me I'm not human anymore. I am one of them, one of the monsters about to fight for our freedom and land. My hair tumbles over my shoulders in drying waves, my magic tattoos seem to move on my skin, and my eyes shine brightly. When the shadows of the room swallow everything else, I shine.

My monsters, my men, are here, waiting for me.

They have been hurt, hunted, and abandoned, and although they just wanted to be left alone and find happiness, they now find themselves in a battle for their lives and the soul of our land because that is what it boils down to.

If the hunters win, there will be nothing but death and destruction. This world will never recover from the senseless murder and slaughter that will ensue. We have to stop it. We have to save our people and theirs too—humans and monsters alike.

There will be so much death, yet none of us can stop this now. I feel like we have reached the point of no return, and I almost choke on my panic of what I will do and become.

Can I pay the price?

As my men step into the mirror's reflection behind me, I know I can. I have to so I can keep them safe.

"Let us help you prepare," Dade murmurs, and I incline my head, afraid if I speak, I will either scream or cry.

I am just a girl from the Shadow Lands. I was meant for nothing other than to work the fields, have a family, and die in the very house I grew up in, yet here I stand, defending monsters and glowing with ancient magic, prepared to wage war.

If my father could see me now . . .

My lips curve up at that.

Dade kneels as Weyland moves to my side. Carefully, he detangles my hair with his claws and starts to braid it. Kaito moves to my left, kneeling opposite Dade, and I glance down to see them tugging up some leather pants. Once they are settled on my hips, they fasten up the sides which are laced. The color is a deep brown, almost black, and when I move, they move with me like a second skin while also feeling thick and padded.

Rook stands behind me, meeting my eyes in the mirror as they dress me, his hands settling on my hips.

Weyland drapes my now braided hair over my shoulder and ties it off before he nods and steps back, grabbing something else. Dade and Kaito stand and help me into a white peasant blouse before pulling on my breastplate made of Nero's scales and then adding my thick-soled, knee-high boots. I watch them the entire time as they transform me from a lowly peasant girl to a warrior.

They add armor to my thighs and arms before slipping daggers into their holsters and securing a sword at my hip. When they stop, I look at us together as I reach for them. I take their hands before meeting Rook's eyes.

"It is time, my little oblivion."

I nod once more, sparing myself another glance before turning away.

When I look at myself again, there will be a stranger there, one capable of taking life, but I will be alive, as will my monsters. I have to believe that.

Cora and her mates are waiting for us when we emerge just beyond the old king's throne room. For a moment, when she turns to me, I still. She looks every inch the queen she is. Her crown sits atop her tightly secured hair, and she wears gold and black armor, matching her mates. She has a sword at each hip, and her hands glow with magic. She stands tall, and when I join her, I realize we complement each other.

The glowing golden queen and her shadow.

She squeezes my hand as our mates spread out behind us. "Are you ready for this?" she murmurs quietly just for us.

"No, are you?" I ask, turning my head to meet her gaze. Gone is the sobbing woman from last night who mourned the death that will occur today. Now, she stands tall today under the pressure, and I am awed by my sister's strength.

"No," she admits, "but fake it until you make it, right?"

Smiling, I squeeze her hand. "I will follow you to the very end, Cora. I need you to know that. Whatever happens, I will remain at your side where I belong."

Tears form in her eyes, even as her smile curls up. "And so will I, my dear Kai. Let us end this the way it started—with two sisters."

The doors open without command, and I keep my hand clutched in Cora's as we stride into the waiting throne room. Monsters line the walls, but I note some humans amongst them—either staff from the castle or those who will fight at our side.

The room glitters with gold as we walk confidently down the middle of the amassed crowd. As we pass, they drop to their knees, their heads bowed in respect.

Swallowing my nerves, I keep my eyes forward, and when we reach the open doors at the end, Cora turns us until we face them. She keeps hold of my hand as her voice echoes around the hall.

A war cry of a queen.

"All children are to be taken to the cellars for safety. Any woman or man who wishes to fight is free to do so. I will not demand it of you. You are free to do as you wish but know this. They will come, and if we lose, they will kill every monster, slaughtering women, men, and children. They are soulless killers, and in their eyes, we are monsters, so let us show them what monsters are capable of!"

The echoing cry is caught up by hundreds, maybe even thousands.

It soon quiets, though, when the ground below us begins to rumble and shake. I glance behind me to the open door, knowing it is from their approaching army. They are prepared to destroy all that we are.

So it begins.

FIFTY-NINE

We wait at the top of a small hill on the field beyond the castle, backed by its glistening structure. The flames burn brightly behind the approaching army, which covers the ground on the other side of the field, heading toward us, their hateful chants brought to us on the wind.

"Kill the monsters! End the darkness! Kill them all! Kill them all!"

I stand beside Cora, our men at our sides. Monsters spread out behind us, and more spill from the walls. Half-breeds poured from the sewers as we marched through the Gilded Lands, and monsters spilled from every dark shadow. Even some humans emerged with handmade weapons. They stand behind us now, bristling and waiting.

The scent of fear and anticipation chokes me as I try to take deep breaths, and my heart thunders more than the sound of approaching footsteps.

"There are so many of them," I whisper, eyeing their ranks. Most are from the Shadow Lands, and some are from the Gilded Lands, but all are angry and holding weapons, ready to spill blood.

"It is not the number. It is the determination," Cora murmurs. "I am determined to win." She glances at me. "I will not let our freedom be taken again. I will bleed for it." She pulls her sword out then, and flames lick along its edges. "Prepare!" she calls.

I pull my own sword, my hand shaking as I hold it before me. I hear some cries behind us, but when I glance back, I see sure, blank faces of monsters ready to fight. Wings flap above us as Razcorr commands the winged monsters. They will attack from above, while we fight from the front. Relying on our monstrous strength is our only hope of winning.

Magic pours through our ranks, seeming to seep up from the earth and into us. It's a comforting promise from this land to help us where it can.

The hunters stop across from us, and the world is silent for a moment as we peer at each other. For a second, I think one of them will make a grand speech and condemn us all with their words, until they raise their hands and a cry follows.

They charge right at us.

"To the end! For our freedom!" Cora cries, and then without waiting another moment, she races to meet them head-on.

I follow her. I can't do anything but.

I glance back as the earth shakes with a roar and see the monsters chasing after us. My eyes glance up as wind blows through us, almost knocking me over as our monsters blot out the sun and dive straight toward the hunters.

I hope it's enough.

When our two armies meet, there is an audible clash. Screams fill the air within seconds, and I lose sight of Cora. Only flashes of gold between bodies let me know she is still alive. Rook's shadows crawl along the ground, turning the golden sunlight dark before wrapping around hunters. Their screams can be heard from within.

Weyland howls and rips people to shreds with claws and teeth, blood matting his fur. Kaito stays at my side and rips off the heads of anyone who gets too close. Dade has transformed, his hooves burning the ground as he lowers his head and charges at those who approach us, spiking them on his horn until blood runs down his face.

I turn, horrified, but quickly duck as a hunter's arrow whizzes over my head. Turning back, I bring up my sword with a shout as a human charges me. Our eyes meet, both wide and horrified as I fall to my back.

He's speared on my sword, his mouth moving as blood bubbles from his lips, and as he falls, he impales on it farther, coughing blood all over me. With a cry, I kick him away and jump back to my feet, staring at his unmoving body.

I killed someone.

I don't have time to process that as something sharp cuts my cheek, making me hiss as my magic lashes out in response. It throws a group of hunters away, the lightning crackling over them, and as I watch, their eyes burst, the sockets blacken, and their mouths open on silent screams of horror as they burn from the inside out.

A hand grips my hair, yanking me back, and I scream. The pressure disappears, and I whirl to find Rook's hand bursting through the man's chest, his heart in his hand. As he yanks it back, Rook tosses the heart into the shadows swirling around us, and he blows me a kiss before fading into mist with screams following him.

My cheeks are wet, and I lift my hand to touch them. When I pull my fingers away, I see my tears glistening there along with blood. I turn away from the dismembered bodies falling to the ground around me and search.

I see Cora battling five hunters with a wide smile as she uses her magic to destroy them. Her mates surround her, carving a path through their midst.

Razcorr dives from the sky, grabbing a hunter by his shoulders. The human screams and kicks, fighting as he's lifted higher and higher until he is thrown like a weapon right at a group of hunters fighting their way through our monsters.

Oh, shadows.

What have they made us into?

My heart aches, and my soul screams as I turn, yet I bring my sword up and slice across the neck of a hunter trying to sneak up on Kaito who's battling three humans. I end his life, and when he falls to my feet, all I feel is regret and pain so deep, I know it comes from more than just me.

It's from the very earth itself. Each boy that falls is another drop of pain in the bucket. I feel every life that is taken, as if it takes a piece of my soul, even if it isn't by my hand.

I stand here amongst the onslaught and I sob.

My men falter around me, keeping the humans back but not killing them, noticing my reactions.

I seek out Cora again to see her pushing forward.

Blood covers the once golden field, and the sky is black with shadows and death. So many blurry faces run past us, and there is so much agony, anger, and death.

I can't do this.

The tip of my sword drops, blood coating the blade and dulling it. I feel specks of it on my face and across my hands, and I want to be sick.

Call me weak or naïve, but I can't.

The horror and bloodshed make me queasy. My powers cry out inside me, protesting being used for taking life when it wants to give it. I even feel the earth below me crying out at the blood spilled across it. It wants life and happiness, not death.

I scan the clashing bodies, and tears spill from my eyes. So many are dead already, and so many are dying.

Their cries fill the air, monsters and humans alike, and without thinking, I drop the sword and lower to my knees beside the first body I come across. It's not until I take the hand that I realize it's a hunter, but it doesn't stop me.

"Please," he begs. He's so young, so very young, and tears flow down his face. His intestines are on the outside, and the scents of death and shit make me wince. He is pale and on death's door. "Please, I don't want to die," he begs. "I don't want to die. I'm sorry."

Swallowing my pain, I close my eyes and do what I was made for. I heal.

When I open my eyes, nothing but a scar remains on his stomach, but he can breathe now, and color fills his cheeks once more. "Thank you, thank you," he sobs, clutching my hand. "Thank you for saving me. I'm so sorry—"

I stand and nod. "Go home," I demand, "or help us. Your choice. You have been given a second chance. Do not waste it."

Sometimes, you have to forgive and help an enemy in order to help your own cause.

With that, I turn to the next voice crying out for help, determined to heal as many as I can. Humans, monsters, hunters, and my people —I will save them all.

I wasn't made to take life.

I was made to give it.

They can call me a monster, but they won't make me one.

CHAPTER

SIXTY

KAI

I don't know how many I heal as I move through the battlefield. I hurry from body to body, uncaring if they are hunter or monster. My lightning crackles along my skin, at ease now that I'm using it for what it's meant for rather than perverting it.

The war rages on around me despite my efforts. Those I heal hesitate between leaving the battlefield and joining our cause, their conscience telling them not to fight any longer after a monster healed them. A few of them join us out of obligation, but most leave the fight altogether. My men move around me, protecting me as I kneel beside the injured. Those I must heal add up, but I can't heal what's dead.

I lose track of time as I work. I'm covered in blood, but a healer's hands are always the most stained. I don't keep count of how many I help or how many leave the battle, but I do take note of those who revert right back to their original state.

"Don't touch me, monster whore!" a man coughing up blood shouts at me.

I don't respond as I kneel beside him, my lightning crackling along my fingers. This man has a slice across the chest, his rib bones showing through the wound. Something with claws downed him, but despite his rapidly approaching death, he doesn't want me to touch him. Too bad for him because he can't move to stop me.

"No!" he rasps, his voice thick with the blood dribbling from his lips. "Don't touch me."

My lightning jumps out and kisses him, stitching his skin back together. I don't recognize this man, but he appears to be from the Gilded Lands rather than the Shadow Lands. I looked through unseeing eyes during my time within the king's castle, so I can't say I know him. As I heal him, his words get stronger, more direct and cutting.

"The king should have broken you when he had the chance," he sneers, reaching up to grab my wrist. "He should have let the guards take turns."

Ah, so this one was a guard. I yank at my wrist, but he doesn't let go, and when he's completely healed, he leaps up with a yell, holding his sword high.

"You fucking monster whore! I'm going to finish the job for—"

He never finishes his sentence. Mid swing, in which he intended to kill me after his cruel words, he stops and looks down in shock. Sticking from his heart is a horn. When he drops, Dade is standing behind him, his black coat shimmering with blood and gore.

You can't change all their hearts, Kai. Remember that, he whispers in my mind. *Not even you can save the damned.*

I nod and move on, but I don't pick and choose. I trust my men to protect me should they attack once healed, but it's a rare occurrence. Most are thankful and don't want to harm the side that healed them. They think we are monsters, but they are the ones acting like monsters.

In the distance, I catch sight of Cora, her bloodstained golden armor flashing in the light. She barks orders and leads the attacks, her own mates surrounding her. She's beautiful, regal, and fierce, and I can't help but watch her for a moment, pausing to simply take her in.

My brilliant sister.

Because I'm watching and admiring her strength, I witness something I hoped to never see.

"Cora, watch out!" I cry as I spy the old man who'd been with Merryl suddenly swinging at Cora from behind. I'm sprinting before I even finish the sentence, uncaring of those still fighting around me. My men, seeing my trajectory, help clear a path.

But I'm too late.

I watch in horror as he stabs a sword through Cora's spine, the blade bursting from her stomach. She looks down in surprise, and the roars around her echo through the air. My blood chills as Grimus turns, sees what transpired, and then turns toward the man still holding the blade. Nero catches Cora before she can fall, his eyes wide and afraid as she goes limp, trying to say words that don't make sense. I slide to a stop just as the first trickle of blood slips from the corner of her lips.

My horrified scream echoes across the battlefield, filled with grief and agony.

My lightning travels down my arms and immediately jumps to her skin.

I will not lose her.

Not today, not any day.

I can save anyone, and my ability has never been more necessary than it is now.

My sister saved me, and it's time I repay the favor.

"Stay with me, Cora," I beg, fresh tears tumbling over my lashes, my lips trembling despite my determination. "Don't you dare die on me! Stay with me!"

Grimus growls at the hunter in his hands and squeezes his neck. "If she dies, your death will be a brutal reminder of what the monsters are capable of," he warns the man whose face is starting to turn blue.

"Come on," I rasp, my lightning dancing along her skin. "Someone needs to pull the sword out."

Bracken kneels, his face far more serious than I've ever seen it. He grabs the hilt of the sword and presses a kiss to Cora's forehead. "I'm sorry, Goldie. You can make me pay for this later." He yanks the sword out with one movement, but Cora doesn't react.

She can't feel it.

Her eyes are almost unseeing as she gazes up at me, her hand shakily cupping my cheek, but it's cold to the touch.

My lightning immediately jumps into the wound, and Cora's back bows, a scream wrenching from her lips as my magic spreads through her body. Despite her severed spine, she can feel the gut-wrenching pain my magic causes as it heals the severe, fatal wound she suffered. Light flashes around us so bright, I have to close my eyes. Those around us pause at the sudden brilliant light around us, curious even in war.

I ignore them all. All that matters is Cora.

My body forces out more magic, more energy, until I'm alive with it, humming with awareness and power. Cora continues to scream for long minutes, all while Nero cradles her in his arms and her other mates reach out to touch her while mine protect us.

The power is too great for my body. I'm channeling so much of it that I can't stop the cascade. As I push to save Cora and hope that my power can mend a severed spine, the power begins to pulse out of me in large, constant explosions. It echoes across the battlefield and traces the face of every monster and hunter. It picks out my monsters and takes note of their small wounds and their exhaustion. How long have we been fighting? How many have been lost?

With a large, final pulse fueled by fear and anger, my power explodes outward, and my back bows with the force of it. I gasp and clutch my chest, as if to remind myself I'm alive.

The fighting stops so suddenly, the sounds of war halting into sudden silence, that I can do nothing but stare as my power fades and I push to my feet.

"You're glowing," Kaito whispers, "like a beacon."

I can feel the warmth of the glow. I stand in the middle of this battle, worn and weary, my heart aching for it all. The light behind me fades, and Cora, my brave Cora, emerges from within to take my hand. There's no time to celebrate and thank whatever god may have given me these powers because we must face two sides of this battle.

The war has paused, but it will resume unless we can stop it. We almost lost a queen today, and we won't lose anyone else.

Those closest to us gasp at Cora's sudden health, as many of them had witnessed one of their own kill her. The man in Grimus's hold curses at the sight, fighting to free himself, but the minotaur is relentless.

"No more!" I shout, looking out over their surprised faces. Monsters and humans alike stare at the two sisters and those closest to us who had been healed simply from being close to the blast. "Look around you! Look at the death!" My voice booms across the silent battlefield, drawing every eye in our direction. Cora watches me with bright eyes, a single strand of orange flickering in her hair after so much of my magic went into her. For a moment, I thank the gods and the shadows for letting me save her. I will break later. "Is this worth it? When we are done, there will be nothing left to fight for!"

Cora blinks. She's covered in gore, her body painted with death from this war. Still, she shines brightly. There's no mistaking her for anything but a queen.

"You're right," she whispers, her eyes wide. "Kai, you're right." She turns and releases my hand, stepping forward. "Monsters, lay your weapons down and put away your claws. This war ends now." She holds up her sword. "No more bloodshed. None of us will win if we carry on this way. All that will be left is our dead."

For a moment, nothing happens, but as the last of her voice echoes across the battlefield, I watch as the monsters begin to do as she asks. Dade transforms back to his human form, as does Weyland. Kaito drops the blades he used. Rook draws his shadows back inside, leaving the area around him unusually bright. Cora's monsters follow suit, laying their weapons down even if their gazes are harsh on those around them, daring them to take action against the queen —for some of the monsters are the weapons themselves.

The monsters set their weapons down, leading by example, and the humans around them watch in surprise. For a moment, I think this isn't going to work, that the humans will choose to be the monsters and attack now that we are vulnerable.

Merryl appears from the crowd, his sword in his hand as he stares at me. I meet his gaze, my chin held high. I don't back down. I am not afraid of my past.

"I loved you once," he rasps, his eyes taking me in.

"I know you think you did," I acknowledge, "but believe me, it was not love." I look toward my mates, my monsters. "Love never abandons you. Love never judges you. Love is steadfast and strong, even in the face of death. Love is love." I meet Merryl's eyes. "And what we had wasn't love. Not really."

He studies me, looks between my monsters and me, and in a move that shocks me, he tosses his sword at my feet.

"Perhaps," he responds.

The humans around him, seeing his acceptance, toss their weapons down, and it travels like a wave through the battlefield, human after human dropping their weapons and stopping this horrible bloodshed. Countless lives have been lost. This war will stain our history with blood, but I hope it will be a reminder of the strength we're capable of.

Cora turns back to me with a smile on her face, and the scene flickers between this Cora, her battle worn and bloodstained armor reflecting the sun, and a Cora from long ago who shot me a smile despite the fact that she was about to walk through the wall into the Dead Lands. She'd been terrified then, but because of me, she smiled. This time, I won't let her go alone. I won't lose her again.

With a gasp, I run toward her and fly into her arms, and we embrace in the middle of the battlefield.

Three lands and two sisters.
Monsters and men as one.
A new future is born.

Happiness and hope spread through the battlefield, touching everyone with their intoxicating tendrils. No more bloodshed. No more death. We can begin to grow and learn to work together.

"What about this one?" Grimus snarls, holding up the man who stabbed Cora. "He does not deserve to live."

Krug nods. "He will continue to sow his hatred through his people as long as he lives."

Rook grins. "You're welcome to give him to me. My shadows will make sure his death is painful."

"No," Cora declares. "No more death."

"But he tried to kill you," Bracken whines. "We can at least kill him a little back."

"And then what example would we set?" Cora asks, her eyes bright and clear. "Let him go"—she meets the man's eyes—"with a warning. If he ever takes up arms against our kind again, he will rot at their feet."

The man bares his teeth at Cora despite her mercy as Grimus

drops him on his feet. He stumbles and catches himself before eyeing all the monsters who stand over him like great, hulking beasts.

"Monster whore," he sneers. "You don't deserve this land."

"That may be," Cora replies, "but neither do you."

He takes a step toward the nearest human. For a moment, I truly think this is over and that this is the end. I'm happy and relieved. There is so much blood on my hands that I know I'll never be able to scrub them clean again. Feeling relieved, I let my guard down, stepping back from Cora and smiling, not paying attention to those around me.

The man crouches suddenly. "Merryl, now!"

I turn with wide eyes and watch as the man I once thought I loved lunges toward me. He holds a dagger in his hand, one he must have had on his belt. His eyes are no longer clear. They are full of hatred as he throws himself toward me, intending to stab me. Kill the healer, take away the hope—I understand the strategy well. I'm the target now, not Cora.

No other humans move, and the world slows as Merryl flies closer, the sun catching on a dagger I recognize. The ornate handle inlaid with jewels is one I saw slide across my skin, the one the king wore on his belt everywhere he went.

He intends to kill me with the blade from my prison.

White-hot fury fills me. This man is no man I could have ever loved. I don't believe he changed so drastically—this hateful monster was hiding beneath his skin all along.

Before I can react, Weyland steps before me, protecting me, and the dagger slams into his shoulder, missing anything important. My lightning is already trailing along his skin, healing him as he yanks the dagger out and drops it to the ground with a snarl. I feel another tattoo bloom on my arm at that but do not spare it a look. Merryl's eyes go round, but before he can turn to leave, Kaito is there with his hand around his throat, sliding a sword into his belly.

"Where do you think you're going, human?" Kaito asks, his eyes narrowed.

Merryl gasps at the blade in his body, but it doesn't match the horror in his eyes as I step around Weyland and come closer, my lightning dancing across my skin.

"You call us monsters," I hiss, grabbing the hilt of the sword and wrapping my hand around Kaito's. "But the monster has always been you." Someone hands me the king's dagger, and when I look down, I see shadows trailing over the blade. As I wrap my fingers around it, my lightning infuses it, and with a feral snarl, I slam the blade into Merryl's heart before I can think better of it. "There's no room for your hatred here," I spit. "Take it with you to the afterlife."

Merryl's eyes widen, and then he slumps in Kaito's hold, his vessel no longer needed. My power explodes out of me as fury, anger, hope, and revolution fuel it, and Merryl begins to disintegrate before my eyes. It takes from him and gives to those who are still injured, healing the individuals with hope in their hearts. I give and give until my power finds no more souls capable of being saved and every injury is healed. Merryl is gone, and the man who commanded him is dead at Grimus's feet. Those remaining bow their heads, agreeing to end the war and deciding to end the pattern of bloodshed our lands are known for.

My power takes from me until there's nothing left but more ink spilling across my arm, as if a mark of the souls I have saved, and I can do nothing but collapse into my monsters' arms. They surround me, reassuring me that I've done the right thing.

The war is over. Hope blankets the three lands, begging for a chance.

Now comes the hard part—we must rebuild.

CHAPTER
SIXTY-TWO
KAI

I don't know what I expected once the blood dried and the soldiers, monsters, and humans left, but it wasn't the bone-deep exhaustion and pain I feel.

I stare out at the remains of the battlefield, the earth scarred from death and war, and I weep in my monster's arms.

When I can stand again, I don't leave or rest or relax. We have to bury the dead.

Monsters and humans alike celebrate, feast, drink, and dance. They trade war stories, but I don't feel their happiness or mirth. All I feel is grief. My heart is filled with it as I help lay the last body to rest. The field where the battle took place has become their gravesite, and they will be entombed there as a reminder of those we have lost.

Darkness surrounds us, the fires at the village and castle brightening the night sky.

Cora's hand slips into mine as we stare at the overturned earth. Our monsters, our mates, are moving around the field, filling the holes we have placed bodies in. The mourning howls of mothers, daughters, sons, and wives fill the air around us, echoing the pain inside my soul.

I took a life, one I promised to love forever. I know I had no choice. The war had to stop, and for that, hatred must be eradicated. Merryl became a symbol, a promise, but it doesn't stop the pain I feel at knowing I killed a man I once held in my arms.

"Without you, this would have been much worse." I glance over to meet Cora's sad eyes, the orange strand of her hair blowing in the wind. She wears it proudly. "The death toll would have been unimaginable. I was so blinded by my own hatred, my own need to protect our people, that I saw no other way, but you did. Even after everything humans have done to you, you didn't let it corrupt you. You chose hope. You chose to heal rather than hurt. You broke the cycle, Kai. You are a hero."

"I don't feel like one," I admit.

"Nor do I feel like a queen right now," she replies. Her face is streaked with drying blood, and there are bags under her eyes, showing her exhaustion. We are all tired.

"How about we try again tomorrow?" I joke, and a sad smile curves her lips.

"Tomorrow. Tonight, let us just be two sisters, both hurting and tired." Cora nods before wrapping me in her arms, and I hold her tight. "Thank you for saving me, Kai."

"Always," I whisper. "I should have done it back then, but I was weak and afraid. I'm not now," I tell her as I pull back.

"You were never weak," Cora replies, cupping my face. "You were and still are the strongest person I know. You looked at this world, and as fucked up as it was, you still saw hope. You saw love and happiness and strove for it. You saw something worth fighting for even when I didn't. That is not weak." She kisses my cheek and flits back over to her mates.

I watch her go as I stand alone in the field, my arms and legs heavy, burdened like my heart. My use of power drained me, and I know before long, I will need to rest, but for now, I wait like a sentinel standing above the dead, ensuring they are all offered respect and dignity as they pass onto their next life where it's hopefully better for them.

A deep warmth gradually grows on my arm, and I glance down in surprise.

I trace the new smoky ink crawling along my skin. I didn't notice it until after my skin dimmed. It shows two interlinked crowns—one for Cora, one for me, no doubt from me healing her.

She carries me in her hair, and I carry her on my skin.

"Kai." I don't know how long someone has been calling my name, but I jerk my head up to meet Weyland's worried eyes. "Are you okay?"

"Just tired," I reply, glancing behind him. "Are they all buried?"

"Yes, every single one. We made sure." Kaito joins him, wiping off his dirt-covered hands.

Rook and Dade appear together, both just as covered in dirt and blood, and I hold out my hand. "Then let's go home."

IT TURNS out I'm more exhausted than I thought I was, so by the time we get back to the castle, I'm nearly dragging my feet. Dade ignores my protests and picks me up, carrying me up the stairs. I press my nose to his neck and inhale his dark scent, filling my lungs with it as I relax.

Once we're in our room, he carries me straight to the bathroom and turns on the tub to fill it. I'm grateful because I don't want to climb into bed covered in dirt and blood. In fact, I want it gone. It feels like a scar, a reminder of what I did.

They help me remove the armor without speaking, no doubt realizing how fragile I feel right now. When I sink into the scalding hot water, I close my eyes and dunk myself under to chase away the chill permeating my bones, staying under for a moment before resurfacing with a gasp.

"Better?" Rook asks.

"Better." I sigh.

Grabbing a cloth from the side as they climb in, I start to wash my body. With the first swipe, the white cloth turns red and brown, and I dunk it under, swallowing at the evidence of the murder that was committed.

Scrubbing my skin quickly, I keep dunking and washing, trying to get it all off me.

It's still there, though, like the blood is stuck to my skin and can never be removed. I start to panic, scrubbing my hands and arms.

"It won't come off!" I sob.

"Shh, I have you." Kaito covers my hands, and when I glance up with tear-filled eyes, he leans in and kisses me. "Let us help you."

Nodding, I let him take one hand while Weyland takes the other, and they slowly and carefully wash each one, scrubbing my nails and hands before moving up my arms. Dade moves behind me, washing my back, while Rook takes careful control of my legs, determined to erase every inch of what happened today.

When they finish, I'm cleaner than I have ever been, but I don't feel it.

I bury my face into Kaito's shoulder as I cry.

I feel the water moving around me before arms lock me against them, their warmth holding me as they kneel in the cooling water and let me cry. "Let it out. That's it, my love, just cry. We have you. We will always have you. It's okay."

They all offer comforting words, their hands sliding across my body as I cry, and when I can't cry anymore, they wash my hair, their touches soft and loving. They do not leave one inch of me unwashed and unloved.

Lifting me from the bath, they work together to dry me off and dress me in an oversized shirt before I'm carried to bed.

For a moment, a flame of desire fills me before I squash it. I need to rest, but more than that, I need them to hold me and remind me that I am a good person, and they do.

All night.

CHAPTER
SIXTY-THREE

CORA

The castle is quiet as everyone rests after a long, trying day. My monsters are waiting for me in our bed. I can feel their eyes on me as I linger before the open balcony doors of our room.

They almost lost me today, and it terrified them. If it wasn't for Kai, I would be dead. They know it, and I know it, yet I'm strangely calm about it all. Them? Not so much. I feel their anger, their need to assure themselves that I'm alive and well, and I know there won't be any rest for me tonight.

My lips curve at that, but for now, I stare at my lands.

There has been so much death and destruction. Even now, the Dead Lands still burn, bathed in embers of what the human hunters did, and I know our lands and souls will forever be changed and scarred by what transpired. Now, it is up to us to make it worthwhile and make every death, every act of sacrifice and bravery, mean something.

We must do better than our past. I will ensure it, with Kai at my side.

She is my moral compass. She is true and strong, and the heart o this world and life itself breathes through her. I saw that today. She is life, and I am magic—together, we will be unstoppable. We will protect our lands and people. We will usher in a new age, and while she heals what has been done, I will prowl the darkness with my monsters, ready to stop anyone who dares to threaten what we are building here.

For a moment, my magic travels through the castle and touches upon my sister. Knowing she is safe makes my tension ease, even as my hand lifts to the strand of copper hair that now stands out at the front—a small price to pay for my life.

Kai is magnificent.

She always was, but now she sees it. She stands taller with confidence and shines brightly with life despite everything she has been through.

She fights for her beliefs with conviction.

She's here with me.

For so long, a part of my soul rested at the bottom of this castle where she plummeted, but now it lingers in the shadows of her room, whole once more.

Smiling to myself, I blink my eyes back into focus and stare across the lands before me. Fires are burning low in the Shadow Lands and Gilded Lands, a reminder of the lives we saved, and I smile. In the darkness between nightfall and dawn, people are resting, celebrating, and hoping.

As am I.

Turning away, I head back to my mates, knowing tomorrow can only be better than today.

And the next day.

And the one after that.

We write our own stories, and ours is just beginning.

CHAPTER
SIXTY-FOUR

KAI

In my dreams, I see war and victory. I see us putting the battle and bias to bed, bringing monster and man together. I see my monsters standing around me, and then I feel a soft touch along my hip, like a feather trailing along my skin.

How strange. There's no feather in my dream.

The sensation continues to grow and another joins it, then another, until I'm blinking my eyes open in confusion. The dream fades away and is replaced by the sight of Dade hovering above me, his bright red eyes vivid in the pale morning light.

"Good morning," he murmurs as he leans down to press a kiss against my forehead. His deadly horn shimmers in the light, reminding me just how terrible it can be when he's in his warhorse form on the battlefield.

I stretch, throwing my hands up over my head and groaning at the feeling. "Good morning," I reply, smiling up at him.

Reaching up to cup his jaw, I smooth my fingers along his face, taking in the oily sheen his skin always appears to have. Dade is as beautiful now as he was when we first met, when the dread unicorn first appeared in the forest and spoke to me. As he holds himself over me, his corded muscles flexing, I can't help but smile brightly up at him despite the lingering threads of sleep. He presses his face against my hand, and the juxtaposition between now and when he first did the same thing in warhorse form is so strong, I blink, seeing both at once.

I don't realize I'm glowing until Dade comments on it.

"So perfect," he says, leaning down to run his lips along my collarbone. He's careful not to nick me with his horn, turning so that he can trail his kisses along my body. He sinks down my form, exploring it, before he settles his shoulders between my legs. That's when I realize the others are lounging around us, watching.

Rook stands against the wall beside the bed, his shadows spreading throughout the room and countering the sunshine. Kaito is at the end of the bed, observing with bright, sensual eyes. Weyland is grinning from the other corner of the bed.

"What?" I ask until Dade presses his lips against my core, and I arch at the touch.

Weyland's smile widens. "I'm just admiring the masterpiece that is my mate," he replies, tilting his head. "I'm admiring her pleasure as one of her other mates tastes her arousal."

Why do those words go straight to my core and drive me mad? I reach down and run my hand through Dade's hair before wrapping my fingers around the base of his horn. His shoulders tense, but he doesn't stop his ministrations, even as I begin to stroke. I assumed it was like bone and that it wouldn't have any feeling, but as I slide my hand along his horn, he shivers against me before growing more brutal with his lips. I gasp as he strokes me with his tongue, driving me mad with pleasure. My legs begin to shake, and my other hand clenches in the sheets to keep me from floating away. He hums against my core, and my body tenses in anticipation.

Shadows appear over the edge of the bed, crawling with aching slowness. I watch them draw closer, my body tense and on the verge of exploding, eager to see what they will do. I glance at Rook, see the desire in his eyes, and grow desperate to know what my mates have planned for me.

They trail along my stomach, and when I think they'll target my core, they trail along Dade's shoulder instead, moving down his back, around his waist, and—

Dade jerks against me and pulls back to narrow his eyes on Rook.

"What's the matter, warhorse?" Rook teases. "Shadow got your cock?"

The laughter bursts out of me. There's no way to stop it from happening as it bubbles up and out, and I start to laugh so hard, tears come to my eyes. They all join in, their eyes brightening with my mirth. My lightning dances along my skin with my laughter, and I feel light, happy, and whole.

They all come toward me then, leaving their posts to move closer and absorb my lightning. It jumps from my skin to theirs as they prowl onto the bed and close in, like they are predators and I'm their prey. I'll happily be eaten by them as long as they continue to hold me so close.

"Little oblivion," Rook purrs. "Your effervescence is intoxicating." He leans down to press a kiss to my lips, his cool shadows touching my skin.

Dade presses back between my thighs, and my body tightens again, ready despite the interruption. Weyland strokes my body on one side, careful not to nick me with his claws as he caresses my breast. Kaito, on the other side, strokes my hip bone, my stomach, and then brushes his fingers beneath my breasts, driving me insane with need.

With all their hands on me, it isn't long before my body tightens and releases, an ebb and flow that's almost a gentle orgasm, like the ocean waves on a beach. My toes curl, my back arches, and I moan as I shiver with it, but they don't stop.

Dade moves up my body, and the others give him room as he comes over me, his hard length pressing against my entrance. Fierce need flows through me at the feel of his large head there.

"So perfect," he murmurs before easing inside me with a slow roll. He's far more gentle than I expect, but I realize it's only for my benefit, since his jaw is clenched and his eyes are tight with restraint.

I reach up to loop my hands around his neck before I feel the shadows moving along me again, heading for where Dade and I meet. When they reach the base of Dade's cock, he jerks, slamming against my hips hard with the force of his thrust. I cry out, even as Dade snarls at Rook, tiny curls of smoke coming from his nostrils.

"She doesn't need gentle," Rook tells him. "She wants you as you are."

Dade pauses for a second before looking down at me. When I nod my head, he glares up at Rook again before picking up his pace. His thrusts become brutal, animalistic, and possessive. He throws my legs up over his shoulders, bettering the angle, and I start to gasp in pleasure as he brutally pounds inside me, dragging his huge cock along those nerves that have me seeing stars. Weyland moves closer, kneeling at my head, his own cock out and in his hand. A glistening bead of moisture hovers on his tip, and I lick my lips as he moves closer, teasing me with his length while Dade fucks me.

"Do you want this, mate?" Weyland growls, running his hand along his length. I can't help but clench around Dade, which makes him growl as he thrusts into me, his hands pushing my legs higher until I'm almost off the bed with the angle.

"Yes," I answer truthfully, desire lacing my tone.

He runs the tip of his length along my lips before pressing inside my mouth, stroking gently so as not to hurt me. I moan around his cock, his taste exploding across my tongue and making me suck greedily. Dade's actions drive me insane, even as I enjoy Weyland in my mouth. They work me between them, the feel of them both claiming me at the same time driving me wild until I'm lifting my hips and sucking harder, needing everything they can give me.

Someone else presses their cock into my hand on the other side, the velvety soft length making me grip automatically as the connection slithers between us. I can't turn my head to look, but judging by the shape, it's Kaito. I'd know him anywhere. I'd know him in the dark. I know them all right down to their souls.

Rook is still satisfied playing with his shadows, stroking them along my nipples until they grow sore and achy, a line of pleasure arching directly from them to my clit as I throb. I grow so slick, I feel it dripping from me, and I become so crazed with need, I roll against them for more. I stroke my hand along Kaito's length, working him harshly. When his moan echoes around us as my lightning crawls along my arm and onto his skin, it makes me want to smile.

I can't though. My mouth is busy, stretched wide around Weyland's girth. His growls vibrate my skin as he forces himself deep into my throat.

Pleasure grows in my body, called by them.

Their hands brand my skin, and their mouths leave their marks as they call their pleasure into the air.

All of their focus is on me, their power feeding my own.

My body is a live wire as they tend to me. I rise and fall, my body convulsing, but none of them stop. They continue to pleasure me, switching places every so often. Weyland moves to press inside me, and then Kaito takes his place after that. I can taste myself on them as they thrust inside my mouth, taking turns and winding me higher. Only Rook remains on the edge, his shadows stroking here and there. I don't understand what he's doing until his shadows close in around us. Kaito is between my thighs, his hard length stroking inside me, Dade is running his length against my lips where I can taste myself, and Weyland is running his hands along my body even as I stroke him with my own.

The shadows close in, tiring of their inaction.

I watch with wide eyes as they curl around us, barely lifting us from the bed. They hold me up, even as they begin to coil around my nipples and clit, and I cry out in surprise and pleasure. The others gasp as the shadows curl around them too, as Rook captures us all in his web like a spider.

Apparently, the boogeyman is ready to play.

Rook hums from his position by the wall, his eyes heated as he watches the show he puppets. His shadows wrap around Kaito and force him to move faster. They reach between us and stroke my clit, even as they circle the base of Kaito's cock and squeeze. Kaito grunts in pleasure, his hands clutching my hips almost painfully as he takes his pleasure and Rook adds to it.

The shadows stroke against my cheek where Dade presses, feeling as he pushes inside my throat until I choke on his length. They curl around his balls and stroke then slither around his cock so they slip past my lips and inside my throat like Dade. His cock jumps with his near release as he snarls and pumps harder.

Weyland groans as the shadows curl around his entire body. They come around my hand where I stroke him, adding more sensation with the coolness. Weyland moans and pumps faster, his fingers pinching my nipples with the shadows.

I'm overloaded and so are they as Rook strokes us all higher. My lightning arches out to meet the shadows, dancing with them until we're surrounded by a beautiful display of darkness and light. I blink against the sight and then close my eyes against the sensations as they overwhelm me. Like climbing the highest mountain, I feel my body wind tightly, on the verge of exploding while they love me.

Shadows caress every inch of my skin. Kaito, Weyland, and Dade drive me mad with need as my body tenses. I gasp, and then I hold my breath, desperate to explode.

"Release," Rook commands. With one growled, dark word, I do.

I convulse with pleasure, crying out as my other three mates tumble after me. Kaito slams inside me and grunts, his cock jumping as he fills me with his warmth and marks me. Dade moans, and his seed splashes against my tongue and down my throat, dribbling from the corners of my lips as he pumps slowly inside, not giving me a chance to swallow. Weyland's cum splashes against my hand and across my chest as he moans his pleasure. I collapse into the shadows, my lightning bright as it dances around me. For a moment, I think that's all there is and that we're finished.

Until the others move away and my boogeyman closes in.

"Little oblivion," Rook purrs, his shadows convulsing around him as if he can feel our pleasure. "Are you at home in the shadows now?"

I nod, my chest rising and falling as he moves around me. The others step away, giving him room but remaining close to watch. If I felt like prey before, I was wrong. With Rook stalking me, his shadows dancing around his shoulders, I've never felt more like prey. I've also never enjoyed it more.

"Good," he replies, grinning. "If I thought your legs could carry you right now, I'd tell you to run so I could give chase." He nuzzles my throat. "Oh, how I would enjoy capturing you, locking you down with my shadows while I fucked you within them."

His shadows wrap around my wrists and ankles to prove his point, tugging me open for him as he looms over me. Slowly, they begin to turn me, until my back is to the boogeyman. He presses against my back, his length hard and ready.

"Imagine how beautiful you'd look pinned against the wall like art," he whispers in my ear. "Imagine how I'd paint you with my need. We could each take turns just like now, driving you mad, our seed mixing and dripping down your inner thighs as you weep your desire for us."

My pussy clenches. "Yes," I hiss, trying to press back against him.

He reaches around and circles my throat with his hand, his claws sharp but never pricking. "All in due time, little oblivion. For now, I'll take my pleasure."

He presses inside me. There's no soft and gentle easing or working up to speed. Rook spears me and immediately starts moving with hard, brutal thrusts that have me crying out in pleasure. His shadows slide down my throat, shaped the same as his length, and I suck them, making him shudder against me. His shadows consume us both, wrapping around us like a shroud and stroking both of us into oblivion.

I shatter and then shatter again, screaming when my back

arches. Rook wrenches my head back, his teeth at my throat as he takes his fill. He slaps against me so hard, I know I'll wear his bruises later, but that's okay. I'm screaming in pleasure, my hands clenching against his shadows as they hold me still for him. I can't move, can't fight it, so I give into the darkness. My body glows with each release, my lightning flashing, and when he trails his tongue along the edge of my ear, I hover on the precipice of an explosion.

"Come for me, little oblivion," he growls. "Shatter my shadows with your lightning."

I'm helpless to fight it, so I do as he says, my lightning exploding out of me and eating away at his shadows like they are clouds. I scream in pleasure, my body convulsing even as Rook snarls and bites down on my shoulder, his cock jumping inside me as his warmth mixes with Kaito's. We both shiver and jerk against each other as the shadows recede back into Rook, the others watching with wide eyes.

We collapse to the bed together in a pile of limbs. I'm panting, my chest rising and falling rapidly. Rook's does the same.

"Wow," Weyland rasps. His cock is hard again as he strokes himself.

The others look much the same.

Rook chuckles in my ear, his claws trailing along my skin. "Looks like you're not done yet, little oblivion."

Despite my panting, I chuckle and reach for my mates until we're a tangle of limbs and there's no way to know where I end and they begin.

Just as our hearts are tied together, so are we.

CHAPTER
SIXTY-FIVE

KAI

The lands are healing with aching slowness. The fire in the Dead Lands has finally begun to ebb, revealing the charred remains of the forest I once thought of as home. It will take a long time for things to return, but I have hope.

We all do.

There is no separation between the Shadow Lands and Gilded Lands now. The golden streets spill into the gray ones, creating a gradual change that is almost poetic. We set to work in the Shadow Lands, repairing houses that were little more than shanties and building new homes that are all the same, none better than the other.

As I stroll through the streets, healing those who have grown sick or who are still injured from the war, I take it all in. I heal everyone I'm able to, but even I have my limits. I go to the direst situations first, and then I work my way through.

A man stumbles into the street on shaky legs—not because he's injured, but because he stands before me.

I tilt my head in confusion. "Are you well, sir?" I ask, pausing m

He swallows and then reaches to the side. Three small children come running from a house. That's when I recognize him. I saw his face on the battlefield, his body shutting down as he neared death, and I healed him in a desperate attempt to stop the bloodshed. A woman trails out after the children, her belly round with a fourth child, and I blink in surprise and then realization.

"Thank you," the man rasps, his throat thick with emotion. "I haven't gotten a chance to tell you before now. I can never repay—"

"Stop," I croak, my fingers clenching my skirts. "You have no reason to thank me."

"I do," he says, his eyes bright with gratefulness. His wife comes forward, and he wraps his arm around her waist. "If not for you, I would have died on that battlefield. I never would have seen my children again. I owe much to you."

He had been a hunter, but he stands before me now simply as a man who loves his children and wife. There are many like him who've realized the foolishness of the war, and now I'm faced with what I've done.

The wife comes forward and takes my hand. Her eyes are bright with unshed tears as she stares into mine. "We are at your service, Kai Black," she murmurs. "I always knew you and your sister would be something great, ever since I saw the two of you sneaking around the cornfields as children." She smiles and bows her head.

The children dance around me, their excitement at meeting me palpable.

"Do the power!" the little girl screams.

"Yeah, make your lightning!" the boys add. "We want to see the lightning!"

I smile and kneel, holding out my hand. Lightning springs to life on my palm, earning shouts of excitement from them. They clap their hands, delighted by the magic and eager for their own. Perhaps they'll have it. The lands are changing, merging, and becoming one. Perhaps the magic will return to everyone.

I can only hope.

"If you think this is cool," I tell them, looking over my shoulder to gesture for Kaito. My men are never far behind. Despite my newfound confidence, they will always protect my back, and I love them for that. I can't help but smile as he winks at me. "You should see what Kaito can do with water."

Kaito smiles and takes a seat beside me, crossing his legs. The children seem scared at first until he holds out his hand and a tiny fish made of water begins to swim around his palm. That's all it takes. They squeal in excitement and leap forward, eagerly watching as Kaito creates animal after animal, taking their requests with ease. He grins with excitement, happy to make them smile. My sweet monster.

I stand and grin at the others. Many fear them, but they are able to walk freely through the streets. All beasts are. There is no violence allowed here, which is a rule that Cora passed immediately.

I feel a tug on my skirt, and I look down at the little girl, her bright eyes wide. "Aren't you scared?" she asks as she glances at Rook.

"Oh no," I say, kneeling to her level. "I don't fear them."

"Why not?" she asks, curiosity in her eyes.

I point at her heart. "We all carry magic in our hearts, so you see, we are the same. How can I fear myself?" My eyes crinkle. "Besides, they love me."

The little girl smiles. "I hope someone looks at me the way they look at you one day."

"They will." I nod. "Someday, perhaps you'll have your own monster who loves you." I tilt my head. "What's your name?"

She flashes a bright smile at me. "Delilah."

"Delilah," I repeat, chucking her on the chin. "One day, these lands will echo with your name, Delilah, just as they do the queen's."

"Just as they say yours?" she asks.

I nod. "Just like that."

I stand and meet her parents' eyes again while Kaito entertains the kids. "You're raising beautiful children. I hope they have all the freedom any of us have ever wanted."

The wife smiles. "Thanks to you, they will."

I flush but glance back at my monsters. "I didn't do it alone."

"No," she says. "But you and Cora took the first steps so the rest of us could follow, and for that, we are forever grateful."

I can feel it then—hope and healing. We'll be okay. The Shadow Lands, Dead Lands, and Gilded Lands are no longer separated by hate.

Hope fills me, and as Kaito makes tiny water animals and Rook joins in with his shadows, the last traces of darkness in my heart heal.

I am whole.

I am Kai.

CHAPTER

SIXTY-SIX

KAITO

Our feet dangle in the water, the saltiness of the mixed river making me feel at home as my magic surges through me, but my entire focus is on my mate sitting next to me. She's kicking her own feet idly in the very river where we first met.

Where she came to die.

"What if this isn't the right choice?" she muses out loud after sitting in nervous silence for far too long, but I have learned not to push Kai, and when she is ready, she will share.

She gnaws on her bottom lip, her eyes on the water even as her hand anxiously plays with mine.

She is so adorable. After everything we faced, this is what she's worried about?

"What if it is?" I counter.

She lets out a sigh and meets my loving gaze. "I'm nobody, Kaito. I wasn't meant to be queen."

"I can't think of a single other person who is more suited," I tell her honestly. "You were willing to die for your lands and people, but you also heal them every single day. You offer them hope, happiness, and love. Right now, we all need something good to lighten our moods and spark hope for the future. You and Cora are it." I kiss the back of her hand as she leans into me. "You will make a magnificent queen, and what did your sister say?"

She sighs, glancing back at the water. "That she couldn't lead without me at her side, and that we are two halves of the same whole—mercy and power, hope and protection. She said our lands need both of us." She swallows hard, and I know she wants to cry again as she recalls her sister's confession last night. She called upon our room late, took Kai for a walk, and asked her to lead with her.

It seems Cora doesn't plan to ever let Kai go again and instead is binding her to this land and her side. Whether she knows it or not, I think Cora worries that without purpose, Kai may relapse, but she was right.

Kai was born to lead with her, and I will be right there at her side where I belong, always ready to catch her when she falls.

"Stop fussing, my love." I smirk as I take her hands, which are twisting the fabric of her gown. "You look magnificent. You look like a queen, but moreover, you look like our mate."

Her face softens. "Are you sure?" she asks. Kai has always been too kind, but she worries she isn't enough, even now.

If she could only see herself through my eyes, she would never ask that question again. Her hair hangs down past her shoulders, her orange streaks bright with her power. Her eyes glow like they always seem to with her, and her skin takes on the same sheen. Her lips are painted a deep, burnt orange to match her hair, and her eyes have been darkened with magical makeup supplied by a pixie. Her magical ink crawls along her exposed arms, showing her gift.

Her dress is a simple black silhouette, but as she moves, it lights from within with her power. The deep, plunging V neckline almost makes me growl possessively, and the jeweled necklace circling her throat makes me recall last night, when my hand was there. Across her tiny waist, cinching it in more, is an orange, glowing belt.

She looks every inch the dark monster queen she was always meant to be.

She also looks every inch mine, which she is. That was cemented last night under the full blood moon.

We had an intimate ceremony last night where we swore our eternal love for one another, but today won't only be the coronation, but a binding marriage for Cora and her mates, as well as Kai and us, for the whole of the kingdom to witness.

Cupping her face, unable to resist, I rest my forehead against hers. "I am just a mere monster, my love." I shush her when she goes to interrupt. "And every day I wake to you feels like a dream. I have been blessed. You're a being who wasn't made for this world, and we all know it. You are kindness, hope, and love. You are healing. You were made to be queen, and you were made to be ours, but if you get nervous today, just look at us. Find us and see how much we love you, how proud of you we are. Find us and remember you are ours, and we are yours, and that will never change. Whether we live in a tiny cottage or a huge palace. You are still Kai, and I am still Weyland."

Shadows stroke across her comfortingly, and I know Rook must be close, but he offers us privacy. It's hard learning to share, but we are figuring it out.

"I love you," she whispers, her eyes glassy with tears.

"I love you forever, Kai. Now go show them what a true queen looks like." I kiss her head and step back as Dade offers her his arm. We fought for the right, and he won. He looks smug as he winks at her, but it makes her giggle, and I can't deny what a pair they make. Instead, I step behind her.

Kaito walks before her, and Rook lingers behind in the shadows.

When the trumpets sound, the doors open of their own accord, and I smile brightly at the sight awaiting us.

Awaiting her.

My queen.

My mate.

～

I HOLD my mate's arm proudly as we step into the golden throne room—the very room where a disgraced king once stole my mate's innocence and hope. Now it stands as a symbol of forgiveness and the future we hold.

I have never been so proud to belong to someone.

Thousands line the city walls, and as many as possible are squished into the throne room here in the castle, all vying for their first look. Monsters and humans alike gather together, and when we appear, gasps spread quickly through the crowd.

I feel Rook's shadows wind through my legs and roll my eyes, but I can't deny that when he wraps them around her like dancing tendrils, the effect is stunning.

We walk slowly down the aisle, the golden carpet crushing under our feet as we head toward the waiting throne—or should I say thrones, since there are now two. Both are a stunning mix of gold, gray, and black.

Cora waits for her sister, the crown atop her head blindingly gold. Her dress sways with her movements, gold where Kai's is black, yet she holds out her hand and I release my grip, letting Kai pass from me to her. Their hands clasp as they face the thrones and bow before turning to face the people gathered.

We step back to the side, watching proudly as Kai lifts her chin, steadying herself.

"Today, we gather to welcome a new era, a new ruler, and a new way of life. So many were lost due to hatred, but from now on, we lead with love and a little iron fist when needed." Cora winks as the crowd laughs. "Many know my sister as the hero of the golden fields who saved thousands of lives. Some know her as the little girl from the Shadow Lands who always had a smile on her face. Some know her from the time the king stole her away and tried to break her, yet here she stands. She had every opportunity to let hatred and anger corrupt her. Instead, she chose life and forgiveness. I couldn't think of anyone better to lead our people with me, to correct me when I am wrong, and to soften me. Since the day I was born, Kai and I have been inseparable, and that won't change. We simply got lost for a little while in the middle. Now, we stand before you, claiming our mates in marriage and claiming these thrones in hope. We beg for your compassion, we hope for your love, and we promise you protection, from now until the day we go to the grave together." Cora turns and picks up a crown, then she smiles softly at Kai. "My sister, my best friend, I have always looked up to you. Your kindness inspires me, your hope is infectious, and I have my own now because of you. I hope we stand together for a very long time and we both get the life we deserve. Kneel."

Kai does, sinking down effortlessly, and my heart aches for my beauty.

She promised never to be on her knees again, but she goes willingly for her sister.

"Do you promise to lead with the same values by which you live? Do you swear to honor people while offering new ways for the future? Do you vow to stand by my side and protect the kingdom until our last breath?"

"I do. I promise. I swear. I vow." Kai bows her head.

"Then I, Cora, queen of the lands, declare you Queen Kai." She places the crown atop Kai's hair, and it settles there like it's always belonged. Cora helps her to her feet, and they stand side by side.

Gold and black.

Blonde and orange.

Two halves of the same soul.

With the black crown placed upon her head and the smile she shoots Cora, I feel my knees weaken.

My girl is phenomenal. More so, she is the perfect queen, and I will follow her forever.

As they rise as one, my shadows retreat to allow them this moment.

They shine brightly together, filled with a magic so strong, it makes them shine. These two sisters were born into anger and pain, but they found their way to love and happiness. They weren't given opportunities or hope, yet here they are, and now they fight for everyone like them.

Kai winks at me and turns to face the crowd once more. "I thank you for your kindness. I will try with everything in me to deserve this honor, and it is an honor, but know this—we may wear crowns, but it's all of you who are the heart of this land. You are the reason we stand here. You are the future. You are the hope."

"Now, let's celebrate!" Cora calls, and chants and shouts break out as both sisters laugh.

Cora leans in, kisses her sister's cheek, and offers her hand to us before turning to her own mates. I hurry over before the others can, stepping to my little oblivion's side where I belong.

She takes my arm and leans in. "I want you to fuck me with your shadows later while I wear only this crown."

I almost stumble as I lead her from the throne room, my head whipping around to meet her laughing eyes. She winks at me, and the growl that erupts from me is pure beast as her head is thrown back with mirth. I wrap the shadows around us and bend down, quickly hoisting her over my shoulder and speeding from the room with them chasing after us.

Her laughter echoes across the kingdom, her hands gripping my back, and a smile curves my lips—one only she can put there.

She made the boogeyman fall and made the shadows whole once more, and as the kingdom breaks out in celebration, so do we. `

As one.

As mates.

As forever.

EPILOGUE

KAI

Months later...

Our lands are still healing. War and hatred can't be erased overnight. There are still those against the unification of monsters and humans, and we make sure we always address that, but for the most part, people just want to get on with their lives.

As soon as they realized the monsters were not here to pillage and kill, most even started to accept them. Monster-run businesses are booming across the lands, and some humans even live in the newly healing Dead Lands, exploring it and mapping what was once uncharted.

Matings between humans and monsters have also increased, with the motto love is love becoming an almost kingdom-wide mantra.

And us?

I can't complain. I have four mates who love me no matter what. They hold me when the nightmares invade, sing me back to sleep, and stand by my side every day. I don't know what the future holds, but I know it's bright, and for the first time since I stood on that tower, I don't regret living.

I'm glad I did.

I would have missed so much.

Maybe it's my memories that bring me here, but I find myself in the Shadow Lands, standing right before the place where our house once stood.

I don't know what happened to my mother or father, and I suppose that should worry me, but it doesn't. As I stare at the brand-new house standing where our shack once did, all I feel is happiness. I am happy it's gone and glad they are gone too.

They were never parents. My mother was a weak, scared woman who wouldn't even risk herself to protect her daughters, and my father was a cruel man. It's better that they are gone and forgotten, and as I turn away from the new house holding a hopeful family, I vow it will be the last time I think of them.

I have my own family now, a real one, and Cora and I never needed them anyway. Sometimes, you can't forgive, but it doesn't mean you can't forget. You can move on without forgiveness, and that is what I do.

Turning away, I take my mates' hands and walk proudly toward our future, never once looking back.

My eyes scan the words, even as my heart knows them better than my own name.

". . . and so it ended the way it began, with two sisters, their hearts filled with love and hope for the future. The end."

Shutting the gilded book that Kaito and I meticulously wrote and illustrated, I lift my eyes to the gathered children before me. I often come into the lands to heal and, yes, sometimes read, and today is one of those days.

"Again, Queen Kai!" they plead as their parents watch on with happy smiles where we are gathered in the little square in the Shadow Lands.

Chuckling, I stand, holding the book to my heart. My gaze lands on my mates at the back of the crowd, and my grin grows. Cora blows me a kiss where she stands with her own mates. We like to visit where we came from, and we even have a house here.

We may be queens, but we will always be peasant girls who grew up running through these fields, and that's okay. I accept that about me. I accept every part of myself.

Scars and all.

"What happens next?" another child calls, pulling my attention from my family and back to the cross-legged children gathered eagerly before me.

My smile blooms so brightly, I am surprised my lightning doesn't crackle. "I guess we'll find out," I say, looking out over the lands we rule. "We will see what tomorrow brings."

THE END, MONSTER FUCKERS.

ABOUT K.A. KNIGHT

K.A Knight is an USA Today bestselling indie author trying to get all of the stories and characters out of her head, writing the monsters that you love to hate. She loves reading and devours every book she can get her hands on, and she also has a worrying caffeine addiction.

She leads her double life in a sleepy English town, where she spends her days writing like a crazy person.

Read more at K.A Knight's website or join her Facebook Reader Group.

Sign up for exclusive content and my newsletter here

http://eepurl.com/drLLoj

ALSO BY K.A. KNIGHT

THEIR CHAMPION SERIES *Dystopian RH*

The Wasteland

The Summit

The Cities

The Nations

Their Champion Coloring Book

Their Champion - the omnibus

The Forgotten

The Lost

The Damned

Their Champion Companion - the omnibus

DAWNBREAKER SERIES *SCI FI RH*

Voyage to Ayama

Dreaming of Ayama

THE LOST COVEN SERIES *PNR RH*

Aurora's Coven

Aurora's Betrayal

HER MONSTERS SERIES *PNR RH*

Rage

Hate

Book 3 *coming soon..*

THE FALLEN GODS SERIES *PNR*

Pretty Painful

Pretty Bloody

Pretty Stormy

Pretty Wild

Pretty Hot

Pretty Faces

Pretty Spelled

Fallen Gods - the omnibus 1

Fallen Gods - the omnibus 2

COURTS AND KINGS *PNR RH*

Court of Nightmares

Court of Death

Court of Beasts *coming soon..*

FORBIDDEN READS *(STANDALONES)*

Daddy's Angel *CONTEMPORARY*

Stepbrothers' Darling *CONTEMPORARY RH*

LEGENDS AND LOVE *CONTEMPORARY*

Revolt

Rebel *coming soon..*

PRETTY LIARS *CONTEMPORARY RH*

Unstoppable

Unbreakable

FORGOTTEN CITY *PNR*

Monstrous Lies

Monstrous Truths

Monstrous Ends

DEN OF VIPERS UNIVERSE STANDALONES

Scarlett Limerence *CONTEMPORARY*

Nadia's Salvation *CONTEMPORARY*

Alena's Revenge *CONTEMPORARY*

Den of Vipers *CONTEMPORARY RH*

Gangsters and Guns (Co-Write with Loxley Savage) *CONTEMPORARY RH*

STANDALONES

The Standby *CONTEMPORARY*

Diver's Heart *CONTEMPORARY RH*

Crown of Stars *SCI FI RH*

AUDIOBOOKS

The Wasteland

The Summit

Rage

Hate

Den of Vipers *(From Podium Audio)*

Gangsters and Guns *(From Podium Audio)*

Daddy's Angel *(From Podium Audio)*

Stepbrothers' Darling *(From Podium Audio)*

Blade of Iris *(From Podium Audio)*

Deadly Affair *(From Podium Audio)*

Deadly Match *(From Podium Audio)*

Deadly Encounter *(From Podium Audio)*

Stolen Trophy *(From Podium Audio)*

Crown of Stars *(From Podium Audio)*

Monstrous Lies *(From Podium Audio)*

Monstrous Truth *(From Podium Audio)*

Monstrous Ends *(From Podium Audio)*

Court of Nightmares *(From Podium Audio)*

Unstoppable *(From Podium Audio)*

Unbreakable *(From Podium Audio)*

Fractured Shadows *(From Podium Audio)*

SHARED WORLD PROJECTS

Blade of Iris - Mafia Wars *CONTEMPORARY RH*

CO-AUTHOR PROJECTS - *Erin O'Kane*

HER FREAKS SERIES *PNR Dystopian RH*

Circus Save Me

Taming The Ringmaster

Walking the Tightrope

Her Freaks Series - the omnibus

STANDALONES

The Hero Complex *PNR RH*

Dark Temptations *Collection of Short Stories, ft. One Night Only & Circus Saves Christmas*

THE WILD BOYS SERIES *CONTEMPORARY RH*

The Wild Interview

The Wild Tour

The Wild Finale

The Wild Boys - the omnibus

CO-AUTHOR PROJECTS - *Ivy Fox*

Deadly Love Series *CONTEMPORARY*

Deadly Affair

Deadly Match

Deadly Encounter

CO-AUTHOR PROJECTS - *Kendra Moreno*

STANDALONES

Stolen Trophy *CONTEMPORARY RH*

Fractured Shadows *PNR RH*

Burn Me *PNR*

CO-AUTHOR PROJECTS - *Loxley Savage*

THE FORSAKEN SERIES *SCI FI RH*

Capturing Carmen

Stealing Shiloh

Harboring Harlow

STANDALONES

Gangsters and Guns *CONTEMPORARY*, IN DEN OF VIPERS' UNIVERSE

OTHER CO-WRITES

Shipwreck Souls *(with Kendra Moreno & Poppy Woods)*

The Horror Emporium *(with Kendra Moreno & Poppy Woods)*

About Kendra Moreno

Kendra Moreno is secretly a spy but when she's not dealing in secrets and espionage, you can find her writing her latest adventure. She lives in Texas where the summer days will make you melt, and southern charm comes free with every meal. She's a recovering Road Rager (kind of) and slowly overcoming her Star Wars addiction (nope!), and she definitely didn't pass on her addiction to her son (she did). She has one hellhound named Mayhem who got tired of guarding the Gates of Hell and now guards her home against monsters. She's a geek, a mother, a scuba diver, a tyrannosaurus rex, and a wordsmith who sometimes switches out her pen for a sword.

If you see Kendra on the streets, don't worry: you can distract her with talks about Kylo Ren or Loki.
#LokiLives #BringBackBenSolo

To find out more about Kendra, you can check her out on her website or join her
Facebook group, Kendra's World of Wonder.
Sign up for Kendra's Newsletter:
https://mailchi.mp/feb46d2b29ad/babbleandquill

facebook.com/AuthorKendraMoreno

x.com/KendramorenoA

instagram.com/kendramorenoauthor

bookbub.com/authors/kendra-moreno

tiktok.com/@kendramorenoauther

Also by Kendra

Sons Of Wonderland

Book 1 - Mad as a Hatter

Book 2 - Late as a Rabbit

Book 3 - Feral as a Cat

Companion novel - Cruel as a Queen

Daughters Of Neverland

Book 1 - Vicious as a Darling

Book 2 - Fierce As A Tiger Lily

Book 3 - Wicked As A Pixie

Companion Novel - Monstrous As A Croc

The Heirs Of Oz

Book 1 - Heartless as a Tin Man

Book 2 - Empty as a Scarecrow

Book 3 - Cowardly as a Lion

Companion Novel - Vengeful as a Beauty

The Lords of Grimm

Book 1 - Cunning as a Trickster

Book 2 - Bitter as a Captain

Book 3 - Twisted as a Princess

Companion Novel - Hateful as a Sister

The Keepers of Enchantment

Book 1 - Charming as a Killer

Book 2 - Ethereal as a Swan

Book 3 - Tricky as a Thief

PREY ISLAND

Book 1 - Prey Island

Book 2 - Predator Point

CLOCKWORK ALMANAC

Book 1 - Clockwork Butterfly

Book 2 - Clockwork Octopus

THE VALHALLA MECHANISM

Book 1 - Gears of Mischief

Book 2 - Gears of Thunder

Book 3 - Gears of Ragnarök

RACE GAMES

Book 1 - Blood and Honey

Book 2 - Teeth and Wings

Book 3 - Jewels and Feathers

Book 3 - Fur and Claws

STAND-ALONES

Treble Maker

Pharaoh-mones

Philomena And The Seven Deaths

CO-WRITES

WITH K.A KNIGHT

Stolen Trophy

Fractured Shadows

Shadowed Heart

Burn Me

*WITH **K.A KNIGHT** AND **POPPY WOODS***

Shipwreck Souls

The Horror Emporium

*WITH **POPPY WOODS***

THE BLOOMING COURTS

Book 1 - Resurrect

Book 2 - Sprout

Book 3 - Flourish

Book 4 - Emerge

Book 5 - Blossom

THE DINOVERSE

(SHARED UNIVERSE WITH POPPY WOODS)

Book 1 – Dances with Raptors by Poppy Woods

Book 2 – Rexes & Robbers by Kendra Moreno

Head Case: A Dark Twist on a Classic

FIND AN ERROR?

Please email this information to thenuttyformatter1@gmail.com:

- *the author name*
- *title of the book*
- *screenshot of the error*
- *suggested correction*